THE
SHALLOWS

BOOKS BY MATT GOLDMAN

Gone to Dust

Broken Ice

The Shallows

MATT GOLDMAN

THE SHALLOWS

A Tom Doherty Associates Book / New York

THE SHALLOWS

Copyright © 2019 by Matt Goldman

A Forge Book
Published by Tom Doherty Associates
175 Fifth Avenue
New York, NY 10010

www.tor-forge.com

Forge® is a registered trademark of Macmillan Publishing Group, LLC.

The Library of Congress Cataloging-in-Publication Data is available upon request.

ISBN 978-1-250-19131-1 (hardcover)
ISBN 978-1-250-19132-8 (ebook)

Our books may be purchased in bulk for promotional, educational, or business use. Please contact your local bookseller or the Macmillan Corporate and Premium Sales Department at 1-800-221-7945, extension 5442, or by email at MacmillanSpecialMarkets@macmillan.com.

First Edition: June 2019

Printed in the United States of America

0 9 8 7 6 5 4 3 2 1

For Elsa and Riley—

*You make me laugh and kvell, fill my goblet with gratitude,
and give me great hope for our species. I pronounce
myself the luckiest dad on the planet.*

THE
SHALLOWS

1

Police floodlights lit the backyard, insects flew crazy squiggles in the faux daylight, and I followed a lackluster cop down to Christmas Lake.

We stepped onto a dock of fiberglass planks. It jiggled underfoot. A red rowing shell lay at the end, overturned and chained to a galvanized post. It was 4:30 A.M. The eastern sky had lightened to gray with a breath of purple. I looked down. Todd Rabinowitz's body lay on the sandy lake bottom under a couple feet of water. It wore khaki pants and a white T-shirt. He looked like he'd lived to about fifty. Fish nibbled on dead Todd's face and fingertips.

I said, "You're leaving him in the water?"

Detective Mike Norton said, "There's a complication." Norton was midfifties, tall, white, and doughy. He had light brown hair and a forehead so big he could rent it out as a billboard. Dress pants and a dress shirt but without jacket and tie. A badge hung on his belt. He said, "When Mrs. Rabinowitz found her husband, she wasn't sure he was dead. She was using her phone as a flashlight. That's how she spotted him. So she ran into the water and tried to pull him up on shore. She moved him a couple of feet then the body stopped. It was hung up on something. She was freaking out, which hey, you can't blame her for. She wanted to see what he was caught on but didn't want to look too close. Most people don't spend a lot of time around dead bodies."

"I thought you said she didn't know if her husband was dead."

"Yeah, well. I'm just telling you what she told me. So, Mrs. Rabinowitz walks out closer to the body and sees there's a cord underwater that leads to the dock."

I looked at the dock. A red nylon cord was tied to a post.

Norton said, "Only it's not exactly a cord."

"Looks like a fish stringer."

"Yep. But instead of the spike running into a fish's mouth and out its gill, it runs it into the vic's mouth, under his tongue, and out his lower jaw. The killer then ran the spike through the ring-end and tied the cord to the dock."

"Like a caught fish."

"Yep."

"But Mrs. Rabinowitz didn't untie him?"

"Nope," said Norton. "She said she was too upset. And by then she was pretty sure her husband was dead. That's when she called nine-one-one."

I wiped the back of my hand across my face. The August air was so humid I couldn't tell if I was sweating or moisture had condensed on my skin like I was a hunk of cheese. I said, "Get him out of the lake."

"We're holding off, Mr. Shapiro. CSU is unloading now. We're waiting for them so it's done right. We don't want to mess up any evidence."

I watched the fish feeding on Todd Rabinowitz's body. Sunfish, crappies, perch, and pike. Might have been a few small trout in there. Then the body rolled faceup.

"Shit!" said Norton. He jumped back. "Sorry. Just surprised me."

"Like you said: most people don't spend a lot of time around dead bodies." I glanced without favor at the country club cop. Then I returned my attention to the water. Todd Rabinowitz stared at the starry sky. The fish had eaten away his eyelids.

My day started at 3:27 A.M. with Anders Ellegaard's phone call. He was my best friend and business partner, although "partner" is a misleading term. Ellegaard ran our private investigative firm. He assumed the important responsibilities like paying bills, bringing in new business, and purchasing our health insurance. I assumed other tasks like, during one of our slower weeks, making a catapult out of coffee stir sticks and a rubber band.

Ellegaard told me his wife, Molly, had just received a call from a friend named Robin Rabinowitz. Robin found her husband dead in their lake, and she requested I go out to see her. Not anyone from the firm. Me. Robin insisted it be me.

When Ellegaard called, I was sleeping next to my ex-wife.

We had a bad habit of falling into bed together. For her, it seemed just that. Bed. But for me, Micaela was a spring trap—I'd have to chew my heart out to get away. I'd tried cutting off all contact. That lasted a year and did nothing to help me move on. So, for the past six months, I woke in her bed as often as my own. We had both just turned forty. I'd heard women hit their sexual peak in their forties. Based on our recent frequency, that appeared to be true. Happy birthday to us.

Everything you need to know about Micaela Stahl you could tell by looking at her side of the bed. It looked more sat-on than slept-in. No strewn sheets. No twisted duvet. No mangled pillows. Micaela slept rock-still, her dreams and worries never creating enough turmoil to toss or turn her. When she told me about a dream, even a bad one, even right after waking, she'd already analyzed it. It was as if she'd not experienced the dream but had seen it like a movie and had written the review before it ended.

Her low stress level helped Micaela succeed at whatever she set her mind to. Or maybe it was the other way around. The companies she ran. Her foundation providing apartments for homeless women and children. And she was a black belt in yoga, or whatever the hell they call a person who's really good at yoga.

Micaela's one failure was her marriage to me, but perhaps failure was my definition. To her the marriage was a house she never quite felt comfortable in or a pair of eyeglasses her eyes never adjusted to. It made perfect sense to move on. Except we didn't move on, not at night, anyway.

I put on my jeans, entered Micaela's master bathroom, brushed my teeth, and pushed my hair around. The face in the mirror did not care for what it saw. Forty Minnesota summers and winters had taken their toll. On my way back through the bedroom, I stopped to look at my ex-wife. She'd get up soon for an early flight to New York. Meetings with money people, she said. I did not kiss her good-bye. There was no point.

Christmas Lake sits across the road from St. Alban's Bay. One of dozens of bays that make up Lake Minnetonka. Unlike its gigantic neighbor, Christmas Lake is small and cold. Trout breathe in its oxygen-rich depths. Wealthy people live around it and commute half an hour to work. Or their money works for them, and they commute nowhere at all.

The Greater Lake Minnetonka Police Department protected and served a handful of municipalities near the lake. They had secured the area. Yellow police tape crossed the narrow street. A GLMPD uniform stood next to it with a clipboard.

I rolled down my window. "Nils Shapiro. I'm a private."

"Got you at the top of my list, Mr. Shapiro. Mrs. Rabinowitz and the detectives are expecting you."

No argument. No attitude. Just welcome aboard. Once in a lifetime it goes like that. She moved the yellow tape, and I drove the half mile to the Rabinowitz house. It was low, long, modern, and sided with white stucco. Big windows revealed an interior of wooden antiques and overstuffed white couches and artsy chandeliers, the kind with a lot of glass balls filled with vintage-style filament bulbs. It looked homey and happy, but if that were true, I wouldn't be there. A flashlight with an orange cone told me where to park. I did, and walked around back to the lake side of the house. That's where I met Detective Norton, who led me down to the dock and showed me the body.

Detective Norton and I left Todd Rabinowitz underwater. I followed him up from the lake and toward the house on a path of crushed limestone. The white-blue LED floods revealed a lawn of deep green. Hydrangeas and lilies grew in planting beds topped with mulched cedar. It smelled fresh and good. The frogs and crickets couldn't stop singing about it.

Norton led me to a screened-in porch attached to the back of the house. Inside, a man and woman sat on big furniture made of more white cushions. A dozen single-filament bulbs hung from individual cords and illuminated the porch in a soft yellowish-gold. The people inside looked hazy through the screens, like in an old photograph.

Detective Norton opened the porch door and said, "Mrs. Rabinowitz, Nils Shapiro is here."

A woman's voice said, "Please send him in." A man stood. Another Greater Lake Minnetonka PD detective.

Detective Dale Irving said, "Thank you for driving out, Mr. Shapiro." Midthirties, dressed like his partner, and had orange hair. Why do they call it red hair? It's orange. Get the big box of Crayola crayons and find the one that matches. It'll have the word "orange" on it. Not red. Red is for punk rockers and baristas and kids who are pissed at their parents. "Please let us know what we can do to help. Anything at all."

Weird. The cops acted like they were working for me.

I turned my attention toward the woman, who had remained seated. Norton the Forehead said, "Nils, this is Robin Rabinowitz."

Robin Rabinowitz looked up at me and said, "Hello, Nils. Thanks for coming out here so quickly." Her brown eyes met mine then looked away. She said nothing more, as if it had taken great effort just to greet me. She swallowed, and I wondered if she was in shock.

I said, "It wasn't any trouble. I understand you're a friend of Molly Ellegaard."

She brought a hand to her cheek and felt it, as if she'd just been to the dentist and her face was still numb. "Yes," she said. "I know Molly. I called her to ask for you." Robin turned toward me again then stood. Thin and tan with short hair and long, lithe fingers.

Ellegaard would have brought a contract and insisted on receiving a retainer before getting further involved. I didn't have his business skills. I said, "How and when did you find him?"

She looked at me again. High cheekbones seemed to push up the bottoms of her eyes, elongating them into something Asian. But she wasn't Asian. Just a dark-haired Jewish woman who'd received a perfect complement of Semitic genes. If anything, she looked like a model who was supposed to pass for Native American while wearing something made of calfskin and fringe by Ralph Lauren.

"Todd was home last night," said Robin. "We ate dinner, then he worked in his study for a couple hours. I went into the bedroom to read. I fell asleep early, but I woke when he came in."

"Do you know what time that was?"

"A little after ten thirty. Then I woke up again around two, and Todd was gone. I didn't think anything of it. But I heard a motorboat on the lake, which is unusual after midnight. Then I heard a bang, like a gunshot. I told myself the motor just backfired, but something felt wrong. So I left the bedroom to look for Todd. He wasn't anywhere in the house."

Robin walked over to the screen, and looked out on the lake.

She wore old jeans and a white gauze top. "Sometimes when Todd can't sleep, he takes out his rowing shell . . ." She paused. ". . . *took* out his rowing shell." She walked back toward me. Her neck looked longer than her head. She didn't wear a necklace. A necklace would have wrecked everything. She said, "Todd liked to row when the water was glass. So I walked down to the dock to see if his shell was there." Robin spoke evenly and in a matter-of-fact tone. "That's when I found him." She shook her head as if discovering her husband dead was more of an inconvenience than a tragedy.

I said, "What were you wearing when you tried to get your husband out of the water?"

"Excuse me?" said Robin.

"Detective Norton said you told him you tried to drag your husband out of the water but were stopped by the stringer. What were you wearing when that happened?"

"Oh," said Robin. "Just a T-shirt. That's what I sleep in."

"Where is it?"

"It's in the laundry room sink. Why?"

"Irving, have CSU check it for blood and pay attention to whether it's a smear or a splatter or nothing. If there's no blood, I want to know if just the bottom of the shirt is wet or if it's all wet. You know, like she washed it."

Irving nodded.

Robin said, "What?"

"Why didn't you untie the stringer from the dock, then pull your husband up on shore? Oh, and, Mrs. Rabinowitz, I'm going to need a five-thousand-dollar retainer if you want me to work for you." I guess Ellegaard had rubbed off on me more than I realized.

Robin Rabinowitz sat down and said, "Did you just imply that I killed my husband then ask me for five thousand dollars?"

"I didn't imply anything. I'm trying to clear you as a suspect. Not that you couldn't have hired someone to kill your husband, but I assume you asked Molly Ellegaard to send me here because you want this solved sooner than later."

Robin squeezed her knees together with her hands then took a deep breath. I'd made her uncomfortable so I continued. "You could want the case closed because you have a keen sense of justice or you loved your husband or you want suicide ruled out ASAP so you can collect the life insurance. Or it could be because you know you'll be a suspect."

She stared at me without expression. Detective Irving fidgeted with his watch. Voices carried from the dock to the house the way voices do around lakes before daybreak. CSU officers pulled Todd Rabinowitz out of the water, barking instructions to be careful with each other's end as if they were moving a couch.

Robin said, "Huh. Molly said you were nice."

"I am nice. But I'm a private detective, not your lawyer. If I were your lawyer I would have told you the police will look hard at you and not to lie about anything because you've left a trail whether you realize it or not. Lawyers give good advice like that, so if you have one, you may want to give him or her a call. You know, after you settle down and aren't crying so hard about your dead husband."

Officer Irving scratched the back of his orange-haired head and looked at Robin Rabinowitz with expectation. He'd become my toady and had that *yeah what he said* look. I was a bit hard on the new widow—the bizarre crime scene stirred up something in me. The only reason to tie a dead man to his dock by a fishing stringer through his jaw is you have something to say. I guess I was trying to ferret out if Robin had something to say.

She stood, stared something cold at me, and walked into the house.

2

"So Irving," I said, "why's your chief not here? This is a bigger deal than a boat going on the wrong side of a channel buoy or whatever usually gets you out of the station."

"Chief's gone."

"Gone where?"

"He ran off with his girlfriend. She worked in the D.A.'s office. The GLMPD governing committee is mad as hell. I'm surprised you haven't heard. Everyone in town is talking about it."

"I haven't been a very good listener lately. When did he run off?"

"About ten days ago."

"Anyone know where he is?"

"Nicaragua. Guess he bought a place down there but didn't tell anyone. Even his wife. Boy is she pissed."

"I'll bet."

Robin returned, iPhone in hand. She said, "PayPal or Venmo?"

"PayPal."

She asked for my email. A few seconds later my phone dinged to announce Robin Rabinowitz had just sent Stone Arch Investigations five thousand dollars. I accepted the payment and deposited it in the company checking account. And all before the sun rose. I deserved to take the rest of the day off.

Robin said, "And my lawyer will be here in five minutes. She lives two houses down."

I said, "You know how to follow directions. That's good."

"Don't be glib. Someone just murdered my husband, put a stringer through his jaw, and tied him to our dock. For all I know, I'm next." She stared at me in pursuit of sympathy. I didn't give it to her. She placed a hand on Detective Irving's shoulder. "Do you mind leaving us for a few minutes?"

"No," he said. "I need to have CSU check out your shirt anyway. And you'll need to come down to the station soon."

"Of course."

Detective Irving nodded then stood and walked out of the screened-in porch and down to the lake. Robin waited for him to get all the way down to the dock, where the Hennepin County medical examiner had erected a white tent.

She said, "I have nothing to hide. I'll tell everything to you and the police. But I want to tell you first."

I said, "Okay . . ."

"Todd and I were months or even weeks away from separating."

"Then why would you spend a considerable amount of money to help find his killer?"

She lifted her left foot and rested it on her right knee. She wore neither shoes nor socks. That's the way wealthy lake people live. It's nothing but clean white docks, soft green lawns, and maid-cleaned floors. Robin's feet and toes were brown on top, with red-painted nails. A fine gold chain circumnavigated her left ankle. She touched it then said, "I loved Todd. But I wasn't in love with him. We just grew apart."

"How long were you married?"

"Ten years. Second marriage for both of us. Todd has kids from his first. I don't. Never wanted them. He's—he was nine years older than me. And when we met—"

"Are you from here?"

She shook her head. "Montreal. We met at a wedding in Toronto about a year after I got divorced. We had a weekend fling and I figured that was the end of it. But then we found excuses to rendezvous in New York or Boston on weekends. Then I started coming here. We went to Vegas once. Don't need to do that again. Then we spent a week at Ventana in Big Sur. Have you been there?"

"No. Never been to California."

"Northern California is the most beautiful place on the continent. You should go sometime."

"I'll add it to my list."

"Anyway, we were walking in the little town of Carmel and Todd just proposed to me out of the blue. We'd only known each other six months but getting married somehow seemed like a good idea. At least at the time it did. So, we popped into a jewelry store and picked out rings and got married a few months later here in Minneapolis."

"Are you a U.S. citizen?"

"As of last year, I am."

"Welcome to our humble country. You getting close to telling me why you hired me rather than just letting the police do their jobs?"

She pushed her short dark hair behind her ears, which were small and brown and bejeweled with diamonds. "Todd and I fought, mostly about his various causes."

"What kind of causes?"

"Political. I'm sure we would have already split, but it didn't look good in his circle. Especially to some of his clients. He was riding out the marriage for appearance's sake, but I'd made it clear I was done."

"How did he react to that?"

"He didn't, really. He just kind of ignored me. Said we could talk about it more toward the end of the year. I asked why the wait and he said there was no reason not to. I pressed him for a date and he said no sooner than mid-November."

"When did he say that?"

"A month and a half ago, maybe two."

"If you wanted out, why didn't you just leave?"

"My first divorce was ugly. I couldn't take another one like that, so if I could make it amicable by waiting a few months, I'd wait a few months."

I knew how she felt. People ask if I'd ever get married again. My answer is absolutely, but I never want to get divorced again.

Robin said, "So Todd and I cohabited as roommates. It was friendly. There was nothing to fight about. It's not like we could fix things. I just had to be patient until he was ready."

"Did he say he wanted to fix things?"

"No."

"But you noticed when he didn't come to bed last night."

"Yes. Neither of us moved into the guest room. Like I said, we were like roommates. We slept in the same bed, but we hadn't had sex in over a year."

"Did either of you have plans to move out?"

"It hadn't got to that point yet. Plus, that's the problem when you have a nice house. No one wants to leave. But I'd started to look around for either a little cottage in this area or an apartment downtown."

"Were either of you involved with anyone else?"

Robin Rabinowitz leaned back into the cushions and stared at the porch's tongue-and-groove ceiling. Her neck was brown and lined with forty or so years of life. There is no shortage of beautiful women in this world. It's exhausting. Robin said, "I don't know about Todd, but I met someone."

"Does your new friend keep his fish or catch and release?"

She gave me a *that wasn't funny* look even though she then said, "His name is Arndt Kjellgren. He's an artist. He doesn't fish. He's vegan. He won't even wear wool."

"The Arndt Kjellgren who makes the big moving sculptures?"

"How many Arndt Kjellgrens do you think there are?"

"Fair point. Did Todd know about the affair?"

"I don't think so. But I want to be upfront about it. You and the police need to know so you can clear Arndt and me and focus on whoever did this."

I stood and looked down at the lake. A loon cried its echoey low whistle. I spotted the Minnesota state bird in the middle of the lake. I said, "Sometimes when a person vomits information, they're trying to throw me off track. It can be an effective tactic with the police because their bureaucracy dictates they follow up on most leads. But I have no bureaucracy. So, I suggest you get to the point before I send your five grand back."

Robin looked down at the team working near the dock and said more loudly than she needed to, "Let me show you where the bathroom is."

Smart woman. I followed her into the house.

3

We entered the living room. Robin shut the door to the porch then said, "Someone connected to Todd's law firm did this. I'm sure of it."

I looked around the room. A coffee table made of frosted glass was full of coffee table books about fashion. Kate Moss and Tom Ford and Coco Chanel. Two tribal masks sat on opposite ends of the fireplace mantel, a ceramic urn between them. Looked like the Rabinowitzes had visited Africa or Pier 1 Imports. The overall motif was modern with a few antiques mixed in. A fuchsia chair that looked like a potato chip. An eighteenth-century armoire. A chunk of once-molten glass that looked like a giant ice cube hanging from a wire. A collection of teacups purchased at Queen Victoria's garage sale.

I said, "All right . . ."

"These lawyers grew up together or went to camp together or college. One of the senior partners is a woman and they sprinkled in a few more to appear current, but trust me, they're not. They're tight-knit and cliquey. Todd worked at the firm when I married him. They never accepted me. I stopped going to their parties and weekend ski trips because, honestly, they creeped me out." Robin finally looked like she might cry. Her eyes got big and wet then flashed with fear. She shut them and took a few deep breaths. "I don't know why one of them killed Todd, or if all of them did, if Todd stepped out of line or what." She opened her eyes and swung them toward me. "But I'm sure his murder is connected to the firm."

I let that hang, trying to determine if her fear was real or manufactured or misappropriated. Then I said, "That's quite an accusation."

"Go meet them. You'll see."

"Did Todd seem upset about work lately?"

Robin shook her head. "No. That's the weird thing. Everything seemed fine. He spent all his time with them."

"Are you sure that's what he was doing? Because 'honey I have to work late' has been around since some company invented the wheel."

She sighed contempt. "I can't prove it was always work related. But I'm telling you, the lawyers at Halferin Silver were Todd's real family. I hate those people. Every one of them."

The doorbell rang. Robin excused herself and walked toward the front of the house. I turned around and noticed a metal kinetic sculpture in the far corner. It featured squares and triangles painted black and white like a giant mobile for a newborn.

Maybe it was a Stillman, but it could have been one of Arndt Kjellgren's creations. I'd seen them around town. At the Walker Art Center Sculpture Garden, on Minneapolis's Nicollet Mall, on sprawling corporate campuses, and in wealthy people's yards and houses. The moving parts probably moved in the wind but sat motionless in the air-conditioning. If it was a Kjellgren sculpture, featuring it in her husband's living room was one hell of a bold move for Robin Rabinowitz.

She returned and said, "Nils Shapiro, I'd like you to meet my attorney, Nellie Chang." Nellie Chang was gymnast petite, had long black hair, sleep in her eyes, and was ethnically Chinese. I liked her for no other reason than she had a culturally mashed-up name like mine. We'd probably shared similarly confounded looks and had been on the receiving end of similarly terrible jokes.

I shook Nellie's hand. She had a firm grip for a slight person. She spoke softly and somberly out of respect for Robin's dead husband. "Hello, Nils. Nice to meet you. I'm shocked. I don't know what to say. People in this neighborhood don't get murdered."

"The police will take Robin in for formal questioning. Are you a criminal defense attorney?"

Nellie said, "Yes. Four years as a Hennepin County public defender and the last ten at Swenson, Nelson, Lindquist, Lundquist, and Carlson. Do you know the firm?"

"Sounds like the starting line of the Gopher hockey team."

"Oh, yeah." She laughed. "It does." But she stopped laughing when she remembered why she'd come over at 5:00 A.M. She composed herself then said, "We're a good firm. Represent a lot of big clients. I can't say who, of course, but they're big."

Robin looked to me for approval, as if she'd brought me on to manage the whole operation. Everyone seemed to be capitulating to me, and I didn't care for it. I said, "Nellie, maybe you should go introduce yourself to Detectives Irving and Norton. Let them know you're here and that you expect everything to be by the book."

Nellie said, "I was just thinking the same thing." She left and walked down to the lake.

Robin said, "So you think she's good?"

"I have no idea."

"Thanks a lot."

"I'm having a hard time figuring you out. One minute you're all business. The next you're sad. The next you're scared."

"Yeah. I'm all of those. Who wouldn't be?" Her big wet eyes returned, but I couldn't tell if Robin was afraid Todd's fate would be her fate or if she was afraid of something else. Like what she's capable of. Maybe that scared the hell out of her. Robin's intentions were as hazy as the stagnant August air.

I said, "I get that you're afraid, and I know your marriage to Todd was ending, but I'm seeing no reaction to you finding him tied to the dock by a stringer through his jaw while fish nibble off his face."

"Holy shit. Give me a fucking break!" She seemed startled by her outburst, shut her eyes and rubbed her forehead. These are the moments when a decent detective keeps his mouth shut to prolong the awkward pauses that abhor a vacuum. Robin looked at me, hoping I'd fill it. When I didn't she grew calm with resignation and said, "I need you to find out who did this because they might do it to me and because I know the police will suspect I killed my husband or had him killed."

"Did you?"

"Yes. I'm an experienced murderer who's grown bored outsmarting the police so I hired the best private detective in town to make getting away with it more of a challenge."

Her face was twisted up with so much sarcasm I began to like her. I gestured for Robin to follow me. She looked annoyed but did. I needed a moment to think. Robin Rabinowitz was about to split with dead Todd. She told me and she'd tell the police. Then they'd look hard at her for Todd's murder and would stop cooperating with me if they perceived me as making their job more difficult. I led Robin into the kitchen. It had glossy white European-style cabinets that opened from the bottom like garage doors and black synthetic stone countertops. Stainless steel appliances gave the room all the color of a dead fish. How appropriate.

I said, "I'll take this job, but we're going to tell the police I'm not."

"What?"

"I'll make it look like I won't work for you because I think you killed your husband."

"Are you out of your fucking mind?"

"You don't have to hire me."

Robin leaned against the kitchen island. She thought for a minute. Maybe two. I was about to walk away when she said, "Molly mentioned you can be a pain."

"I thought she said I was nice."

"She said you were nice and sometimes a pain."

"That hurts my feelings." She glanced up at me. She was not amused. I said, "Here are the rules: no electronic communication. I'll contact you via snail mail with sympathy cards. You can write me back at the return address. The five grand will cover my rate and expenses. Until it runs out. I'll let you know when that is. Assume your emails, texts, and phone calls are being monitored. Assume you're being followed. Don't meet your boyfriend until further notice."

"I don't like these rules."

"You have two choices. I can not work for you or work for you and tell people I'm not. Your decision. And you need to make it right now."

She stared at me, ran her fingers through her dark hair, then said, "All right. We'll do it your way."

"Good. You look like a quick study. Follow me. And act surprised when I quit." I walked out of the kitchen, through the living room, into the screened-in porch, and exited to the backyard. I continued down the lawn and saw Nellie Chang kneeling on the dock and puking into the water. It was a goddamn smorgasbord for the fish that morning in Christmas Lake.

I entered the white tent. The Hennepin County medical examiner was sixty-something and six feet four or so and that was standing stoop-shouldered. He wore tiny round rimless eyeglasses and was bald on top but had allowed the white-gray hair on the sides of his head to grow. He had pulled it back into a four-inch ponytail. Normally, I'd look for a scissors to snip it off, but when a person reaches sixty, I forgive them certain transgressions.

Dr. Melzer had kind gray eyes and a capillary-ridden nose. He wore a white smock and green latex gloves and examined Todd Rabinowitz's fingernails. Detectives Norton and Irving stood queasy and quiet and pasty, and a CSU photographer snapped photos as if a model were walking down a runway. The M.E. said, "Hello. I'm Dr. Melzer. You must be the P.I." He smiled and looked up from the body, which lay on a stainless-steel table. The red stringer still ran through Todd Rabinowitz's lower jaw, and his lidless eyes stared at the tent ceiling.

I said, "Nils Shapiro. Nice to meet you, Dr. Melzer. Anything yet?"

Melzer glanced at Detectives Irving and Norton. "You boys okay with me sharing?"

"Please," said Norton.

"Our friend here has water in his lungs. I won't know if it's lake water until I get him back to the shop. But assuming it is and he drowned and died in Christmas Lake, and factoring in lake temp, air temp, and body temp, I'd say he died around one A.M. I do know he was still alive when the stringer spike was shoved through his jaw. Must have been unpleasant. The fish have had at him pretty good. Especially the eyelids. Not uncommon. My theory is the eyelashes resemble something the fish like. That draws 'em in and the little buggers take it from there."

"Legs."

"What?"

"The eyelashes look like insect legs. Of mayflies about to hatch or stoneflies about to crawl out of the water."

"No kidding?" said Dr. Melzer. "You some kind of amateur entomologist?"

"Fly-fisherman."

"Ah. Loved *A River Runs Through It*. Ever see that movie?"

Robin said from outside the tent, "Excuse me, Nils?"

Detective Irving said, "Uh, Mrs. Rabinowitz, you probably shouldn't come in here."

"Okay. Um. Is Nils Shapiro in there?" I walked outside but stayed close to the tent. "There you are," she said. "I just saw that you declined my five thousand dollars. What's that about?"

"I can't work for you."

"Why not?"

"I'd rather not say."

"You'd better say. I hear you're the best and there's no point hiring anyone else. I need someone to help the police find Todd's killer."

That last line sounded a little clunky. I'd hoped she'd do better. I said, "I think it's best if I leave."

"No! I'm willing to pay good money! However much you want! I need to know why you won't take the case!"

The inside of the tent had gone silent. I paused for dramatic effect. I felt the cold seep of morning dew as it breeched my Rod Lavers.

"All right," I said in a hushed but audible tone. "I made a few calls, Mrs. Rabinowitz. Woke some people up. Apparently, you haven't been forthcoming with me."

"About what?"

"About you and Todd. About you and a man named Arndt Kjellgren."

"I don't know what you're talking about."

"I think you do. My sources tell the truth." That line was a bit clunky, too. I blamed my early wake-up call.

Robin lowered her voice. "You think I killed him?"

"Probably not personally. I can't picture you pushing that stringer spike under his tongue and out the bottom of his jaw. But you had all the reason in the world to have someone else do it."

"If that's true, why would I be trying to hire you?"

"Appearance? Hubris? You tell me."

"I can't believe this."

"Good-bye, Mrs. Rabinowitz. And good luck. You're going to need it." I walked up the dewy lawn, my soaked socks squeaking in my shoes. God, I hate summer.

4

I got into my still-new-smelling Volvo. The hockey-mom-mobile had two years left on its lease. Ellegaard insisted I get it, saying the car made a more favorable impression than my old, beat-up Volvo, but I looked forward to turning the car in and replacing it with something less maternal. Too many envious looks came my way from people pushing baby carriages.

Stop-and-go rush-hour traffic clogged Highway 7 heading back into the city. I didn't mind the thinking time and when I was done thinking called Annika Brydolf, Stone Arch Investigations's junior investigator. I asked if she could meet me at eight. She requested closer to eight thirty because she had to drop her kids at day camp.

I pulled into my loading dock because I lived in a former

coat factory that still looked like a coat factory except the manufacturing equipment was gone and my crappy furniture was there. The owner of the building had finally acquired permits to renovate my home into retail space with condos above. I had an option to buy one of the condos but the price tag was well out of my range. I'd have to move by October 1.

After coffee and a shower and more coffee I put on jeans, a T-shirt, dry socks, Stan Smiths, and walked to a coffee shop called Moose & Sadie's. It was 8:15 A.M. and eighty degrees and I had thoughts of driving to the North Shore of Lake Superior where the cold waters push away August. I entered Moose & Sadie's with my T-shirt sticking to my back, got in line, ordered two iced teas, then sat down facing the door.

The place had brick walls painted white and old wood floors and a clientele of former hipsters turned professional gentrifiers. Annika Brydolf walked in and found me. She wore shorts and sandals and a linen blouse. Summer hadn't darkened her pale skin. It was so white it couldn't absorb enough light to get jump-started on a tan. Her glacier-blue eyes looked fake but weren't. Her right eye drooped thanks to nerve damage inflicted by her now-incarcerated ex-husband. You noticed it until she smiled and then you saw nothing but wonderful.

She sat and looked at the iced teas. "This one for me?"

"It's for the first person who asked. Congratulations."

She grabbed the tea and took a sip. "You look tired."

"I am. Ellegaard called at three forty-five this morning. Asked me to check out a crime scene."

Annika said, "What happened?"

"A man named Todd Rabinowitz was murdered last night. His wife found him tied to their dock in Christmas Lake with a stringer through his jaw." Annika gave me an incredulous look. "I know. Someone's either trying to send a message, has a flair for the dramatic, or is trying to create a distraction."

"Did the police bring you in?"

"No. The wife."

"Odd."

"They were about to separate. She's having an affair. She knows she'll be a suspect so she wants me to clear her by helping the police figure out who killed him."

"Bold fucking play if she killed him."

Annika didn't used to swear. The job did it to her, and I found it adorable. I said, "I know. And it's possible Robin killed him. Or had him killed. But I'm going to start with her boyfriend and Todd Rabinowitz's law firm. Robin thinks his employer had something to do with it. Or at least that's what she's saying."

"What do you want me to do?"

Two young men sat next to us. They each had gauges in their earlobes, quarter-size rings stretching the skin and cartilage as if it were made of Play-Doh. I wondered what they'd think of their stretched-out earlobes when they were my age. I felt grateful for having no visible markers indicating the decisions I'd made twenty years ago.

I said, "Annika, I want you to just be you. Except with a fake story. You've left Stone Arch Investigations to work freelance. Drop in on Todd's law firm cold. Give them your résumé. See if you can get past the receptionist. Whether you do or don't, tell them you worked with me. Hit my name hard. Let's see what they do."

"I'm not quite sure I understand."

"I want to know if they're interested in hiring you. Do they call me for a reference? If so, do they use the call as an excuse to meet me in person? I want to investigate them, but the goal is for that to happen by them calling me, not me calling them."

Annika Brydolf understood. She smiled. Her right eye perked up.

"So my story is I'm freelance now?"

"Print up some business cards. Say we still hire you on a case-by-case basis but freelance gives you more flexibility with your kids."

That sounded all right to Annika. She asked if she could buy me breakfast. I said yes if it was on the Stone Arch Investigations credit card. The food came, we ate and talked about regular life. She said her kids were getting older and more independent. She could start focusing on what she wanted for herself. I asked what his name was. Annika Brydolf smiled and asked me to pass the salt.

5

The call came just after 2:00 P.M. A woman said, "I have Ian Halferin for Nils Shapiro."

I'd perused the firm's website. Ian Halferin was from Golden Valley. I'd never met him, or at least I never remembered meeting him. I'd heard of a few attorneys at the firm—I either knew their siblings or my siblings knew them—but I didn't know any directly.

A deep, smoky voice on the other end of the phone said, "Is this the famous Nils Shapiro?"

I said, "If you're only famous in Minnesota, you're not famous."

He laughed and said, "Nils Shapiro. How have we not met?"

We went back and forth like that for five boring minutes, Ian

Halferin asking if I was related to a shotgun splatter of Shapiros. I said no to all, then his tone grew more serious and he said, "So Nils, I'm calling because I'm looking at the résumé of an investigator named Annika Brydolf. And according to her résumé, she worked for you at Stone Arch Investigations."

"Yep. I know Annika well. Hell of an investigator. She went freelance to spend more time with her kids, but we hire her whenever she's available."

"That's good to hear. Unfortunately, Nils, a sad and sensitive matter has come up at our firm. I'm not comfortable discussing it over the phone. It would mean a great deal if you could come in so we could continue this conversation in my office."

Ian Halferin had taken the bait. I just needed to play him a bit to land him. "No offense, Ian, but I don't go to meetings unless I know what they're about."

Halferin said nothing. A truck rumbled outside the coat factory—air brakes hammered it to a squeaking stop. It rumble-idled outside my loading dock door. Maybe I wouldn't miss this place, after all.

Halferin cleared his throat then said, "Can we speak in confidence?"

"Of course."

"Thank you. Did you hear about the body found in Christmas Lake today?"

"No. Haven't looked at the news yet."

"The man, God rest his soul, was named Todd Rabinowitz. He was a partner at this law firm."

"I'm sorry."

"Thank you. I'd like to discuss the investigation of his death. And I'd like to do it in person."

"I understand. Let me reschedule a few things. I'll try to be there in an hour."

"You're a mensch, Nils Shapiro."

We hung up. I did not have a few things to reschedule. I could have been there in fifteen minutes. But I didn't want to appear eager, which is a detriment when meeting prospective clients. Same goes for when meeting women, children, and dogs. I showered off another layer of August, shaved, threw on khakis, black wing tips, and a pressed white shirt. I left the shirt untucked for ventilation and to convey a dash of apathy. I clunked down the four cement steps from the factory floor to the loading dock. The steps were sweaty. So was the metal hand railing. I opened the heavy service door and stepped into the August sauna. Some asshole had just poured a bucket of water on the rocks.

It was a four-block walk to enter Minneapolis's skyway system at Parking Lot C near Target Field. The Minneapolis Skyway System is over eleven miles of enclosed bridges connecting downtown buildings to one another on the second and third floors, allowing its citizens to move about, never having to go outside. Just like hamsters in a Habitrail. I walked over a mile through air-conditioned bliss, passing over the homeless and indigent, the only street life that does exist outside the glass enclosures when the weather is too hot or too cold or too wet.

The law firm of Halferin Silver filled a wing of offices on the twentieth floor of some tower on Ninth Street. It was unpretentious as far as downtown law firms go. The walls were neither oak nor crotch mahogany but simple painted sheetrock. Numbered prints made up most of the art collection as opposed to tax-sheltering originals. A receptionist sat behind a curved desk made of cherry wood. It had a 1990s feel to it, and so did she.

The woman had an equine nose and short, jet-black hair teased into something that might have looked good on Joan Jet. She wore heavy makeup and a purple and pink polyester combination of blouse and jacket. A telephone headset seemed to hold everything above her neck in place. The desk spared me the rest of her outfit.

She said, "Good afternoon. How may I help you?"

"Nils Shapiro to see Ian Halferin."

"One moment, please."

She didn't hesitate before she said it, but as she pushed buttons and spoke in her professional, discreet tone, I saw my name register behind her makeup. The Twin Cities' Jewish community is a small, well-greased grid. There is no more than one degree of separation between each of us. We all know someone who helped fund the Coen Brothers' first movie, *Blood Simple*. We all know someone who grew up down the street from former U.S. Senator Al Franken. We all know a relative of Bob Dylan. We all know a descendant of Isadore Blumendfeld, better known as Kid Cann, a Minneapolis gangster and close associate of Al Capone and Meyer Lansky.

I hadn't done much to deserve my notoriety other than solve a few crimes, including the Duluth murders five years ago, but it didn't take much in this community to become talkworthy.

The receptionist said, "Mr. Halferin's assistant will be out momentarily. Can I offer you coffee or water?"

"No, thank you."

She smiled and swiveled away on her rolly chair as if she had something to do. I sat on a couch and looked at the cover of *Minneapolis-St. Paul* magazine. It made noise about the best doctors in town who I bet all just happened to be photogenic. I let it lie.

A large, modern sculpture sat in the corner. Probably another Arndt Kjellgren. Robin Rabinowitz's boyfriend had, apparently, sold a sculpture to Todd Rabinowitz's law firm. The piece was made of metal and had moving triangles, squares, and circles, each painted bright blue, green, or red. It was simple and complex at the same time, just like me. I decided I liked it.

A woman in her early thirties approached. "Hi. Mr. Shapiro. Celeste Sorensen. I'll take you to Mr. Halferin." She spoke bubbly cute and smelled like soap. A good kind of soap they sell at fine gift shops, not the chemical infused olfactory-bombs you can detect passing by a storefront. I stood, shook her hand, then walked with Celeste down hallways and around corners lined with more framed prints. She didn't shut up about the humidity, so my attention wandered. She had green eyes, shoulder-length blond hair, and an exercised body under a sleeveless blue linen dress. Rodin wouldn't have made her arms that defined. She must have had an all-you-can-bend pass at some yoga studio.

She said, "And here we are." She led me into Ian Halferin's office. It, too, was simple and understated. The man collected photography, mostly black and white. The print that caught my eye was a stack of books with the edges sawed off, bits of paper and hardcover scattered around the stack. I thought of thinking about what it meant but I was tired.

Ian Halferin stood six feet tall behind his desk. We shook hands and he said, "Nils. So good of you to come in."

"Happy to do it."

He wore a charcoal suit with a white shirt and baby blue tie. He had olive skin, short-cropped dark hair with a few gray threads, and warm brown eyes that might have smiled, but the solemnity of the day forbade it. His desk was clean and neat. I never trust someone with a clean and neat desk. Celeste and her soapy smell left. She closed the door behind her, and we sat down on opposite sides of Ian Halferin's spotless desk.

"Tough day around here. Will we be billing a lot of hours? I don't think so. Nor should we be. Poor Todd. God rest his soul."

"Tell me about him."

Ian Halferin took a breath, and his brow wrinkled. "Todd Rabinowitz was an excellent lawyer. More importantly, he was a lovely person and wonderful friend. We're like a family here, and I don't think I'd be the only one to say Todd was the favorite son. I'll be honest. I've had quite a cry this morning."

He didn't look like he'd had quite a cry. Maybe he had it on the inside.

"I'll be at the funeral and shivah all day tomorrow so I'm trying to hold myself together and get some things accomplished today, one of which is helping the police find the monster who did this to Todd."

"Oh," I said. "Did you mention he was murdered? I didn't catch that." The only personal effects in Ian Halferin's office were pictures of his family on the otherwise spotless credenza behind him. His wife, one daughter, and one son, each in a silver frame. I felt a twinge of envy mixed with more than a twinge of sadness.

Ian Halferin said, "I don't remember if I mentioned it or not. I'm sorry. Yes, Todd Rabinowitz was murdered. His wife, Robin, found him in the lake, fastened to his dock by a fishing stringer. Quite gruesome."

I said nothing.

Ian Halferin said, "Our firm is small. We don't employ our

own in-house investigator. We hire out for that. Usually it's one of a few independent P.I.s. You probably know them. But in this situation, I feel the most ethical and responsible thing to do is bring in someone new."

"To investigate what?"

"Todd's murder. We want the son of a bitch who did this to pay with his life."

"You're a lawyer, Ian. You must know Minnesota hasn't had the death penalty since 1911."

"Okay, okay, so not literally with his life. But do I want the monster to spend the rest of his days behind bars? Yes. Do I wish him great suffering? Absolutely." Ian Halferin unlocked his fingers so he could shake one at me. "May he wish he were dead."

I didn't know if I believed Ian Halferin. Maybe he was lying or maybe he was just used to talking in lawyer speak or salesman speak so you couldn't get a bead on what he was saying.

Halferin said, "And am I concerned that Todd's murder is related to a case he was working on? Absolutely. Because that could put everyone who works at this firm in danger." Halferin looked out the window and frowned. "I have one additional motive. And it's a sensitive one." He interlocked his fingers and placed his locked hands on his desk. "This firm represents Karin Tressler. Ah, I see by your expression maybe you don't like her or agree with her politics."

I wished there was something on Halferin's desk I could pick up and play with. Even a pen or nameplate or dish full of paper clips. But there was nothing. Ian Halferin's desk was unnatural. I said, "I don't care about Karin Tressler's politics."

He nodded. "My point is this: a partner at Halferin Silver has been murdered. It will draw attention to the firm. From the media, of course, but more importantly, from our clients. Do we want this attention? We do not. It could hamper our efforts to get Karin Tressler elected to the United States House of Representatives. So, personal and professional tragedy aside, we'd like this investigation wrapped up as soon as possible."

"You can't force the police to go faster than they're going to go. It's not possible. And I wouldn't advise trying. It will not reflect well on you or the firm or your precious Karin Tressler."

"Ah. You don't care for her."

I noticed a quarter in my right hand. I wondered when I'd fished it out of my pocket. "I don't want to get into a political discussion, but a lot of people don't care for her. People on both sides." I set the quarter on edge then gave it a flick with my left index finger. It spun like a top across Ian Halferin's too-clean desk you should clutter it up with some obstacles. I said, "Moving on."

Ian Halferin tried his best to ignore the spinning coin. He said, "All right. We'll move on. So this morning, after I stop grieving long enough to think, I wonder where we can find an independent investigator on short notice. Then as luck would have it, Annika Brydolf walks in and drops off her résumé. The Lord works in wonderful and mysterious ways." The quarter spun off the desk and made a soft thud on the carpet. I did not pick it up. Halferin said, "I think, could this Annika Brydolf be our outside investigator? I look at her references and see your name. Of course, I've heard of you. And I think, is Nils Shapiro the investigator I want to hire?"

It had happened before. A subject I was investigating tried to hire me. It's an excellent way to serve your client and an excellent way to lose your P.I. license. Especially if you're double-agenting a lawyer who knows the rules and how to have them enforced.

I said, "I'm in deep on a couple cases I can't abandon right now. I can't in good conscience take on another client. I just wouldn't be able to do my best."

"I see . . ."

"But if you hire Annika, I will, as a favor to you, consult with her on a daily basis. Annika and I have a shorthand so I can make time to do that. And I will investigate directly if my schedule clears up. No guarantees. And only as a favor to you and this firm and out of respect for your loss. I will not accept payment. Nor can I enter into a written or verbal contract. Again, I'm just not available to do so."

Ian Halferin stared down at his desk and said, "So my choices are to either hire Annika Brydolf and get your experience and wisdom on the side, or to hire someone else."

"Yes."

"I'll have to think about that."

"Please do. And hey, I have a question. Is that sculpture in your reception area an original Arndt Kjellgren?"

"It is. Why do you ask?"

"I just noticed most of the other art pieces here are signed reproductions. Does the sculpture belong to the firm or one of the partners?"

"The firm. We purchased it ten years ago. Bought it before Kjellgren got famous. Probably the best investment we've made. If you're here enough, you may get to meet him."

"Kjellgren? Is he a client or a lawyer?"

Ian Halferin smiled. "Neither. Because his sculptures have moving parts, he services them a few times a year. Does the work himself. Says he doesn't trust anyone else to do it right."

"They're giant mobiles, not particle accelerators."

"I know, but he's an artist. What are you going to do? His sculptures are all over the country. I don't know how he gets to them all."

I said, "Artists don't have to go to meetings. That frees up all sorts of time."

He laughed, then realized our meeting had gone on for quite some time. He thanked me for coming in, shook my hand, and walked me out of Halferin Silver.

6

I left Halferin Silver and meandered the skyways to see if I could discover something new then find my way back without a map. It was a game I played as a kid and often lost. The theme of that game turned into my job. And my life. But I still liked trying to get lost in the skyways, and pretended my survival was at stake despite passing dozens of restaurants, sundry shops, and pharmacies.

I had long given up at the game when I spotted her from the second floor of the IDS Crystal Court. The second floor is like a catwalk circumnavigating the block-large building. It's lined with shops and restaurants and open to the granite-floored courtyard below. I'd just walked out of Starbucks sucking iced-coffee through a straw and had stopped at the railing to look down. The Crystal Court hadn't changed much in thirty years. Trees grew out of big planters, fed by daylight filtered through the glass ceiling. Kiosks dotted the space as if it were the center of a shopping mall or a park in Manhattan.

Micaela Stahl walked out of the store that sells Minnesota souvenirs—cutting boards shaped like Minnesota, candy named after and resembling wildlife droppings, wild rice, loon-embossed T-shirts, and other must-haves. Her strawberry-blond frizz was pulled back into a ponytail. That's how she secured it on hot, humid days. She wore jeans, a cream linen top, and carried a paper bag, as if she were a tourist visiting from a distant land like North Dakota. She had told me she was going to New York for the day on business. Either there had been a change of plans or she'd lied.

Micaela headed for the doors on Nicollet Mall, which is not an indoor mall but a street for pedestrians, taxis, and busses. No regular cars allowed. The game of trying to get lost was over. It was time to play a new game.

I dropped my iced-coffee in a garbage can and jumped on the escalator, quick-stepping my way down, weaving through content standers-still. Micaela exited the building and took a left on the mall toward Eighth Street. I jogged to the door to catch up, got spit out of the revolving door, and spotted her waiting at the light to cross. I jogged a few more steps then slowed to a walk and hung back twenty feet, close enough to see her strawberry-blond ponytail but far enough to duck behind a giant Scandinavian if she turned around.

The light turned green. Micaela crossed Eighth Street, passed Men's Warehouse and Panera—maybe Nicollet Mall was like a shopping mall—then turned left into the Medical Arts Building. I followed. The building is a 1920s masterpiece. The first floor is stone and gold with a wide marble swirly staircase and hanging chandeliers. It's art deco or a precursor to that style but it's in mint condition and beautiful and maybe that's why it hadn't been knocked down and replaced by a big box filled with blue-white lights shining on disposable merchandise.

Micaela turned a corner into a narrow bay lined with elevators. There were a dozen or so other people perusing the directory or waiting to go up. The space was too tight to blend in unnoticed, so I turned around, rounded the corner, and waited to hear the ding signaling an arriving elevator.

My ex-wife and current bed partner was in town but told me she was going to New York. It was an unnecessary lie. We rarely talk during the day. I would have assumed she was working and if I happened to run into her downtown she could have easily said she had driven down from her Linden Hills office for lunch. Or a meeting. Or a doctor's appointment. I wouldn't have questioned it. Her lie made no sense.

I heard a ding then peeked around the corner. Micaela entered the third elevator on the left with a scrum of others. I waited for the elevator doors to close, then walked toward it and looked up at the numbered lights above.

The elevator stopped at floors 4, 9, 12, and 20 before heading back down. I made a note in my phone and headed over to the directory, took a picture, made sure it was readable when zoomed in, then headed toward home.

Ten minutes later, my phone rang. It was Annika.

She said, "Halferin Silver just called. They want me to come in at five."

"Good. Just treat it like a normal job. Straight investigation. I'll check with Ellie to make sure he can stomach the questionable ethics of this. But we'll do our jobs, and hopefully, both our clients will find out who killed Todd Rabinowitz, whether they like the answer or not."

"Got it."

"Tell Halferin we haven't had a chance to talk. I'm on a stakeout and couldn't be reached. See what he says. We'll compare notes later."

"Okay," said Annika. "Hey, should I tell Ellegaard if I see him before I go over to Halferin Silver?"

"Let me speak to him first. He isn't going to like this, and I'd like to spare you the blowback."

"I have no problem with that."

My call-waiting buzzed. I glanced at the screen. "Shit. That's him now. Consider him told."

I stopped in the skyway just past City Center, looked northeast up Hennepin Avenue, and took Ellegaard's call. "Hey. Get some sleep?"

He said, "Enough, yeah. Listen. I have to ask you for an unusual favor."

"Good. Because I'm about to ask you for one, too."

"I don't like the sound of that."

"It's not that bad." Then I told him what happened with Robin Rabinowitz and her suspicion of Halferin Silver, and how I helped get Annika hired there working the same case but for a different client.

"Dang it, Shap. We'll get in real trouble if they find out."

"Only if someone files a complaint. And if neither killed Todd Rabinowitz—"

"Whoa, whoa," said Ellegaard.

"Hear me out. If neither murdered him, and we find the killer, they'll both get what they hired us to do. And if one of them did it, the guilty client will be in no position to file a complaint, and the other client will have no reason to complain."

"Shap, you're making my stomach hurt."

"You should be used to that by now."

Two cops rousted a sleeping vagrant on the street below. They sat him up and leaned him back against the wall of the ugliest building in town. One cop produced a pouch of juice like the kind kids drink, poked a straw into it, and handed it to the homeless man.

Ellegaard said, "Why do you put us in situations like this? It's like you don't think."

"It seemed like a good idea at the time. Still does."

"That's the kind of answer I get from my daughters, which is a perfect segue into the favor I'm going to ask you."

I said nothing and could feel Ellegaard's hesitation.

"Molly and I are having problems with Emma. She's making some bad choices. It's like she's just not thinking. Sound familiar?"

The cops helped the vagrant to his feet, handed him a bag of what looked like trail mix, and sent him on his way.

I said, "How can I help?"

"Sit down with her. Talk to her. She likes you. You two will communicate in the same language. Molly and I do not speak it."

"What do you want me to say to her?"

"Does it matter what I want?"

I saw my reflection in the skyway glass. I had a stupid smile on my face. Fucking Ellegaard. The guy knew me. "I'm happy to talk to Emma. I get the gist of what she needs to hear."

"Thanks, Shap. Molly and I need you on this. Our concern for Emma is number one. But she's also the oldest of three girls and setting an example for Olivia and Maisy whether she realizes it or not. We have to get her straightened out."

"When's a good time?"

"Tonight. Take her to dinner. Anywhere you want. On me."

"You sure? We're going to drink a lot of whiskey and you know I like the good stuff."

Ellegaard laughed. We talked a little more about Emma, then he agreed to look the other way when it came to how Annika and I investigated the murder of Todd Rabinowitz.

I will ruin him yet.

7

I walked back to the coat factory, opened my laptop, and looked up the offices on floors 4, 9, 12, and 20 of the Medical Arts Building. I found podiatrists, oncologists, ophthalmologists, cardiologists, endocrinologists, ENTs, dentists, and everything in between. Micaela could have visited any of them, and I wasn't even sure she visited as a patient. She could have gone to support a patient. She could have a doctor or nurse friend and was meeting him or her for coffee. She could have been meeting someone in the medical field on business.

My chance sighting of Micaela Stahl had led to a dead end. If I wanted to know what she was doing in the Medical Arts Building and why she hadn't gone to New York like she'd said,

I'd have to flat-out ask her. But it wasn't any of my business. I was her bed partner. Nothing more.

I changed out of my big-boy clothes then threw on an old green T-shirt, a pair of shorts, and Stan Smiths. I don't wear sandals. I'd rather have white feet and keep my toes to myself. Besides, I was going to visit a metal sculptor. Open-toed shoes could be a hazard.

Arndt Kjellgren lived and worked in an orange-bricked building near the corner of Hennepin and Stinson in Northeast Minneapolis. It's the kind of neighborhood where roads dip under metal train trellises covered in rust and graffiti. I parked the Volvo in a gravel lot and walked around back to enter the building near a loading dock not unlike the coat factory's. Whatever the building had been—maybe a coat factory of its own—it wasn't anymore. I walked in search of a directory and passed offices for small, trendy ad agencies, branding agencies, web developers, and other businesses I didn't understand. I found one toward the front entrance. A TV monitor mounted on the wall listed the building's tenants. It didn't speak well of the businesses that they were listed on a monitor as if they came and went as often as airplanes.

Arndt Kjellgren's studio wasn't listed, so I wandered the concrete-floored hallways looking for anything that resembled an art studio. I didn't find it but spotted a guy hand-trucking two gas cylinders toward the loading dock near where I'd entered. He wore a Polaris trucker's hat, solid in front and mesh in back, a long brown ponytail jutting out above the hat's plastic adjustment strip, and a heavy beard. He wore blue coveralls, the sleeves pushed up revealing scars enveloping both forearms. Probably not uncommon in the welding business.

It's not polite to stare, so I looked up at the man's smiling brown eyes. A welding gas delivery man is the perfect way to find a metal sculptor.

I said, "Excuse me. You wouldn't by any chance be taking those to a metal sculptor, would you?"

He stopped and looked me up and down as if he was considering asking me out. "No, man. These are his empties. Taking them back." His voice was hoarse and weak. Maybe he talked too much or took an iron bar in the larynx while welding.

"Oh," I said. "Do you know which space is Arndt Kjellgren's? He wrote it down for me on a piece of scrap paper but I think I washed it—can't find it anywhere."

"Been there," he said. It sounded like it hurt him to talk. But he smiled, displaying a perfect set of teeth. Maybe it was time for me to try some of that tooth-whitening stuff. Even coveralls-wearing guys with trucker hats and beards were upping the teeth bar.

"I checked the directory but Kjellgren isn't listed."

"Yeah," said the guy. "He's a bit weird."

"Nothing against the arts, but they do attract their share of atypical personalities."

He chuckled. "No shit."

"My boss is a collector. We're commissioning Kjellgren on a piece." I laughed. "That is if I can find his fucking studio. Dude ever hear of putting up a sign?"

The gas guy considered my plight for a few seconds then said, "Far northwest corner of the building. Gray door. Paper over the window."

"Thanks." I navigated to the northwest corner of the building, where I found one closed gray steel door next to a sidelight window covered with newspaper from the inside. I saw no sign informing me who the door belonged to. No welcome mat. Nothing but a muffled blast of music from within. It was Neutral Milk Hotel's "Holland, 45." It made me pre-like Arndt Kjellgren, and I wasn't happy about it.

I knocked and waited. Nothing. Knocked again. Still nothing. I grabbed the doorknob. It turned. I pushed the door open. The music pounded clear from a hi-fi system against a brick wall. A stack of McIntosh electronics with their blue and green lights powered gigantic wooden vintage speakers. A turntable sat on top of the rack. Long, high shelves filled with record albums extended both left and right of the electronics stack. Thousands of records. Dude was analogue. The son of a bitch was making my job hard.

He wore white jeans and a white shirt, both splotched with paint as if he were the mixing palette. His face hid behind a welding mask, torch in hand, connecting or cutting metal—I couldn't tell which. I looked away from the flame made silent by the music. Then the song ended, the last on the record's side. The man set down the torch and lifted his mask, revealing a thirtyish-year-old face, clean-shaven, shiny with sweat. He started toward the stereo, I assumed to change the vinyl.

I said, "Excuse me." He stopped, turned and looked.

He said, "Hey, man," then continued toward the turntable.

"You got a minute?"

"You the P.I.?"

"How'd you know?"

"Lucky guess." He removed the vinyl disc from the turntable and returned it to its sleeve then slipped the sleeve inside the cardboard jacket. He said, "New York Dolls, Aretha, or Leonard Cohen?"

"You got a few minutes first?"

"Depends which one you pick."

Arndt Kjellgren insisted on playing a game on his field with his ball by his rules. And that's pretty much all I needed to know about Arndt Kjellgren. He offered excellent choices, but that was part of the fix. I said, "I'd rather hear a little Hot 8 Brass Band if you got it."

"What?"

"Hot 8 Brass Band. You probably don't have it. Throw on whatever."

He looked confused then turned toward the shelf, removed an iPad, and said, "Is that Hot or Haute?"

"Hot. H-O-T."

He tapped the screen then changed the input on the pre-amp. A few seconds later the room filled with the rhythmic sounds of bass drum, snare, and tuba. He listened, nodded, then looked at me and said, "Dope band. Right on." He lowered the volume then walked up to me and shook my hand. "Arndt."

"Nils."

"Kombucha?"

"Why not?"

Arndt Kjellgren had a makeshift kitchen like mine but with newer and better appliances. He walked over to a double refrigerator, removed two bottles of red kombucha, then led me to a sitting area of ultra-modern couches and chairs that looked like blocks but were upholstered in some kind of all-weather canvas. They surrounded a coffee table made of shattered glass over tangled metal. I guessed it was high-end patio furniture, probably to withstand the odors and potential friendly fire mishaps of indoor welding and painting.

"So," he said, "you probably want to know all about me and Robin. The police did when they were here a couple hours ago."

"The only difference is I work for Robin."

He laughed. "Really. I figured you guys all work for Truth and the Good of Mankind."

"You obviously don't know many of us."

"Right. You're in it for the money."

"I don't think that's true. But if I make some, I'll let you know."

He smiled then wiped his cold bottle across his forehead. "Fire away, man."

I guessed he was ten years younger than Robin. Twenty years younger than Todd Rabinowitz. Arndt Kjellgren still had a lot of boy in him. He looked like a kid making stuff in his garage. Another mark in the plus column. I said, "How did you meet Robin?"

"Charity event at the Walker. Rich people paid for a private tour and to meet a few artists. I was in the sculpture garden with one of my pieces. We talked for a while. The tour moved on but Robin stayed behind."

"Love in the garden."

"Not at first. But I've been making sculptures since I was sixteen. The job's got some perks and one of them is women who fantasize about being with an artist. I'm not a fucking priest or anything so if I'm interested I invite 'em over to see the studio."

"So this place is a Venus flytrap."

He sighed. "Dude, it's not that predatory. I don't lure women in. They're chasing something. And I'll be honest, most aren't that thrilled after they catch it. But Robin's different."

I twisted off the cap of my kombucha. A pink foam bubbled to the top. "How long ago did this chance meeting happen?"

"About two years ago."

"So it's a coincidence one of your sculptures is in the reception area where Todd Rabinowitz worked."

"Yeah," said Kjellgren, "but not that big of a coincidence. My sculptures are all over this town. It's not like I make Post-it notes, but my work's in a lot of offices."

"All right. Tell me about Robin."

"So, wait," he said. "*She* hired *you*, right?"

"Right."

"Then why do you sound like you're investigating her?"

I sipped my kombucha. Strawberry. "Robin hired me because she knows you two will be suspects and she wants me to help clear your names by finding whoever killed Todd. The more I know about Robin the better I can do that."

"Ah. Like if she has a tendency to fuck artists, maybe any collectible asshole could have killed Robin's husband." The boyish twinkle was gone from Arndt Kjellgren's eyes. I'd struck some sort of nerve, and it wasn't a good one.

I let whatever irked him simmer for a tick then said, "Yeah. Something like that." He couldn't hide his surprise. I didn't give him the conventional Minnesota denial. I didn't pretend we were all nice decent folks who didn't understand ulterior motive. Yet, he still seemed to hold out hope for just that. Something to rebel against. Maybe Minnesota nice, or his rejection of it, fueled his artmaking. But he wasn't going to get it from me. I knew when to play that card, and this wasn't the time. I said, "If Robin's fucking her way through artists, or if you have a habit of falling for wealthy, married Semitic-looking women ten years older than you, it's good for me to know. Maybe Robin's the one who finally stole your heart but she hadn't worked up the courage to leave Christmas Lake and her Audi Q7 for something more Bohemian. And maybe you'd lost patience. It happens."

He said, "Look. The thing you got to understand is Robin did not hate Todd. Sometimes she said she did, but the truth is they'd just grown apart. He was re-upping his membership in the old boys' club, and she had grown into a more thoughtful place. I don't mean considerate. I mean full of thought. The house on the lake doesn't mean anything to her. She has a fucking inner life. She doesn't care about everyday bullshit."

"Did she want to divorce Todd because of you?"

Kjellgren took a gulp of kombucha then said, "Nah, man. They had grown apart, and his politics embarrassed her. I'd even say his politics disgusted her. Guess it's happened to a lot of couples. My parents almost split up over a few issues. People fall for the shit they see on TV and dig in. A waste of energy if you ask me."

"Did Todd's politics anger Robin?"

"Dude, that is a stupid question. His politics offended her. She lost respect for him and his money. No more love. No more romance. That is all. And that's how I know she didn't kill Todd."

"Or have him killed?"

"Never. No need. She didn't give a shit about that life. And don't be a fucking dick and judge my net worth 'cause I'm covered in paint. I shit out a piece of metal and get fifty grand. Robin was just trying to . . . what's that bullshit word . . . de-couple. In like a constructive way. You know what I mean?"

"Did you ever meet Todd?"

"No. Robin invited me to a party at the house. We were still just friends then, but I knew how I felt about her and didn't want anyone, especially Todd, to pick up on that. I'm not skilled at hiding how I feel. I didn't expect anything would happen between us, but I didn't want to send the wrong message."

He wiped his forehead with his arm and said, "Fuck it's hot. Between the torch and shitty air-conditioning . . . I hate this fucking time of year."

"It won't last. It never does." Arndt Kjellgren took no solace in my Buddhist tagline. "What do you do for fun besides make art and see Robin?"

He looked at me with contempt. "What, are you writing my online dating profile?"

"If you don't want to cooperate then don't cooperate. I don't care. Just doing my job."

"You know, dude? You're kind of an asshole."

I guessed what he'd said was true—he really couldn't hide his feelings. I said, "Really? I don't get that much. But I'll take it."

He said, "I don't know what else you want to hear."

"Nothing," I said. I stood. "I've heard plenty. Thanks for the kombucha. Good luck with your next visit from the cops." I turned and walked away.

Arndt Kjellgren said, "Wait. What next visit from the cops?"

I opened the door and walked out.

8

I was thinking about my Micaela sighting and obnoxious artists while blasting The Suicide Commandos in my hockey mom mobile as I pulled into my loading dock. I shut off the Volvo then pressed a button on the car's ceiling. The loading dock door shut behind me. I got out of the car, and she was standing there. She said, "I need a drink."

"How did you get in here?"

"I walked in when you drove in. You didn't seem to notice."

"Yeah well," I said, "I have a bit of a space-out problem. Didn't we agree on rules of contact? And the rules were no contact?"

Robin Rabinowitz wore white shorts, white Birkenstocks, and a pink sleeveless top with a deep V-neck. She said, "I take your rules as a suggestion. A suggestion I don't like very much. I can't be alone, not after what happened to Todd."

"You must have friends."

"None who can protect me."

"Didn't the police offer to post someone outside your house?"

"Yes, but then I'd be trapped there, and I hate feeling trapped." Her eyes got big again. I couldn't tell if it was genuine fear or a trick she'd learned to gain sympathy. Robin was a little too smooth, too coquettish, although the play seemed less for love and more for things like getting out of a speeding ticket or convincing a private detective he should be her bodyguard. "And I can't be sequestered from Arndt."

"That explains how your boyfriend knew who I was."

"I heard about your visit."

"When? I was there ten minutes ago."

"He called right after you left. Said he didn't like you very much."

"Huh. I adore him."

She smiled and twisted her Birkenstock's cork sole on the concrete floor. "Can we sit down and talk?"

"I thought you needed a drink."

"You don't have anything here?"

"I have alcohol. I don't have air-conditioning."

"I don't mind."

"Really? It's so hot in here a camel would mind. But all right. Come on."

I led her up the sweaty concrete steps and into the kitchen. She said, "Awesome place."

"It's home. At least for a little while longer. So, I have Irish whiskey, gin, vodka, and this." I opened my industrial fridge. I had a few bottles of sauvignon blanc. Micaela's drink of choice— too sweet for me—but I kept them in case we ever ended up at my place. We never had. I pulled out a bottle and showed it to her.

She said, "Cold wine sounds good. What are you having?"

I looked at the clock. 5:30. I don't like to drink before the sun sets. It's easy in the winter when the weak ball of fire disappears in the afternoon, but not so easy in the summer when Minnesota's northern latitude keeps the sky light until 10:00 P.M. I said, "I'll have a little Irish whiskey. You sure you don't want to go somewhere with air-conditioning?"

"I don't mind the heat," said Robin. "I'm good here."

I poured the wine and Irish then we sat on the soft furniture in my makeshift living room, an assortment of Craigslist finds and what I had in the tiny shitbox I moved out of almost two years ago. I said, "I hear Todd's funeral is tomorrow."

"It was supposed to be. But they won't release his body until the autopsy is done."

"What about shivah?"

"It's at Todd's parents'. His ex-wife and kids will be there. The family never embraced me. I don't want to go, but I suppose that would look bad." I agreed with a glance. "This is a mess. I'm not going to have a normal life for a long time."

The sounds of afternoon rush hour filtered in through the coat factory's high awning windows. Robin slipped out of her Birkenstocks and said, "Is it okay if I put my feet up?"

"Have you had your shots?" She smiled. "For your protection. I don't know where most of this furniture has been."

She said, "I'll take my chances." She set her brown feet and painted toes on a sage green corduroy ottoman, the fine gold chain still around one ankle. She sipped her wine and said, "Good *vino*."

"I never touch the stuff. I'll take your word for it. How did it go with the police today?"

"Well, it wasn't anything like what I've seen on *Law and Order*. They were nice. No one slugged me in the stomach or threw me against the wall. They asked basic questions. I told them everything I told you."

I felt flushed from the heat, humidity, and whiskey. I took off my shoes.

"How did they respond when you told them about Arndt?"

"They were interested, that's for sure. They'd already talked to him. Cute ankle socks."

"Thank you. Do you think the police were harder on Arndt than they were with you?"

"He didn't think they were bad."

"How did he take the news that I asked you not to see him for a while?"

"He wasn't thrilled about it." She raised her empty wineglass. "Do you mind if I get a refill?"

"I'll get it."

"No. You sit."

The widow of fourteen hours walked toward the kitchen then disappeared behind a wall of books, which was the only interior wall other than the few in the corner that defined the bedroom and bathroom. I heard the fridge open and a moment later she returned with the bottle of sauvignon blanc and my bottle of Redbreast. "I hate having a second alone." She poured the drinks and reclaimed her spot, bare feet up on the ottoman.

"Two's my limit. I have dinner with a young lady tonight."

"Oh? Someone special?"

"Emma Ellegaard."

"Molly's daughter?"

"She's going through some teenage stuff. They asked if I'd talk to her."

"'Cause it takes one to know one?"

"I suppose."

We talked for another hour. I asked Robin how her attorney, Nellie Chang, did at her meeting with the police. Robin thought she did fine. Everyone was so pleasant. Robin didn't stop talking and didn't stop drinking—she killed the bottle of wine. Finally, after a silence of a few minutes, she said, "Well, I guess I should go to that goddamn shivah."

I said, "You're not driving anywhere. Take a Lyft or a cab."

"Maybe I'll just call and say I'm too upset. I can't keep it together. I need the funeral before I can face people."

"I'd buy it."

Robin's eyes got big and wet again. She said, "Can I stay here while you're gone?"

She was tired, drunk, and scared. Of what, I'm not sure, but she was scared. I couldn't send her out into the world that way. I said, "Of course. I have cheese and crackers and takeout menus. Or I can order you something when I'm at dinner with Emma and bring it back. I doubt we'll be there long."

"You know," said Robin, "I think I just want to shut my eyes."

I stood, walked over to her, and held out an open palm. She placed her hand on top of mine. I said, "Thank you. But I want your keys."

She shut her eyes. "They're in my purse in the kitchen. Help yourself."

I told her where the bathroom was and to make herself at home, took the keys from Robin's purse, then left to meet Emma Ellegaard.

9

I slugged through traffic crawling west on 394 to meet Emma Ellegaard at Crave, a decent link in a chain restaurant with a varied menu leaving little for a fifteen-year-old to complain about. I considered using my road time to call Micaela and confront her about her non-trip to New York but decided I'd wait for her to contact me. I did connect with Ellegaard to tell him about my visits with Arndt Kjellgren and Robin Rabinowitz. We planned to meet for breakfast with Molly so I could give them my uneducated assessment of their daughter, then at the office to catch up with Annika.

St. Louis Park's shopping and eating area called the West End is not on the west end of anything, including St. Louis Park. It's in the middle of the first-ring suburb. It's an outdoor mall, which contains restaurants, shops, a multiplex, and monstrous parking ramps. Across the road is a Home Depot and a Costco and a fake pond with an aeration fountain that attracts geese and ducks year-round.

Emma Ellegaard was standing by the hostess stand when I walked in. She had her mother's smile and dark hair and her father's blue eyes and gawky limbs. She wore old jeans and a denim work shirt.

"Hi, Mr. Shapiro." She gave me a hug.

"Emma, stop growing. It's getting embarrassing." She smiled. I said, "And I know your parents make you call me Mr. Shapiro, but I've never liked that, so tonight please call me Nils or Shap or hey you. Cool?"

She nodded, then the hostess walked us to our table. We caught up with small talk about school and volleyball then ordered dinner from a perky young woman with a Miss Minnesota smile who'd gotten too much sun over the weekend, her peeling skin splotched pink within the tan. I've had plenty of three-hour dinners, but didn't want to have one with a fifteen-year-old, so I jumped right in when the server left. "So, Emma, your parents are pretty upset. Do you think whatever's going on with you is as big of a deal as they do?"

She shook her head and twisted her mouth into what was both somehow a smile and frown. "They're so weird. I don't get it."

"Well, you know their concern isn't because they hate you, right? It's not their goal to make you miserable."

"Yeah . . ." She shook her head again.

"But what?"

"They want me to be just like them. It's so not fair. Olivia's like them, and good for her, but I'm different. They don't get me. They think I'm . . ." She paused, searched for the word, then said, "messed up."

"You can swear if you want. I don't care."

"Really? I think that would be weird."

"I'm not saying you have to swear, just that you can. I won't think any less of you."

"Would you swear around me?"

"If you started it, hell yes."

She laughed and said, "You're weird, Shap."

"I've been called worse. So, I know you stay out past curfew sometimes. What else are they upset about?"

"Ugh. Like everything. My hair. My clothes. I like thrift shop stuff. My mom thinks it's gross. The music I listen to. The people I hang with. My Twitter and Instagram. My fingernail polish. It's like stop. Enough."

Someone brought a basket of bread that also contained chip-like cracker things that stood high and pointed like stalagmites. I took one and broke off a piece then said, "Are you drinking?"

She looked away then shrugged and said, "I've tried it."

"Pot?"

"Tried it."

"X?"

"No."

"Anything else? Coke? Meth? Speed?"

"No. Just had a few beers and smoked pot two times."

"Did you like it?"

She shrugged. "It was okay."

"All right."

Curiosity all over her face. She said, "All right?"

"Are you a drug addict?"

"No."

"A drunk?"

"No way."

"Then all right."

"I don't get it."

"When you get your driver's license, no drinking and drugs if you have to get behind the wheel. No exceptions."

"I know."

"I believe you. Let me ask you this, Emma. How would you want your mom and dad to behave if it were up to you?"

"What?"

"If you were the boss of everything, how would things be different at home?"

She looked down and shook her head. "I don't know."

"What do you want them to understand better?"

When she looked up, her eyes were wet. "I just want them to not make such a big deal out of everything."

"Yeah," I said. "I get that. That's fair. But what would you do if one of your sisters was doing something that concerned you? I know they're younger, but what if they were hanging with the wrong crowd or just fucking something up that they shouldn't? Or they were just being mysterious or evasive? What if you found a joint in Olivia's jacket pocket? Would you let it go? Would you say something to her?"

She nodded.

"You'd probably be way cooler about it than your mom and dad. Probably take Olivia to a restaurant like this and have a talk with her."

She laughed and wiped away her tears. The waitress brought

our meals, sensed the gravity of our conversation, and left. We ate for a while without talking about anything other than the food, then Emma said, "Everything just sucks."

I said, "Agreed."

"Really?"

"Hell yeah. But that's life. It's about the journey. You know where you are. You see where you want to get to. But life doesn't make it easy. So you got to deal with shit. So what? What else do you have to do?"

"That's your philosophy?"

"At the moment, it is," I said. "Listen, I'm the oldest of three kids. I tried not to get in trouble because that would open my parents' eyes to a long list of possible wrongdoings and make it a lot harder on my brother and sister. You know what I'm saying?"

"Yeah. Don't get in trouble."

"More like don't get caught."

She laughed. "Oh my God, I can't believe that's the advice you're giving me."

"And as far as school goes," I said, "the reason to do well is not because your parents want you to. The reason to do well is so you have choices when you're older. If you end up emptying those portable toilets at construction sites for a living, then great. But do it because you want to, not because you have to."

Emma thought about that for a full minute, took another forkful of stir-fry, then said, "Thanks, Shap. I mean, seriously."

"I don't know much, Emma. Ask anyone. But I do know if you try to pretend to be someone you're not, it'll mess you up in all sorts of ways. So be who you are, but be nice about it. You don't realize it yet, but you got really lucky in the parent lottery.

And whether you like it or not, your sisters look up to you. Look out for yourself like you'd look out for them."

She started to say something, but stopped, nodded, smiled, and wiped away another tear.

We ordered chocolate globs for dessert, ate them while bullshitting about this and that, then I drove Emma home to Plymouth. I didn't go in, but texted Ellegaard and Molly it went well, and I'd fill them in during breakfast.

I returned home and found Robin passed out on my couch. Her face was swollen, and her eyeliner smeared. She'd worked her way through a second bottle of sauvignon blanc and was either drunk or in a diabetic coma. I wondered who this woman was and why she was in my coat factory. She might have been so used to playing the pretty-girl card that she couldn't stop herself. Maybe she thought if she could just keep playing that card, she'd be okay, whether or not she had anything to do with her husband's death. Playing the pretty-girl card was her go-to move. Her comfort place.

I wedged a proper pillow under her head and covered her with a light blanket then put myself to sleep, leaving a nightlight on in the bathroom in case she needed to find her way.

I woke before Robin and decided to go out for coffee so the Nespresso machine didn't wake her. I descended the sweaty loading dock steps and twisted the service door knob. It turned, but the door wouldn't open. I pushed hard, but it didn't budge, as if the door had somehow been nailed shut. Old building. Old door. Something could have broken. But I had no idea what. I peered out the small, chicken-wired window within the door. Nothing appeared to be blocking it. It didn't make sense.

I no longer cared if I woke Robin. I walked into the garage part of the dock and pressed the button mounted on the wall to open the bay door. The motor jolted and hummed, but the bay door didn't budge. I hit the button again to stop the motor, then manually released the door from the drivetrain and tried to lift the door. I could not. Weird.

There were no other exits. I was locked inside my own home.

10

"What's going on?" I walked up the loading dock stairs to see Robin Rabinowitz, sleepy-eyed, wearing only bra and panties. She had no goddamn tan lines and no goddamn shame. Either she was born that way or Christmas Lake was more exciting than I thought.

I said, "I think we're locked in."

"What do you mean?"

"I mean the doors won't open. They're not locked. They just won't open."

"What about a window?"

"They don't start until twelve feet up. I could climb up to one, slip out, hang and fall. But I'd land on concrete. I hope I've established how delicate I am and . . . Hold on." I called Ellegaard.

"Ellie, it's me. I'm locked in the coat factory . . . No, locked *in*. The doorknob turns, but the door won't budge and neither will the bay door. Wondering if you and Molly can swing by and look at the doors from the outside . . . No, it's a twelve-foot drop . . . That's fine. Thanks." I hung up and turned on the coffee machine. "They have to run the girls to activities and won't be here for forty-five minutes. Coffee?"

"Please," said Robin. "Is it going to look bad I'm here?"

"Yep."

"Really?"

"Yeah, really. A day-old widow almost naked in her private detective's house after having spent the night, empty wine bottles scattered like bowling pins. It doesn't look great. You might want to hide in the bedroom."

"You're probably right. Especially if Molly is coming over. Shit."

She got up and walked down the loading dock steps, leaving the blanket behind. She looked out the thin strip of chicken-wired glass in the service door. "Oh, fuck."

"What?"

"I was worried Molly would see my car. It's a red Audi SUV. Kind of a giveaway. But either someone stole it or it got towed."

"You parked on the street?"

"That was bad?"

"Depends on how much money you put in the meter. They're enforced until midnight."

"What?! I've never heard of such a thing."

"Welcome to the city. And at least we know where your car is."

Robin slugged back up the stairs like a kid who just lost her dog. I made a couple of coffees by pushing a couple of buttons.

I cooked scrambled eggs with scallions and blistered cherry tomatoes with ginger and garlic and toasted four slices of rye. We drank coffee and ate and talked. Robin didn't put on her clothes. She was comfortable with her near nudity like a teenager in a bikini, which made me uncomfortable. She said, "What's with you and Irish stuff? Your whiskey. Your butter. I was looking at some of your vinyl last night. So much Van Morrison and The Pogues and Chieftans. I thought you were Jewish."

"I am. It's weird, I know."

She chewed a few seconds then started to cry. That made two meals in a row with a crying woman. She said, "Todd must have suffered so much. I used to be in love with him. I didn't want to be married to him anymore but I did care about him. Such a violent death. He was only fifty years old. He never got to have grandchildren. He'd talk about how much he looked forward to that. To seeing life continue . . ." She broke down and wailed like a child, either out of grief or guilt or both. I was pretty sure Robin Rabinowitz didn't physically kill Todd. But if she had him killed, perhaps it happened in a way she didn't expect. In a more violent and ugly way.

I let her cry for a couple minutes, but when my plate was empty, I got bored. I said, "Maybe Arndt Kjellgren isn't the gentle artist you think he is."

She shook her head. "Arndt's sensitive. He wouldn't kill someone. Arndt wanted me to leave Todd even if I didn't end up with Arndt. That's what he said. He wanted me to leave for my sake, not his."

"Those are easy words to say."

"You think he was lying?"

"I don't know, but I think Arndt Kjellgren welded us in here."

"What?" She said it while chewing with her mouth open. I didn't care for that.

"It's just a guess. I can't see outside, but the doorknob turns. Both the service door and bay door are just stuck. They're metal doors with metal frames. Well within a welder's wheelhouse. Did you tell him you were coming over here?"

She thought for a moment. "No. I don't think so. Besides, how would he know you live here?"

"The internet. He wasn't too pleased with me when I left so maybe he came by to finish the conversation. But he saw your red SUV parked outside. Then he came back later, saw your car was still here, freaked out, and welded us in here. Or maybe he just wedged shims between the doors and frames. Something. I don't know." Robin Rabinowitz looked sick. She stood and carried her plate to the sink. I got a text from Ellegaard. I said, "You should probably go hide now. The Ellegaards will be here in a minute."

Robin rinsed her plate, put it and her fork in the dishwasher, then said, "Thank you, Nils. I feel safe here. I couldn't have stayed by myself last night."

"Ask a friend to stay with you tonight."

She looked hurt, turned and walked into the living room. She grabbed her purse, clothes, sandals, pillow, and blanket then disappeared into the bedroom.

My phone rang a few minutes later. "Hey, Ellie."

"We're standing outside. Someone taped you in."

"Taped?"

"There's a metallic tape going around your service door and the same tape running along the bottom and up the sides of your bay door."

"So peel it off."

"I tried. It doesn't move."

Molly said in the background, "Tell him my key can't even scratch it."

"Molly tried—"

"I heard."

Ellegaard said, "The tape is made of metal. It looks like aluminum or steel. I'll have to call someone to cut you out."

I walked down the loading dock steps and saw Ellie through the narrow window in the service door. He waved. I walked back up the steps and to the bedroom, where I gave Robin an update on our confinement.

Forty-five minutes later, Ellegaard called again. He'd found a guy who said he could cut the tape with an acetylene torch. I asked if there were any other options. Apparently not. I said cut away and hoped the owner of the building planned on replacing the ground-level doors, because my meager security deposit wouldn't cover what was about to happen.

I heard the hiss of the torch and smelled burning metal. A few minutes later, Ellegaard and The Guy opened the door and entered. The Guy was large, wearing Gumby green coveralls and work boots. His long beard seemed like a bad idea for someone who worked with an open flame, but any portrayed lack of intelligence was counteracted by his ice-blue horn-rimmed eyeglasses. Ellegaard introduced him as Jim. I asked Jim what the hell was with the tape.

"Oh yeah well sure," said Jim, in a thick northern Minnesota accent, "it's metal-on-metal tape. Stuff's almost as strong as a weld or rivets. You see it on some buildings there. You know, like on the art gallery at the U, the one done by that big shot architect who makes buildings out of shiny metal, you know, what's his name?"

"Frank Geary," I said.

"Oh, yeah. That's him. This tape is the real deal. 3M makes it. It's good stuff." Jim stroked his beard, a clear sign he was thinking. "Kind of sucks some a-hole taped you in though. Kind of a dirty trick if you ask me."

Ellegaard said, "So who uses this tape, other than Frank Geary?"

"Oh, I don't know, lots of folks. Mostly industrial. It's a lot faster for bonding metal than rivets or welding. It comes in different kinds. You got your one-sided aluminum-looking stuff like on your doors and you got the double-sided kind. That'd be good for building something out of metal to make sure it's right before you start welding. 'Cause you know, a day of welding then cutting up your mistakes, heck that's no good. But a little spot of double-sided tape between two big pieces. You can break those apart okay if you have to, especially if your pieces aren't totally face-to-face and you got some leverage."

I said, "So maybe someone who makes large sculptures out of metal would be familiar with this tape?"

"Oh yeah," said Jim. "The tape would sure work great for that."

Ellegaard said, "I guess that makes cutting you out of here a Stone Arch expense." He handed Jim the company credit card.

Jim inserted a white plastic square into his phone then swiped the credit card. I tipped him a twenty. After Jim the welder left, Ellegaard said, "So who's hiding in the bedroom?"

I shook my head and said, "Dammit. Detectives are annoying."

"Yes, we are."

"A woman spent the night, but on the couch. I slept in my room. Nothing more happened."

"You're not mixing business and pleasure, are you, buddy?"

"There was nothing pleasurable about it. I promise."

"All right, then," said Ellie. "Meet us for breakfast in half an hour? Molly's already there catching up on emails."

"Give me an hour."

Ellegaard gave me a look his daughter Emma must have seen a thousand times. He nodded then left. I showered then got in the Volvo with Robin and headed to the impound lot. On the drive I said, "So, Mrs. Rabinowitz, it appears your boyfriend knows you spent the night. So does Ellegaard. And I bet the police showed up at shivah and saw you weren't there. Your behavior has been nothing but suspicious."

Robin looked out her side window. My phone rang. Micaela's name popped up on the Volvo's touch screen. Even if Robin hadn't been in the car, I had no desire to talk to my ex-wife. My curiosity about her non-trip to New York had morphed into resentment just as our relationship had morphed into dysfunction. I had become an alcoholic except instead of alcohol being my poison, it was Micaela Stahl. For me, no amount of her was healthy. One drop could lead to something lethal. I had tried to quit her then fell off the wagon. I had to try again. Maybe I could find some kind of twelve-step program. There is nothing I hate more than joining a group that meets on a regular basis with crappy snacks, but apparently, I needed help. Step one is admitting you have a problem. So far, so good. I touched the image of the red phone to decline Micaela's call.

Robin said, "Sorry I'm cramping your phone call time."

"It's not a problem."

She turned toward me and said, "Do you really think the police suspect me of killing Todd?"

"They do if they're good at their job."

She thought about that for a minute then said, "You know I had nothing to do with it, right?"

I looked right at her and said, "I am definitely good at my job."

11

At breakfast, I gave Molly and Ellegaard a report on my dinner with Emma, then Ellie and I headed to the office.

Six months ago, Stone Arch Investigations moved from our expensive, ugly offices to an old building on SE Main Street, just across the Mississippi River from downtown. It was on a cobblestone street, had old high-gloss wooden floors, and rough-hewn stone walls. I convinced Ellegaard to have *Stone Arch Investigations* stenciled in gold paint on our glass door in honor of the private detectives of the 1930s and '40s. I then pressed him for a receptionist with Veronica Lake hair who had to use an old rotary phone and intercom boxes. He said sure, as long as we wore suits to work every day, so I dropped it.

We met in the conference room. It had four walls made of

glass, a conference table, and six chairs. The constant push of cool air through the exposed ductwork created a whispery hum of deadness. It was the only thing I didn't like about the place. The conference room cone-of-silenced us from an empty office. Our receptionist had ditched us for law school. We were looking for a new one but had yet to fill the vacancy.

Ellegaard was getting jittery about us working the same murder investigation for different clients. He said, "We're walking a tightrope on this one. We have to be careful."

"Well," said Annika. She took a breath. When she had felt like an underling, she knew her role. But Ellegaard and I had been giving her more responsibility, and it sometimes made her nervous. "Yesterday I met with Ian Halferin and a few of the other partners, including Silver."

I said, "What's he like? I haven't met him."

"He's a her," said Annika.

The air conditioning whispered disparaging remarks in my direction. I said, "Sorry. I heard the firm was an old boys' club."

"It is," said Annika, "except for Susan Silver. She's in her fifties. Pleasant and tough. She and Halferin told me all about Todd, his business, and asked me to start by reading partially redacted summaries of his current and recent cases to see if I thought anything or anyone looked suspicious. So, one of the assistants set me up in a small conference room with a stack of files. Her name is Celeste."

I said, "Did she have ripped arms and smell like soap?"

"Yes," said Annika. "How'd you know?"

"She wore a sleeveless dress and smelled soapy when I was there yesterday. Blond?"

"That's her," said Annika.

"So do you think the soapy smell comes from actual soap or does she use soapy-smelling perfume?"

"Doesn't matter," said Ellegaard, "she smells like soap. I get it. What about her, Annika?"

"I was going through the files. Celeste brought me a cup of coffee I didn't ask for, closed the conference room door, and sat down. She said she was glad the firm hired me. Their other investigators were crusty old men who ate them out of bagels."

The air conditioner turned off and our glass room of silence grew even more quiet.

Annika said, "Then she just sat there, so I asked if she'd brought me all the files or if she was going to bring in more. She said I had all of them and that she and I should grab coffee or a drink sometime."

I said, "She hit on you?"

"No. It didn't have that vibe."

Ellegaard said, "What'd you say?"

"I said yes. Told her I could use a break and it sounded fun."

I said, "Hey, our little investigator is growing up. Nice job, Annika. When are you going to see her?"

"Tonight. We're going to happy hour at Keegan's."

"Good. See if she talks when she gets a few in her. Shouldn't take much. She can't weigh more than a hundred pounds."

Ellegaard said, "Did Celeste seem nervous or upset?"

Annika tilted her head. "I wouldn't say nervous, upset, or scared. To me she seemed more frustrated. Like she'd had it with whatever is going on and needed to vent."

I said, "When you go to happy hour, give the server your credit card the moment you sit down. Tell Celeste you insist on paying. Even though you're working for Halferin Silver, you'll write off drinks as a Stone Arch Investigations expense. Order food. Say we can afford it and badmouth us. We work you too hard. Don't pay you enough. We're an old boys' club and won't give you a seat at the table. Maybe she can relate and you two will bond and she'll be more willing to share."

Annika said, "Seriously?"

Ellegaard said, "Yeah. Shap's right. Make us the bad guy. That could help with the camaraderie."

Annika's phone rang. She looked at the screen and said, "It's Halferin."

I said, "Put it on speaker."

She answered her phone. "Hello."

"Annika?"

"Yes. Mr. Halferin?"

"I wonder if you could come in today. I just received an unpleasant phone call from a man named Arndt Kjellgren."

"What was unpleasant about it?"

"Well, for one thing, he sounded unhinged. I know he's an artist. We have one of his sculptures in our reception area. But all artists aren't crazy, right? He flat-out accused us of killing Todd Rabinowitz. Said he had proof and all sorts of nutjob things."

"What does he have to do with Todd Rabinowitz?" said Annika, even though she knew exactly how Arndt Kjellgren tied to Todd Rabinowitz.

"No idea," said Ian Halferin. "That's the extra crazy part. I don't know if he knew Todd or just saw Todd died on the news and is high on drugs or something. Because Arndt Kjellgren is a somewhat famous person in the area, I'd like to nip this before he jumps on social media or goes to the press and rumors get started."

"Of course. What time would you like me to come in?"

"As soon as possible. I'm here all day."

"I'll head over shortly."

"Thank you. And one more thing. I know it's unlikely, but I thought I'd just ask if Nils Shapiro can join us today."

Annika looked at me. I held up a finger. Annika said, "Let me try to find him. Hold on. . . ." Annika muted her phone and said, "What do you want to do?"

"Tell him I'm out working my other case, but I'll swing by at about eleven." Annika nodded and reached toward her phone. "One more thing. Tell him I'll have Ellegaard with me. Poor guy's spending too much time behind a desk."

"That's the truth," said Ellegaard.

Annika unmuted her phone and told Halferin. He didn't care who joined the conversation as long as I was there. He was in full pursuit of me, and pursuit can blind the pursuer to everything but his object of desire. It's how you trick a fish into biting a hook, and how you trick a lawyer into exposing himself to a murder investigation.

12

Ellegaard and I sat in the reception area of Halferin Silver on a leather couch near the coffee table smeared with magazines. Ellie looked at the Arndt Kjellgren sculpture in the corner and said, "What is that supposed to be?"

I said, "A sculpture."

"I know that. But what is it?"

"It's not anything. Just shapes. Shapes that move."

"Guess I'm missing something," said Ellegaard.

"Eye of the beholder."

"Or lack thereof."

I laughed. Ellegaard smiled. We reverted to twelve-year-old boys, making eye contact through suppressed merriment. Rebellion against a world where decisions were made for us because our voices didn't matter. Camaraderie of the marginalized.

The receptionist sat behind the cherrywood desk on her rolly chair and shot us snickering twelve-year-olds a disapproving look, as if she were a middle school librarian. Her teased, jet-black hair nested atop her head above a sleeveless black blouse studded with white polka dots. Her heavily made-up face made her neck, arms, and shoulders look sickly in the overhead fluorescents.

Our silent scolding was interrupted when Karin Tressler entered with three men. She had been all over the news in the last year, but I'd never seen her in person. She was Minnesota royalty, heiress to a fortune made in taconite mining in the Arrowhead during the previous century. Billions, not millions. She had spendy-looking brown hair that fell straight and shiny just past her shoulders, and periwinkle eyes. She stood ramrod erect, as if she were wearing a brace, but her head rotated with ease. Her smile seemed permanent. She wore a navy blazer over a pink blouse, a matching navy skirt, and ivory shoes with a three-inch heel. The receptionist almost sprung out of her rolly chair with excitement.

Karin Tressler beat the incumbent U.S. congressman in the recent primary. She took positions far right of the incumbent, who had staked out moderate positions to hold the purple district for six consecutive terms. Some felt assaulted by Karin Tressler's victory. She outspent the incumbent five to one, made loud, media-attracting speeches, and worst of all for her party, Karin Tressler could lose the upcoming general election. Karin Tressler won the primary but was hated from both ends of the political spectrum.

Ellegaard looked anxious, a rare aberration from his glasslike demeanor. He was one of the voters Karin Tressler had alienated. He shook his head and looked away.

The three men with Karin Tressler wore boring suits and shoes and might have all gotten their hair cut by the same barber. They each had bright complexions from scraping a razor over their face every day. They varied in age from thirties to sixties but shared a common air of sycophancy.

Celeste Sorensen darted into the lobby. Her grin was so big it could have caught bugs. "Ms. Tressler," said Celeste, "so nice to see you! Mr. Halferin and Ms. Silver are dealing with an urgent matter. They'll be with you momentarily."

"That's fine," said Karin in a high-pitched, reedy voice.

Celeste asked if they wanted to wait in Mr. Halferin's office or if they preferred the reception area. Karin Tressler said the reception area was fine. Celeste apologized again for the delay then turned to me and said, "Mr. Halferin asked that I bring you back right away."

Karin Tressler and her team of men remained standing near the reception desk.

I said, "Celesete, this is Anders Ellegaard, my partner at Stone Arch. He's joining the investigation."

"Wonderful!" said Celeste. "Welcome, Mr. Ellegaard." She looked up at my tall, blond-haired, blue-eyed colleague with a reverence she had never offered me. "Right this way."

Celeste started toward the corridor, expecting we'd follow, but I turned to Karin Tressler and said, "You go get 'em in November, Ms. Tressler. We need you. And I'll tell you what irks me. Those damn red and green lights at intersections. Who's the government to tell us when to stop and go? This country is supposed to be about freedom. Our Founding Fathers put their lives on the line for it. It's time we take it back." Karin Tressler's perma-smile didn't budge. The eyes of her male entourage were flat. I affirmed my declaration with a nod and walked away.

Celeste Sorensen didn't acknowledge my statement.

Ellegaard said, "Was that necessary?"

I said, "Absolutely."

Celeste led us through the hall of signed prints and into Ian Halferin's office. Halferin stood behind his desk wearing a charcoal suit and a big heap of worry. Annika sat across from him.

Susan Silver leaned against the credenza, arms crossed over her white blouse. I guessed she was early fifties. She had long wavy gray hair that framed high cheekbones under tiny horn-rimmed glasses. Old-fashioned tortoiseshells of rich browns and golds over milk chocolate eyes. Her skin had a half-century patina, and it suited her.

Ian Halferin thanked me for making time from my other case. We introduced each other to Susan Silver and Ellegaard. Susan managed a smile and spoke in a husky, atonal timbre. "I've heard a lot about you, Mr. Shapiro."

"Hazard of the trade."

She smiled but it didn't last.

Annika said, "Ian and Susan were just talking about the call they received from Arndt Kjellgren this morning."

Susan said, "Are you familiar with him?"

"I've seen his work."

"It's his specificity of language that's most concerning," said Annika. "He seems to have concocted a whole story about how this firm had Todd Rabinowitz killed."

I said, "Did you?"

"Did we what?" asked Susan.

"Have Todd Rabinowitz killed?"

Susan Silver and Ian Halferin looked at each other and then at me. Susan had a most perplexed expression. She said, "No. Of course we didn't have Todd Rabinowitz killed."

"Well good," I said, "let's move on to Arndt Kjellgren. What exactly did he say?"

Ian said, "He accused our firm of funding private militias. Specifically, militias that exist to counter dissent and asylum seekers."

Ellegaard said, "That's quite an accusation."

"It sure is," said Susan, "and it would be illegal if we are. But we're not. What's most relevant is Arndt Kjellgren said Todd discovered what we're allegedly doing, threatened to tell the authorities, and in response, we had him killed."

I sat in the chair next to Annika and said, "How does an artist even know about Todd Rabinowitz? Or that he worked here?" We knew about Arndt Kjellgren's affair with Robin Rabinowitz. But did Susan Silver and Ian Halferin know? Ellegaard's job was to look for the little telltales.

"We have no idea how Arndt Kjellgren knows or for that matter cares about any of that or . . ." Ian Halferin finished his sentence with a shrug.

I looked back at Ellegaard, who was ready and waiting with his answer. Ian Halferin and Susan Silver were full of shit. They were well aware of how Arndt Kjellgren knew about Todd Rabinowitz and Halferin Silver. Robin Rabinowitz's secret affair wasn't so secret after all.

Annika said, "Would you like us to look into Arndt Kjellgren so you better know who you're dealing with?"

"Yes," said Susan. "That's exactly what we want. This firm has suffered a terrible loss with Todd's murder. He was our dear friend. We're all dealing with that on a personal level. Not just the death but the grisliness of the murder. We also lost a colleague, an important cog in what we do here. Every lawyer in this firm is scrambling to cover Todd's workload, which was substantial. If this psycho, Kjellgren, drags our name into the press with wild accusations, it could push us over the edge."

"We need to discredit Kjellgren," said Ian Halferin. "The commodity he trades is just as subject to reputation as ours. We want to dig up so much dirt on him that collectors and institutions cancel commissions, the value of his sculptures plummets, and museums put his pieces into storage. As soon as we're out of this meeting, I'm going to have his sculpture removed from our reception area."

Ellegaard said, "You sound confident there's a lot of dirt out there on Arndt Kjellgren."

"He's an artist," said Halferin. "I've made some calls, and by all accounts, he's a complicated man. That's the nice way of saying it. He's temperamental. He's promiscuous. He doesn't respect the boundaries of our social institutions. I want to bury the son of a bitch."

I mentioned that would open a second front on our investigation. Annika would focus on who might have killed Todd Rabinowitz, and Ellegaard would do background work on Arndt Kjellgren. Susan and Ian approved the added expense. Me working for Robin Rabinowitz just got a degree more messy. More risky. But Ellegaard didn't blink.

Celeste Sorensen reappeared in her cloud of soap and said, "Excuse me. I'm sorry to interrupt."

Halferin said, "Almost done here, Celeste. A few more minutes."

"It's urgent. We just received a bomb threat. Everyone has to clear the building."

13

When Celeste Sorensen said "we just received a bomb threat" she meant Halferin Silver had just received a bomb threat. One firm. But every person in the thirty-story office tower had to evacuate, sending a flood of able-bodied, highly-educated laptop-clutchers down the staircase in a din of their own creation. Leather soles scuffing on concrete coupled with comments and jokes. I heard two neckties say something to the effect of, "Come on, guys. My PowerPoint wasn't *that* bad," followed by genial laughter. The exodus felt like a fire drill in fifth grade. A swirl of excitement over the break in routine mixed with the slight possibility there may actually be a fire. Or in this case a bomb.

The stairwell spit us onto the street, and authorities cattle-drove us a block away from the office tower. Smartphones were held high, documenting the event live on social media. Minneapolis PD and FBI headed the throng of law enforcement agencies that rushed to the scene. The Minneapolis Fire Department sent a long, red truck. Ian Halferin and Susan Silver's wish to avoid attention had not been granted. A threat to blow up their office, in effect, shut down an entire city block, became the lead story on the local news, and shot out to millions via news alert notifications.

A reunion of friends and foes pooled on the corner of Ninth and Marquette. Gabriella Núñez, deputy chief for the Minneapolis PD, was the ranking local cop. Gabriella was the third musketeer to Ellegaard and me at the Minneapolis Police Academy. She invited Annika, Ellegaard, and me inside the yellow tape. My pals from the FBI, Special Agent in Charge Colleen Milton and Special Agent Delvin Peterson, weren't so happy to see me. It'd been almost two years since our skirmish following the Edina murder. Not long enough.

Cameras and microphones surrounded Karin Tressler and her suit-clad goon squad. A reporter asked if the bomb threat was a threat on her life. She said something about death threats not being new to her, and she was confident that the capable men and women in our law enforcement agencies would make their determination after a thorough investigation.

FBI Agent Delvin Peterson finished talking to the rolly chair then turned away and bumped right into me. I said, "Why are you still in Minnesota, Delvin? I thought you were D.C."

"I was, but I'm being punished." He said it as if his plight were my fault. "Five more years in Minnesota before HQ will consider a transfer. Had to move my wife out here. My three kids.

I've spent thousands of dollars on jackets and boots alone. And my Nats never play the Twins. I had season tickets. I miss my Nats, Shapiro. I miss cherry blossoms. And I hate winter."

"Maybe you should take up cross-country skiing or ice hockey. Makes winter more enjoyable."

"I'm from Marietta, Georgia. I don't do winter sports."

"It's your five years, Peterson. I don't care what you do. Mope all you want."

In the interest of expediency, information ricocheted about and was easy to overhear. Celeste Sorensen calmed down enough to explain she had taken the call, which came in to Ian Halferin's direct line. The FBI said the call originated from a Voice over internet Protocol rerouted through so many servers and virtual servers that they doubted they could trace it. The caller used a digitized voice and, according to Celeste, sounded like auto-tune. She couldn't guess whether the caller was male or female, young or old, ethnically distinct in any way. She couldn't even be sure it was human—it sounded like a robot.

Ian Halferin and Susan Silver told the FBI about the call they'd received from Arndt Kjellgren earlier that day. They admitted they told private detectives first in hopes of keeping it quiet for business reasons. They defended their decision, pointing out that Kjellgren made no threats, much less a bomb threat. But they continued throwing around the artist's name, anxious to smear it. They acted as if Karin Tressler hadn't even been in the office when the threat was called in.

The FBI's bomb squad geared up to sweep the Halferin Silver offices. "It's a routine procedure," said Agent Colleen Milton. "We'll send a robot up the elevator to the twentieth floor then drive it through the offices via remote control." She went on to say something about the employees of Halferin Silver probably getting back in their offices by day's end.

Then the bomb exploded.

Glass rained down. Tempered pebbles splitter-splattered off the pavement in the echoing decay of the boom. Law enforcement scrambled. Susan Silver went pale. Ian Halferin looked like he might cry. The fire drill atmosphere ramped up to panic. People moved farther away from the building. We all thought the same thing: if the buildings fell in New York, a building could fall here.

Half a dozen hook-and-ladders arrived, and a squadron of helicopters circled overhead. Chaos is an extrovert's playground. I had no desire to stick around. I found Ellegaard and Annika and suggested we get the hell out of there.

The Mercury Dining Room and Rail in the Soo Line Building had dark wood floors and dark wood wainscoting below off-white walls featuring panels and sconces. The booths and high-tops were full of chattering Minneapolitans who ventured out to gossip about the explosion. Rumors of terrorism, assassination attempts on Karin Tressler, and conspiracies surrounding the murder of Todd Rabinowitz floated in the air with orders for gin and tonics and lunchtime beers.

"Listen," said Ellegaard, "investigating Todd Rabinowitz's murder for both his widow and his employer puts us in ethically murky waters, so let's make sure we stay out of the police's and FBI's way."

I said, "Why are you looking at me?"

"You got to behave on this one, Shap. This situation is now federal and, with Karin Tressler being present, political. If we, or more likely *you*, get in the news, we could alienate half our potential clients. So color within the lines, buddy, professionally and personally."

Annika twisted her mouth into an expression of *good luck*. I nodded to Ellegaard, which signaled my intent to behave. He was about to continue his lecture, but my phone rang. Micaela. She needed to know I was no longer available whenever she felt like reaching out. I declined the call. She called again. I declined again. She texted before I could turn off my phone. She could see the text was delivered. One thing I knew about Micaela: she wouldn't stop.

Annika said, "What's wrong, Nils?"

"Nothing. Just have to make a call. I'll be right back."

I walked out of the restaurant and into the lobby of the Soo Line Building, passed the sales office for the apartments on its upper floors, then climbed the spiral staircase to the second level. I found a quiet spot in the skyway and returned Micaela's call.

She answered. "Are you safe, Nils?"

"Yeah."

She was crying. "I saw you on the news just before the bomb went off then I didn't and I told myself you were okay but I just had this nagging feeling that— Why didn't you answer before?"

"I was talking to the FBI," I said, bending the timeline of events. "We were in the law firm when the bomb threat was called in."

"With Karin fucking Tressler?"

"Not with her, but she was there, too."

"Oh my God, Nils. Oh my God. This country is so crazy. It's just insane."

"I saw I had a message from you. Sorry but I haven't listened to it yet."

"That's okay. Hey . . ." She paused. "Are you free later tonight?"

I wanted one final moment with Micaela Stahl to bust her on her New York lie. I wanted an ugly confrontation to catalyze our split. The final split. I said, "I think so. Not sure what time. I'll have to go in and give a formal statement at some point."

"I don't care how late it is. I just need to see you."

"All right. I'll let you know how the day's playing out."

"Thank you."

"Oh hey," I said, "how was New York yesterday?" I eyed a military helicopter flying directly over Fifth Street. The big fat kind with two rotors.

Micaela said, "Fine. I'll tell you about it tonight."

I said good-bye and walked back downstairs to the restaurant.

Annika's eyes looked heavy with concern. She said, "What's wrong, Nils?"

Goddamn women and their emotional antennas. "Nothing," I said. Annika's silent gaze accused me of lying, and my expression no doubt pleaded guilty.

14

What most people assume are the non-glamourous aspects of investigation are my favorites—the hours researching on the Net, days staked out in a car, nights lying awake hoping the inaccessible part of my brain will tell me the story, weeks waiting for something, anything to happen. Those times are peaceful and profitable.

But the afternoon following the Halferin Silver bombing was none of those things. Annika, Ellegaard, and I spent hours at FBI headquarters in Brooklyn Center. They put us in three different rooms and interrogated us separately.

Special Agent in Charge Colleen Milton led me into her office on the fifth floor of the FBI building. Unlike on my previous visits, she smiled and offered me a beverage. This time, I wasn't the enemy. My case wasn't bumping up against hers. Not yet, anyway.

"Let's forget about two years ago," said Colleen. She'd blonded her brown hair and cut it shorter into a Minnesota mom do. It's an odd combination of color, length, and shape that counteracts a woman's natural beauty, as if she had rotten breath or talked about reality TV. Colleen said, "Tell me about Todd Rabinowitz and how you got involved with the case."

I said, "Todd's widow, Robin, called us after she found him. Right after she called the police. She knows Ellegaard's wife, Molly. Robin was having an affair and rightly assumed she and her lover—do people still use that word? I hope not. Anyway, she assumed they'd be suspects and wanted me to help find Todd's killer."

"So, her motivation in hiring you is selfish."

"Everyone's motivations are selfish. Even altruistic do-gooders. They wouldn't do good if it made them feel bad. But to answer your real question, even though Robin and Todd's marriage was ending, I get the sense she cared for him as a person. Just not as a husband."

"And Todd's life insurance and will?"

"Seventy-five percent of it goes to children from his first marriage. Twenty-five percent to Robin."

Milton stood up and paced behind her desk like a courtroom lawyer. There was a knock on the door, then it opened. A young woman said, "Sorry to interrupt, but *The New York Times* is calling."

Colleen said, "Not available for comment at this time."

The young woman looked at her phone. "What about Politico, Fox News, and MSNBC?"

"Same for any and all of them. Thank you." The young woman left. Colleen resumed her pacing. "What's your gut on Todd Rabinowitz having some piece of evidence at the office that could incriminate Robin or Arndt Kjellgren for his murder?"

"If they wanted to kill Todd but knew there was a piece of incriminating evidence at Todd's office they wouldn't have killed him. At least not until they had that evidence in their hands."

"What if," said Milton, "they realized the incriminating evidence existed after they killed him?"

"I don't think so. Neither Robin nor Arndt Kjellgren seem to think in what I'd call strategic paranoia."

"What's strategic paranoia?"

I wished I hadn't used that term. The language I use to explain the world to myself is best kept internal. Once it's out, I have to justify how I think, and that's an invasion of privacy. I said, "I've observed that people who scheme to get ahead, who take shortcuts, what most people would call cheating, often assume that's what everyone does. It comes from a combination of entitlement and laziness. The strategic paranoids are the kind of people who are often guilty of doing things where the cover-up is as bad as the crime. Which is what bombing a law firm would be for Robin Rabinowitz and Arndt Kjellgren. But they don't strike me as strategic paranoids. That's my gut anyway."

Milton ran that through her logic sieve. I could tell she didn't buy my theory, but didn't want to ruin our little playdate. She said, "Okay. That's interesting. Let's put Robin Rabinowitz and Arndt Kjellgren aside for a moment. Did you arrive at Halferin Silver before or after Karin Tressler and her colleagues?"

"Before. I was in the reception area when they entered."

"Were any of them carrying a package?"

"Not that I noticed."

"Did any of them appear nervous or agitated?"

"Well, the three suits with her weren't all that jovial, but my guess is they were born that way."

"Did any of them frequently check their cell phones?"

"I honestly didn't pay close attention."

"Did any of them leave the reception area?"

"While I was in it? No. But I left the reception area before them. To meet with Ian Halferin and Susan Silver."

Colleen Milton sat down on the edge of her desk. "Karin Tressler said you told her the government should stop interfering with our traffic intersections. Were you being sarcastic?"

"Very."

She smiled then said, "Do you know why Karin Tressler was meeting with Halferin Silver?"

This wasn't an interrogation—it was a conversation. A cordial chat. The bombing of Halferin Silver had somehow given Colleen Milton and the FBI an opportunity, not a crisis. I said, "Come on, Agent Milton. You've already talked to Karin Tressler and Halferin Silver. I think they have a better idea of what they met about than I do."

"That's not why I asked. I asked because if you knew why they were meeting, maybe someone else did, too."

I said, "Because there's no way in hell Karin Tressler's presence during the bomb blast was a coincidence."

Special Agent Colleen Milton moved from the edge of her desk to her chair. "I think it's unlikely to be a coincidence."

"Okay," I said, "let's think that through. If someone wanted to kill Karin Tressler by planting a bomb in a place they'd know she'd be, why call in a threat so she can evacuate before the blast?"

Colleen Milton nodded. Her new hair did not move.

I said, "What kind of bomb was it?"

"We don't know yet."

I smiled and said, "You know if it contained nails or BBs. You know if it was homemade or military grade."

Colleen Milton returned my smile. "I'm sorry, Mr. Shapiro," she said, "you're right. I do know what kind of bomb it was. But I can't tell you. Thank you for your time. Think we can stay on good terms?"

"I hope so. I've been a big fan of the FBI since J. Edgar left to slip into something more comfortable."

"Glad to hear it."

We parted amicably, though both of us knew we could be headed for another head-butting. I hoped not. If that happened, I'd no doubt come out on the losing end. I snuck up on the FBI last time. They wouldn't let it happen a second time.

The information flowed more freely from Gabriella Núñez. We talked in her office, which hadn't changed in the six months since I'd last sat in it. Neither had Gabriella. Her shiny black hair, smooth brown skin, and clear brown eyes made her look ten years younger than the thirty-nine years I knew she was. I walked over to a photograph hanging on the wall. It was of our Minneapolis Police Academy Class. Ellegaard and I looked like boys. Hell, we were boys. Gabriella looked younger than she did now, but the youth expressed itself in her eyes and smile rather than in more common physical markers of age. Her expression in the photograph radiated more hope than resignation.

I said, "Why does our time at the academy feel so special now but it didn't then?"

"Is that a rhetorical question?"

"No. I want an answer. Rhetorical questions are a waste of time, don't you think?"

She smiled, walked over, and stood next to me. I turned my head to watch her study the picture. Gabriella Núñez gleamed and said, "Maybe it's nostalgia."

No. It wasn't nostalgia. Not for me, anyway. I answered my own question as soon as I'd asked it. But I couldn't share the answer with Gabriella. She knew how I felt about Ellegaard. She might think that's how I felt about her.

We walked away from the photo and sat down. Gabriella told me the bomb had been delivered in a package. It detonated in the mail room before it was opened. It was homemade with peroxide and had been packed with dry ice to keep it cold and more stable. A burner phone had been wired to detonate the bomb, which contained no shrapnel. It was apparently intended as an incendiary device. And it worked. Everything in the mail room burned.

I said, "You don't need a bomb to start a fire."

"That's true," said Gabriella. "The bomb was intended to send a message."

"Like tying a murder victim to his dock by a fishing stringer through his jaw."

"Yes," said Gabriella. "We also made that connection. If the murder and bombing were committed by the same party, someone out there is angry about something. We're working with the FBI to stop them from showing that anger again."

Gabriella Núñez and I talked for a few more minutes, then I thanked her for the information and walked out of her office weighted with an inexplicable sadness. I checked my phone and saw seven messages from reporters, three messages from Robin Rabinowitz, and a reminder to visit Micaela.

15

I took a cold shower and changed into fresh jeans and a T-shirt but they didn't feel all that fresh by the time I stepped outside. We needed a thunderstorm to wash away the stagnation. I called Robin on the drive to Micaela's. She answered before I heard a ring.

"Nils, I can't find him."

"Arndt?"

"Yes. I've called, texted, stopped by his place, tried friends. No one knows where he is."

My still-new Volvo exhaled a blast of Swedish winter. I said, "Did you ever think he might be avoiding you?"

"The FBI came to the house today. They had all sorts of

questions about Arndt and Todd. Oh God. This whole mess is my fault."

"Which whole mess are you referring to?"

"I knew our marriage was over five years ago. But I didn't do anything about it. I just let it rot. Staying with Todd was a lie that turned into a thousand lies. Now Todd's dead and Arndt's missing and someone blew up Halferin Silver."

"Hate to break it to you, but there might be bigger forces at play than your and Todd's marriage." She didn't respond. I said, "Arndt knows you slept at my place last night. He doesn't know you slept on the couch. You not finding him might have something to do with that." I approached the Walker Art Center. It looked like the head of a Rock 'Em Sock 'Em Robot. I doubt that's what the Swiss architecture firm had in mind when they designed it. But the resemblance was uncanny, and it made me smile every time I saw it.

Robin said, "Will you help me look for him?"

"Let's see if he turns up tonight, and we'll talk tomorrow."

"I need you to help me look for him tonight."

"I can't tonight. I'm sorry. Have you had any more contact with the police?"

"No. Haven't heard a word."

"What about Nellie, your lawyer? Has she said anything?"

"Not since yesterday. Nils, I can't sleep alone tonight. I don't feel safe."

I clicked the Volvo's fan down a couple notches. My world got quiet. I said, "Call a friend. Or check in to a hotel. I have a personal thing to deal with right now. I'll check in with you later and we'll take it from there."

"I'm so fucking scared right now," said Robin. "There's a crazy person out there. They got Todd. They got Todd's office. I could be next."

"I can send someone out there." She didn't respond. I let her think a few moments then said, "Robin?"

"I'm here. Just . . . just call me later, okay?"

I said good-bye, turned left on the southeast corner of Bde Maka Ska, then drove the half-mile connecting road to Lake Harriet. Traffic was backed up thanks to a concert at the band shell. I rolled down my window but couldn't identify the music makers. It was some sort of soft jazz, which is the last kind of music I associate with my hometown. I was expecting to hear a string quartet, a Semisonic reunion, The Suburbs, or a band of octogenarians playing John Phillip Sousa marches.

I turned off Lake Harriet Parkway, found a parking spot, and walked a half block to Micaela's building. I rarely came empty-handed, but the thought of stopping for a bottle of wine or whiskey hadn't crossed my mind. Maybe it was because Micaela hadn't come clean when I asked her about New York. Maybe it was the sorrow in her voice when we spoke. Maybe I just didn't feel like it.

I rung Micaela's penthouse from the security box. She buzzed the door, and I entered. I had a key, but I never used it if she was there. We didn't have a "honey I'm home" kind of relationship. Since we'd picked up again, the boundaries were clear. We never discussed them, but we both knew what they were. We didn't make plans more than a day in advance. We didn't say "I love you." We didn't talk about our social lives. It was as if we'd created another dimension in which we could hide from reality. Or at least hide from each other's reality. It wasn't a safe place—it was a make-believe place.

I walked toward the trio of elevators off a lobby filled with furniture upholstered in white leather on a floor of four-inch-wide-planks of oak, stained a medium brown and sealed in something shiny. A few area rugs defined the seating areas in case the couches and chairs weren't a strong enough clue. The elevator on the far right dinged then opened. It was Micaela's elevator. Only Micaela's. I stepped inside.

It reopened in the foyer of her penthouse. White walls lit with candlelight. Always candles. The Catholic Church was probably pissed at Micaela for what she did to the supply-and-demand curve. The candles flickered in the currents of air-conditioned air. Micaela Stahl's residence was one beautiful fire hazard. She stood in the kitchen plating sautéed spinach from a pan. I smelled garlic, mushrooms, and greens. She looked at me with the smallest of smiles, her eyes red and puffy from crying or allergies. But Micaela didn't suffer from allergies.

She said in soft, tired voice, "Thanks for coming, Nils."

Sadness wafted over with the aroma of food. Or maybe it wasn't sadness but a heap of emotion that presented like sadness. I said, "I'm always up for free food and good company."

Micaela said, "I guarantee at least one of those. We're having wild trout, mushrooms, and spinach. White, red, or brown?"

"Brown if it's open."

"If it's open," she said with a mock scoff. She walked to a cabinet and removed a bottle of Yellow Spot. She uncorked it and poured two fingers into a lowball. She had already poured herself a glass of white. "Are you ready to eat?"

I helped her carry the plates and drinks over to the bistro table by the window overlooking the lake. We arrived at place settings, water glasses, a full pitcher, and a lit oil lamp. Dinner started with an exchange of facts about our day, mostly from me, since I'd had a newsworthy one. Then I stopped talking and let it get quiet. For over a minute I heard only flatware on ceramics, glassware on the mosaic-tiled table, and the constant exhale of air-conditioning.

Micaela looked at me with round, swollen gray eyes and said, "I have something to tell you, Nils. It's not easy." She lifted her water glass, took a sip, then set it back down. "So please be patient with me." Another sip. She bowed her head. I had never seen her pause to gather her strength. She always seemed invincible. "I've been keeping something from you for the past few weeks."

I pictured Micaela in the elevator bay of the Medical Arts Building. All those doctors on one of the four floors where her elevator stopped. All those doctors trying to treat all those diseases. Glitches in the human body. Glitches that could end life.

She said, "I haven't been feeling like my normal self. I've been tired. And I've noticed some swelling . . ." She trailed off and lifted her water glass but it was empty. She refilled it with the pitcher. The air-conditioning stopped, and the silence gave voice to the tiniest sounds like breathing and, I feared, my squishing ventricles. I sniffled, and that caught Micaela's attention. She said, "What?"

The question confused me. "What do you mean, what?"

She looked at me with curiosity and tilted her head. "Do you know what I'm going to tell you?"

"No. But . . ." I couldn't finish my thought.

Her sadness morphed into a curious indignation. She said, "What do you think I'm going to tell you?"

I got up and walked to the kitchen and grabbed the bottle of Yellow Spot. On my way back I said, "That you're sick."

She said, "What are you talking about?"

"After my meeting at Halferin Silver yesterday, I stopped at Starbucks in the Crystal Court. I saw you walk out of that souvenir store on the first floor. But you told me you were going to New York for the day. Two wrongs don't make a whatever and all that, but I followed you."

"Oh, Nils."

"Just to the lobby of the Medical Arts Building. I know you went to one of four floors, but then I ran out of detective skills."

Her tiny smile returned. "I didn't lie about New York. I was headed for the airport but changed my mind."

I sighed. "God dammit, Micaela."

"I am telling you the truth."

"Like fuck you are," I said. I poured more Irish into my empty glass. "There is no value in hiding shit from me at this point. Regardless of what we've been doing, you—"

"Stop."

I stopped and recorked the bottle. Micaela stood from the bistro table, walked to an antique credenza that had layers of paint partially removed or added. I couldn't tell which. She opened a drawer and pulled out a paper bag, returned to the table, and handed it to me. It was from the Minnesota souvenir store and whatever she'd purchased was still inside. "Open it."

I opened the bag and removed a tiny green knit hat with the Minnesota Wild logo on it. I didn't understand. I looked at her.

Micaela smiled. "Nils," she said, "I'm pregnant."

"What?"

"I took a home test a few weeks ago and on my way to the airport yesterday thought *wow, I should really see a doctor.* So, I canceled my New York meetings and saw an O.B. instead."

"In the Medical Arts Building."

"It is full of obstetricians."

Our eyes had a long conversation in which I learned she wasn't kidding. I think I might have laughed and said something stupid like, "You're pregnant. And drinking wine?"

She pushed her wineglass toward me and said, "I poured wine. I'm not drinking it. It would have been too obvious if I didn't pour it. *I* wanted to tell you, not my wine habit."

"You're pregnant?"

"Yes, Nils. I'm pregnant. You're usually a quicker study than this."

I said, "Are you happy?"

"So happy."

I got up from the table. She stood, and I gave her a long hug. She hugged me tight and said, "Listen . . ."

I didn't let go. I didn't want to see her face. "Is it m—"

"Ugh. I knew you'd ask that. Of course it's yours, you idiot. It could only be yours."

I let go and stepped back. I saw something in her eyes I didn't expect. I saw fear. She said, "We can't do what we've been doing anymore. We need to make this permanent."

I nodded. Micaela's fear all of a sudden made sense because I felt it, too. A flutter in my heart. A light-headedness. I reached for my whiskey but stopped. Whiskey couldn't help this one. Nothing could. Even though it had been my intention on my way over, her initiating the conversation still hurt.

Micaela said, "We have to go back to being just friends."

"Uh-huh. Real exes."

"Yes."

Micaela's wish to end our romantic entanglement surprised

me, but my reaction surprised me even more. After the words were said, I felt happy. No, giddy. Not even a sliver of rejection. I placed my hands on her shoulders and said, "I never expected this would last. And whatever this is, or was, who knows? But it's always felt temporary. Like summer vacation when you're a kid. It's always felt like the good times would end."

She nodded—relief washed away her dread. "I don't want or expect anything from you. Not money or time or anything. But you are the father. If this one sticks, and I so hope it does, you will be part of the kid's life as much as you want."

I hugged her again.

She said, "Kids adapt to their reality, right? This kid will know his or her mother is single but loves a man very much and together they created him or her out of love. Just not . . ." She stopped herself.

"You can say it. It's okay."

". . . just not . . . partnership."

I nodded, then kissed her on the cheek.

She said, "We'll always be in each other's lives, Nils. Until one of us dies. I hope so, anyway."

"Me, too."

She cried tears of happiness or sadness and said, "But you should move on."

16

I left Micaela's around 10:00 P.M. The frogs and crickets were at it again, calling out to their nocturnal predators, "Eat me. Eat me." A mosquito buzzed in my ear, most likely a female out for blood to nourish her young. I waved her away, got in the Volvo, and called Ellegaard. He answered on the first ring.

I said, "I'm glad you're up."

"I was just about to head out to Robin Rabinowitz's house. She's scared to death. Molly thinks I should bring her back here."

"Stay put. I'll go out there."

"You sure?" Ellegaard wasn't questioning my work ethic—he was questioning my boundaries.

"Yeah. And don't worry. The lines are clear on this one."

He said, "You okay? You sound different."

"I have to tell you something. I was calling to see if you wanted to go grab a beverage."

"I would, buddy, but—"

"I know, I know. Robin. I'm on my way. But can you stay on the phone a minute?"

"Of course."

I turned left on Lake Street. "I just had dinner with Micaela. She's pregnant." Ellegaard said nothing. I realized he was missing a big piece of information. "Oh," I said, "right. Um, last spring we started up again. Now she's pregnant. We didn't try to prevent it because we didn't think it was possible."

"And . . . ," said Ellegaard, "how do you feel about it?"

"I'm fucking thrilled, Ellie. I can't even tell you. Ecstatic."

"So, you're getting back together. Fantastic, buddy."

"Actually, we're not."

"But you said—"

"I know. But we're not getting back together."

Ellegaard said nothing for a long time. I could feel him searching for words. He finally said, "Nils, are you okay with that?"

"Yeah, for some reason, I am. At least for now. And it's early. Who knows if—"

"It will, Nils. You guys just had bad luck before. This one will make it. I'm happy for you. For both of you." He said the words. He meant the words. But I heard a not-so-sureness in his voice. A hesitancy. A parental-like worry.

I said, "If Micaela wanted a relationship because of this, I'd be all in. But she doesn't. And the weird thing is I'm good with that. If I push getting back together, it could destroy everything. And *everyone*. I can feel it in my gut, Ellie. Don't ask me how."

"Like on cases."

"Yes."

I could almost hear him smile. "But you're not psychic."

"Not even close."

"You're an outfielder."

"Exactly."

Ellegaard referred to how I explain what sometimes appears to be my psychic intuition. I'm like an outfielder in baseball. As soon as a batter makes contact with the ball, the outfielder, who stands three hundred feet away, knows exactly where to run to make the catch. In what direction. At what speed. At what distance. How does the outfielder know where to go when the ball is still on the bat? It's not intuition or psychic ability. It's experience. Or the data from that experience that gets crunched somewhere in the brain in a fraction of a second.

"Well buddy," Ellegaard said, "I couldn't be happier for you. We will celebrate tomorrow."

I passed Highway 169. The western sky still had a brushstroke of purple that night had yet to paint over. It'd been a long time since my own happiness pushed away everything else. On the remainder of that drive, for fifteen whole minutes, I didn't give a shit who killed Todd Rabinowitz or who blew up Halferin Silver or that Arndt Kjellgren had taped me into the coat factory.

I even assumed the baby had deep enough roots and functional enough chromosomes to be born alive. My fear of a repeat tragedy barely whispered. When Micaela and I lost our first baby, it cracked a marriage that was waiting to crumble. That marriage would never be rebuilt. Instead, my happiness stemmed from the simple idea of becoming a father and the less simple idea of knowing Micaela and I would be connected by something other than joint tax forms and shared utility bills.

I was about to call Robin to tell her I was almost there when Annika Brydolf called.

Annika said, "I just finished having drinks with Celeste Sorensen."

"I forgot that was tonight. Tell me."

"It was weird, Nils. You know how you taught me when something feels wrong, that's when you need to pay attention? I can't put my finger on it. Not even a guess really. But something definitely felt wrong about her."

"Well," I said. "Let's talk it out. Maybe we can narrow it down. What did she say?" I stopped for the red light at the Highway 101 intersection. There were only two other cars. Dead town at 10:10 on a weeknight.

Annika said, "One thing she kept saying was how good it was to talk to a normal person. She kept complimenting me on being normal. She was so happy they finally hired a normal private detective. She said she liked working at Halferin Silver but no one there is normal. She said they're good people. Their hearts are in the right place. Especially Susan Silver. She loves Susan. But she said they're not normal. I'm not kidding. She said the word *normal* a thousand fucking times. What is that about?"

"Did you ask her how she ended up working at Halferin Silver?"

"Yes. Her father got her the job. He's friends with Ian Halferin."

"Huh," I said. "I wonder who her father is."

"I didn't ask, but it's easy enough to find out. She had a few drinks then didn't shut up."

"What did she drink?"

"What do you mean?"

"Wine? Beer? Cocktails?"

"Cosmopolitans."

"At an Irish pub?"

"I know."

"Amateur. And she had a few of them?"

"Three. Why?"

"Oh, boy. Did she drive home?"

"No. Ubered from work and then home."

"She's not a drinker if she's drinking cosmos. Cosmos are a fun night with the girls drink for girls who don't drink all that much." I turned left on Christmas Lake Road then pulled over and parked to continue the conversation. "Any info on Celeste's personal life?"

Annika said, "She's married. Since she was nineteen."

"Hmm . . . Did she ask about your personal life?"

Annika hesitated then said, "Yes. I told her, and she said how sorry she was about my husband. She asked what was going to happen when he gets out of jail. I asked what she meant. She wondered how I thought it would go when he came back home. I said I didn't know because he's never coming back home—I divorced him."

"She looked disappointed, didn't she?"

"How'd you know?"

"What'd she say at the end of the night?"

"She wants to do it again. If drinks are involved, learning more from Celeste Sorensen will not be hard. And it was kind of weird," said Annika. "She invited me to a dinner party. Said there'd be some single men there. She stressed that they're normal men. Good husband material. Kept saying how sorry she was about what happened with my marriage. I think she wants me to give the asshole another chance. So strange."

I put the car in Drive. "Thanks, Annika. I know you didn't get to see your kids tonight."

Annika said, "Once in a while, that's okay. I'm starting to feel like a real detective."

I wanted to tell her about Micaela being pregnant. I don't know why. I would in person, maybe soon, maybe not. I pulled back onto Christmas Lake Road. "You've been a real detective for a while. I—" Red and blue light swept through the car. I checked my rearview mirror. "Annika, I'll talk to you tomorrow."

She started to say something but I hung up. I pulled the Volvo to the side of the road. A police car passed going sixty on the small road. No siren. It continued another hundred yards or so before killing its emergency vehicle lights. A stealth approach. I turned off my lights, hit the gas, and followed.

I called Robin. She answered on the first ring with a whisper. "Nils."

"I'm almost there. Did you call the police?"

"Yes. Someone's outside the house."

"Where are you?"

"In the basement. In the wine cellar."

"Do you know who's outside?"

"No, but they were trying to break in. They tried the front door then tried to jimmy the French doors facing the lake."

"Do the police know where you're hiding?"

"Yes."

"Good. Do not move unless they identify themselves by name. I'm right behind them."

"Nils."

"Yeah?"

"Stay on the phone with me?"

"Of course." I pulled over three houses away from Robin. I turned off the Volvo, reached for the door handle, then stopped. Where was I going? The police were at the scene. It was dark. The dumbest thing I could do was try to help, the most likely outcome being a cop mistaking me for whoever was trying to break into Robin's house. I didn't want to get shot. Not after the arrow I took in the shoulder last year, but especially not after Micaela's news.

"Nils," said Robin, over the car's speaker, "are you still there?"

I took the phone off Bluetooth and held it to my head. "Yes. The police are outside your place now. Stay where you are."

My headlights shot forward, illuminating the road and its border of trees. Maples, oaks, and cottonwoods, each carrying leaves at full capacity to harvest the last months of sunlight before autumn took the leaves away. The headlights kept me safe. No police officer would shoot in their direction. They also made me worthless. Safety was one thing. Being of no value was another. I killed the headlights, then the engine.

Robin said, "What are you doing?"

"Waiting for my eyes to adjust to the dark." I felt for the glove compartment keyhole, unlocked it, and retrieved my Ruger. "I'm covering Christmas Lake Road." At the academy, they taught us to load, unload, and reload our weapons blindfolded. I dropped the clip into my left hand. It felt heavy with six rounds. I popped it back in.

"Hold on," said Robin, "the police are calling."

She clicked over, and I lowered the Volvo's windows. More

crickets and frogs. The August steam bath rushed in and condensed on everything the air-conditioning had touched. I put the call on speaker, rested the device on the center console, and stared into the dark until I could see the edges of the road. Bits of gravel on the shoulder reflected light from somewhere. Just enough to make out the straight piece of gray surface before me.

I heard footsteps, quiet at first, then louder, followed by a shout, "Police! Stop and get down on the ground!" But I saw nothing. No flashlights sweeping the woods or road. Just darkness.

The footsteps grew quicker, louder, closer. Robin's voice startled me. "I'm back. The police said someone's definitely out here and—"

I killed the call, silenced my phone, and shoved it in my pocket. The footsteps were now running and almost to me. I took a breath, then put my right foot on the brake pedal and pushed the Volvo's Start button. The headlights ignited everything in front of me.

A man, blinded by my headlights, shielded his eyes with his hands. He wore black pants and a black T-shirt. My headlights were too bright for him to see anything but white, and when he got five feet in front of me, I pushed the car door open. He smashed into the Volvo's driver-side door panel and collapsed to the pavement. I grabbed a handful of plastic ties from the center console, bolted out of the car, and jumped on top of him.

He said, "Fuck! Get the fuck off me!"

His fist caught the side of my head, and he squirmed out from under me. He scurried like an animal and got back onto his feet. I lunged toward him and caught a few fingers inside his pant leg. He hit the pavement face-first and screamed, "It's not safe, you idiot! It's not safe!"

I rolled him onto his stomach, grabbed his wrists, and zip-tied them together behind his back.

Then I turned around and zip-tied his ankles. The phone rang inside the Volvo. I pulled my phone out of my pocket and took the call off Bluetooth.

"Call the police, Robin. Tell them I've caught the man who was outside your house. He's three houses north on Christmas Lake Road."

17

I've been in plenty of police stations but none more lovely than the Greater Lake Minnetonka Police Station. New carpet (no coffee stains), the pictures on the walls had matching frames, and the office furniture coordinated in a way that suggested furniture store instead of being stolen from other city bureaucracies. Unprecedented in law enforcement. And unnerving. It didn't look like a place in which to fight crime. It looked like a place where you sit across the desk from a business casual to discuss your retirement account.

I sat in a small conference room with Detective Norton. His sad eyes had come to life with the night's excitement, two big orbs under his giant forehead. He and Detective Irving had been outside Robin Rabinowitz's house when Arndt Kjellgren ran into my driver's side door. Norton asked how that happened, and I told him. He seemed too delighted with my answer, as if he were a German shorthaired pointer who had flushed the game-bird for me to shoot out of the sky.

Robin sat in another office talking to Detective Irving. I could see them through the glass walls. Irving's hair looked like Orange Crush in the LED overheads. He couldn't mask his boyish enthusiasm. I made eye contact with Robin. She looked like hell. After completing the formality of taking our stories separately, Irving brought Robin into the conference room.

Before Robin sat down she said, "Tell them, Nils. Tell them to let me see Arndt."

Norton and Irving sat in adjacent chairs at the head of the table like a couple of kids who both wanted to be in charge. I said, "Let her see Arndt."

"I'm sorry," said Norton. "That's not possible right now."

"Why won't you at least tell me if he's asked to see me?" said Robin.

"All right. He has asked to see you," said Irving, "but he wants to see Mr. Shapiro first."

Robin looked at me. I shrugged and said, "Maybe he should see his lawyer first."

Norton said something about Arndt's lawyer being on the way, and the FBI and Minneapolis PD were, too. And that Arndt said he had nothing to do with the bombing at Halferin Silver and that he wasn't trying to break into Mrs. Rabinowitz's house. He claimed he was there to protect her, not harm her, and that he only ran because he was afraid of getting shot by police.

I said, "Well, Detectives, what do you want to do now?"

Irving the Orange said, "Not sure. With no chief of police, we're kind of freewheelin' here."

"Well, I don't know about that," said Detective Norton. "We got this under control." It wasn't just his eyes that looked different. For the first time since I'd met him, Detective Norton wore a necktie. All dressed up for the big occasion.

Irving said, "Detective Norton and I spoke with the head of the coordinating committee, and they have authorized funds to hire you as a consultant, Mr. Shapiro. Just like how Edina hired you a couple years ago."

All those years I struggled for work, then all of a sudden everyone wanted to hire me. And on the same case. Irving looked at me with *what da ya say?* raised eyebrows. Robin looked at me with an unpleasant expectation. I said, "I'm sorry, but I can't work for the police. I'm already working for Robin."

Irving said, "You turned her down. We both heard the conversation."

"Yeah, well. I changed my mind."

"What's the problem with working for Robin and us?" said Norton.

"You have disparate goals."

Norton and Irving looked at each other. They either didn't understand how Robin's goals could be different from theirs or they didn't understand what *disparate* meant.

"Well," said Norton. "That puts us in a tough spot." He scratched his huge forehead then fidgeted with the knot of his necktie. I could tell he wasn't used to wearing one. "We can't have you interrogating Kjellgren if you're not working with us."

"That's fine. I don't need to talk to him."

"But you're the one he wants to talk to," said Irving. "Not us. Just you. What are we supposed to do?"

"No idea, but you have a problem. The FBI will be here in a minute. So will Minneapolis PD. They'll know how to deal with him."

Norton said, "We want to question him first."

Robin said, "Couldn't you just work for them for an hour, Nils? That wouldn't be a conflict, would it? That would give you a chance to talk to him before everyone else gets here. He wants to see you. He must have a reason."

I turned to Irving and Norton and said, "What do you think? Hire me for an hour?"

I sat in the Greater Lake Minnetonka Police Station's interrogation room, which looked like it had never been used. I glanced under the table and chairs to see if they still had price tags. Norton led Arndt Kjellgren into the room. His hands were cuffed in front of him, and his face was scraped from when he belly-flopped onto Christmas Lake Road. The officers sat Kjellgren in a chair directly across from me.

Kjellgren looked down, sighed something venomous, then said, "I want to talk to Shapiro alone."

Irving said, "You comfortable with that, Mr. Shapiro?"

"So comfortable I might order room service."

Irving and Norton nodded like boy soldiers then turned and walked out. After the door shut, Arndt Kjellgren looked up and stared at me through the tops of his eyes.

"The FBI will be here any minute," I said, "so if you want to talk, then talk. I assume you're pissed about me slamming you with my car door, so I wouldn't waste your time on that."

"I don't give a shit about that. Are they watching us?"

"Normally, I'd say yes, but with these guys I don't know if they can find the On button."

He nodded, then braced for my answer before he asked the question. "Did you sleep with Robin last night?"

"No. She slept on my couch because she'd had too much to drink."

"Nothing happened between you two?"

"She came over late afternoon. We talked. She drank some wine. Too much wine. She hadn't eaten all day. I went out to dinner. When I returned, she'd drunk more wine and was passed out on my couch. I threw a blanket over her and went to sleep in my room."

Arndt Kjellgren stared at me like I was a bug crawling up a wall, half curious and half like he wanted to squish me. He took a few slow, audible breaths then said, "I want to hire you."

"What?"

"I need you to work for me."

"Get in fucking line."

"I'm serious. I was outside Robin's house, but I swear it was to protect her. Someone was going to break in tonight."

"Who?"

"I don't have a name. They would have hurt her if they needed to. If they wanted to."

"Where are you getting your information?"

"I can't tell you. But I promise you it's the truth. One hundred percent, man. I swear."

"Why couldn't Robin get ahold of you today?"

"I turned off my cell. For her safety."

"I got to tell you, Arndt, you're sounding kind of crazy right now. You say you were lurking outside Robin's house to protect her, but you won't tell me what or who you're protecting her from. Or how you know. I wouldn't take that case even if I were available, which I'm not."

Kjellgren moved his head around as if he was doing a neck-stretching exercise. He kept doing it as he said, "You need to trust me. You need to fucking trust me right now."

"It doesn't matter if I trust you. There are three law enforcement agencies that don't give a damn what I think. One of them is the FBI."

Arndt Kjellgren opened his eyes and said, "I did some shit I'm not proud of."

"Like tape-welding me into my place last night?"

"I don't care about that. I've done other things. I can't talk about them. Unless we can talk in private. With no one listening in."

"That's not up to me." I looked out toward the lobby and saw badges filing in. "Your time's up, Arndt. The FBI is here. I can't help you."

He said, "Look at me. Fucking look at me. I keep records."

"Okay—"

"Listen to me! I keep records. Of my sculptures. Who buys them. It's recorded. I know. Because of the records. I *know*."

"Because you keep records."

"Yes. I have a collection of records."

"Just say what you're trying to tell me, Arndt. You have nothing to lose. Just—"

The door swung open. Detectives Norton and Irving entered, followed by FBI Agents Coleen Milton and Delvin Peterson. Arndt Kjellgren said, "Protect her, Shapiro. Don't leave her alone. Keep her safe!"

Irving escorted me out of the interrogation room and said something about invoicing the department for my time. I told him I wouldn't do it, and he had a mini meltdown, saying I promised and have to invoice them or they could get in trouble for allowing me to interrogate a person of interest, especially in the interrogation room. I asked who they'd get in trouble with. Irving rubbed his orange hair but didn't answer.

I agreed to drive Robin home, and we left Arndt Kjellgren with the FBI and a handful of Minneapolis cops I didn't know. I opened the passenger-side door for Robin as if she were a date or an infirm person. She gave me a tiny smile as I shut the Volvo's heavy door. I walked around to my side and, in the orange glow of sodium vapor lights, saw what the careening Arndt Kjellgren had done to my driver's side door. Two grapefruit-sized dents disfigured the panel. It had taken almost a year, but my hockey-mom-mobile had finally lost its virginity. It was about time.

We didn't talk much on the short drive back to Christmas Lake. The clock on the dash read 1:04 A.M. when Robin said, "Would you please stay with me tonight?"

I had professional reasons to say yes and professional reasons to say no. Robin's air-conditioning cast the tie-breaking vote. I said, "Of course."

She looked at me with a tiny smile, and her eyes danced in the dash light. She caught a glimmer in mine I hadn't intended for her. It was an accidental discharge and she was in the wrong place at the wrong time.

The glimmer came from my sudden sense of freedom. Micaela's pregnancy uncaged me for the first time in over a dozen years. The counterintuitiveness of the feeling floored and delighted me. Having a child with someone is supposed to make you love the person more. Plenty of greeting cards and religions say so. I don't believe in destiny, but if I did, I'd say something stupid like Micaela and I were meant to have a child together. That was why we couldn't let go of each other, a simple preprogrammed biological drive to procreate. Like salmon swimming upstream. Unwavering. Now I was free to leave like a stag or grizzly bear or golden retriever who'd been used for stud. It felt wrong that it didn't feel wrong. It could only mean one thing: Micaela Stahl wasn't my person. Now, I was free to find her, whomever she was.

"You seem happy," said Robin, interrupting my wonderment.

"Well," I said, "I've always wanted to catch a fugitive with my car door."

Robin laughed then said, "No. You're thinking about something else." Her tone shifted to serene. "Or maybe *someone* else?"

"Life can be surprising and weird sometimes."

"You're telling me . . ." Robin looked out the passenger window at the blackness along the road. I watched her reflection in the glass. She said, "Do you think Arndt's telling the truth?"

"I don't know. He's a strange dude, your boyfriend."

"What did he say to you?"

I wasn't sure I should share the information with her, but since I had no idea what Arndt had meant, it was worth the risk if Robin could fill in the missing pieces. A risk of what, I wasn't sure. "Arndt said he was outside your house to protect you. That someone was going to break in. And he said he keeps records of who buys his sculptures. He kept talking about the records, that they are the reason he knows. He said records so much I wasn't sure if he meant his files and bills of sale for his sculptures or the thousands of vinyl records in his studio. Do you have any idea what he meant by that?"

"None."

"Maybe he hides documents in the record jackets with the vinyl? I don't know . . ."

She looked away from the dark and turned her shoulders toward me. "Is he going crazy? Like Van Gogh or something?"

"Maybe. Check your mail for an ear."

Robin half-smiled. I pulled into her driveway and stopped my freshly dented Volvo just shy of the garage. She said, "Thank you for staying."

"It's my turn on the couch."

She opened her door and stepped out of the car. I did the same and followed her over the pebbled pavement. She was about to put her key in the lock then stopped and looked at me in the soft gold glow of a filament bulb hanging above the front door. She said, "There's no need for you to sleep on the couch."

I had no idea if she said that because, unlike me, she lived in a real house with a guest bedroom, or maybe she wanted me to sleep in her bed. But I had no intention of doing that. Her husband had been dead forty-eight hours. Her boyfriend, an apparent lunatic, was in jail. But all I managed to say was, "Your house. Your rules."

We walked inside. She said, "Wine? I'm opening a bottle." She saw my hesitation. "We also have—*I* also have scotch, vodka, gin . . ."

"Scotch." She told me where it was, and I retrieved a bottle of Old Pulteney. Never opened. I couldn't find a proper whiskey glass so I poured a couple ounces into a stemless wine glass, bemoaned the improper vessel, then joined Robin in the living room, sitting on the other wing of an L-shaped sofa. We drank and didn't say much then Robin said, "Time for bed." I answered with a nod. She finished the last of her wine, set the glass on a big low coffee table made of frosted glass, stood, and walked over to me. "This is kind of awkward, but with all that's happened, I wouldn't mind you sleeping in my bed."

I said, "I'm not comfortable with that."

She said, "Too weird?"

I looked up at Robin. She'd missed a button on her blouse, and I could see her dark summer-tanned stomach and the underswell of her breast. Either she hadn't worn a bra all night or had slipped it off when I went hunting for the scotch.

I said, "I'll take the room closest to yours."

"Please," she said. "I just need a person next to me." Robin turned and walked away. There was a slim chance Arndt Kjellgren wasn't crazy. He said, "Protect her, Shapiro. Don't leave her alone. Keep her safe." A slim chance indeed. I followed her into the bedroom.

18

Robin and dead Todd's master suite overlooked Christmas Lake via a wall of glass with two sliding doors that led to a deck. Porch lights and dock lights showed the lake's edge, a black oval in the middle. A single reading lamp on one nightstand diffused a soft glow into the cavernous room. The modern minimalism gave extra depth to the negative space. A step-counter would beep with delight if you tried vacuuming the place.

Two nightstands, a king-sized bed, and small seating area near the wall of windows were the only furniture. The nightstands had digital clocks, votives made of handblown glass, and one paperback: Michael Chabon's *The Amazing Adventures of Kavalier & Clay*. I guessed it might have been Todd's. Not finishing it added an extra layer of tragedy to his death. Everything else was hidden by built-in drawers—a whole wall of them—just like in a morgue.

Robin hit a button on the wall. A sheer shade lowered from above the windows, its electric motor humming as it replaced the blackness with a sheet of soft ivory. Robin said, "Let me get you a toothbrush." She disappeared into a closet and reappeared half a minute later with an electric toothbrush head, its bristles blanketed in a squirt of toothpaste. "This is new. You can use Todd's bathroom if you're comfortable. There's a handle in there. The police took his toothbrush head yesterday along with most everything else." She head-motioned to a doorway within the suite.

I said, "Thanks," then started my journey toward dead Todd's bathroom. I stepped into the blackness and a motion sensor turned on a light revealing a walk-through closet. The clothes were gone. Ivory carpet and walls. More built-in drawers. I opened a few. Empty. I continued past a comfy-looking chair and ottoman then stepped into Todd's bathroom. A creamy limestone floor under white cabinetry.

Separate bathrooms are the most worthwhile rich-people indulgence. They're even healthier for a relationship than separate vacations. Privacy and personal time when you need it most help avoid shame and bring your best self to the marriage. Todd and Robin had separate suites, starting with their closets and ending with showers, toilets, tubs, and dressing areas.

Todd's bathroom wasn't taped off, so the Greater Lake Minnetonka Police Department had probably checked the drain traps in both the shower and sink. They'd taken his towels and toiletries. Todd's shower contained the kind of metal bar you see in bathrooms for the elderly and disabled, something to hold on to for stability. Only that and the electric toothbrush handle resting on its charger remained. I put on the new toothbrush head, brushed my teeth, returned to the bedroom, removed my shoes, and sat at the foot of the bed.

Robin Rabinowitz stepped out of her closet wearing baby blue gym shorts and a white tank top. She smelled of lotion and astringent. She walked to the left nightstand, removed an LED candle from the votive, turned it on, and set it back inside the votive. She smiled at me and walked around to the other nightstand.

"Electric candles. I would have figured you for real fire."

"You would have figured right," she said, "but Todd was always worried I'd fall asleep with an open flame." She turned on the other candle then turned off the reading lamp. The fake flames danced, lifelike, blurred by the thick bubbled-glass votives.

I said, "Did Todd have any leg or balance problems?"

"No. Why?"

"Did you buy this house from elderly people?"

"We didn't buy it from anyone. We had it built. Why do you ask?"

"Why is there a safety bar in Todd's shower?"

"Oh," she said, "that. Todd's father fell in the shower a few years ago and broke a hip. It was touch and go for a couple of weeks—he almost died. Todd wanted to live in this house for the rest of his life. He had the bar installed so it would be there when he got old and needed it." Robin walked back to the lake side of the bed and sat. "Guess he got his wish."

"What wish?

"To live in this house for the rest of his life." She got under the covers. I crawled up toward the headboard and lay on top of the covers.

She said, "Thank you for being here. I'm just . . . scared."

"Understandable." I shifted to my right side and faced her. She smiled, then turned her back to me and settled in an arm's distance away. I was about to ask her whether she always slept with fake candlelight when she wriggled herself backward like a worm across a sidewalk. She pressed her back into me. She found my left hand, pulled it onto her shoulder, then placed her hand on top of mine. Then she reached behind my back and pulled me into her.

"I can't," I said. "I can't lie in your dead husband's dent and do this."

"We're not doing anything. I just need you close. It's my only chance of getting any sleep."

"Okay." I didn't know what to do with my right arm so I just laid on it until it went numb. I wanted to leave but didn't. It took me a long time to fall asleep on the big bed in the cool air next to the woman who smelled of lotion and astringent.

I woke just after 5:00 A.M., having slept only a couple hours. Gray light filtered in through the ivory shades, voiding the room of color. The loon on Christmas Lake cried its echoey whistle. Robin slept on her stomach, her head facing me. She must have just turned that way because pillow marks creased her cheek. I was contemplating whether or not to wake her when she opened her eyes.

She blinked a couple times then said, "Hello," in a voice weak and scratchy.

"Good morning. I have an early appointment. I have to go."

She nodded, but said nothing.

I said, "I'll talk to you in a few hours."

She nodded one more time. I left, locking the door behind me, drove home and slept in the hot coat factory until nine, when I woke to a ringing phone. I took a sip of lukewarm water from my bedside table then answered.

"Mr. Shapiro, this is Detective Irving of the Greater Lake Minnetonka Police Department. I have some sad news. Arndt Kjellgren and Robin Rabinowitz are dead."

19

"What? Say that again?" I took another sip of water.

Detective Irving said, "You're my first call. It's uh . . . oh, boy . . . shocking. We got a nine-one-one call from Mrs. Rabinowitz's house, but when the operator answered she heard nothing. Just a hang-up. One of our officers went to check on Kjellgren. She thought maybe he got his hands on a cell phone and had made a threatening call to Mrs. Rabinowitz. But instead, uh geez, she noticed Kjellgren had escaped."

The news hurt my heart and swirled my stomach. I sat up on the bed. I heard construction workers outside the coat factory yell a conversation because that's what construction workers do. I said, "What time was the nine-one-one call?"

"Five forty-three A.M."

"And how the hell did Arndt Kjellgren escape?"

"We're looking into it. That's all I can say for now. A couple of uniformed officers went out to check on Mrs. Rabinowitz. Uh, boy. Looks like a murder-suicide."

"God dammit."

"Yeah."

I said, "I'll meet you at the station in half an hour."

"Okay. But actually, we'd appreciate it if you could meet us at the crime scene."

I wasn't sure if Detective Irving called because I was a suspect, a witness, or a private detective. I figured I'd find out when I got there. I took a moment to let the murder of Robin Rabinowitz sink in. I liked her.

I wiped my eyes and blew my nose then called Ellegaard and Annika and asked them to meet me at Christmas Lake. I also asked Annika to call Ian Halferin and tell him the bad news. Then I sobbed in the shower. Cried like a boy, my arms folded over my chest, my head bent in the spray. I cried until I had nothing left. I wasn't in love with Robin Rabinowitz. Not even close. But I abandoned her when she was scared for her safety. I couldn't wait to get the hell out of her house. There was no way to rationalize my failure, and I hated myself for it.

I got dressed, backed out of the coat factory, drove a few blocks, and ramped onto freeway 394. I got up my nerve and called Ellegaard. "Listen. I need to tell you something. I spent last night with Robin."

Ellegaard paused. I pictured him pinching his temples between thumb and forefinger. He said, "Geez, Shap. Really? After our conversation?"

"I told you there would be nothing physical between us and

there wasn't. She was scared to spend the night alone, and apparently for good reason. But she wanted me to sleep next to her. So, I'm sure they'll find a hair or two of mine on the pillow. I know I shouldn't have slept next to her, but I did. Actually, I take that back. What I shouldn't have done is left. I'll tell the police. Just wanted you to hear it first." Ellegaard didn't respond. There was little traffic heading west on 394. Sometimes this city feels empty. "Ellie, you there?"

"Yeah . . . Listen, Shap. Don't tell the police when Annika's around. She thinks the world of you."

"I suppose it looks pretty bad, huh?"

"Yeah, buddy. Pretty bad. Hey, I should call Molly and tell her about Robin."

"Of course," I said, not sure if Ellegaard really wanted to call Molly or just get off the phone with me. I'd disappointed him. It wasn't the first time, but it was the first time it stemmed from a dumb move on my part rather than from a difference in personality or style. I hated feeling his disappointment. I said, "I'll see you out there."

I drove down Christmas Lake Road, past the spot where I'd dropped Arndt Kjellgren with my car door. I'd had less than twelve hours of bliss—not even my awkward sleepover with Robin Rabinowitz had nipped away at Micaela's good news. Our good news. Then Irving called this morning and took it away.

The same uniform I'd seen a few nights earlier stood by another strip of yellow police tape. I stopped and rolled down my window. She said, "Welcome back, Mr. Shapiro." She scrunched her face. "I suppose that sounds weird."

"A bit. Yeah." I managed a courtesy smile, and she pulled away the tape. I drove forward and into the Rabinowitzes' driveway.

The house built for the oft-entertaining, child-free couple had a big enough driveway for three squad cars, two unmarked cars, an ambulance, county coroner's van, and my dented hockey-mom mobile. I got out of the Volvo, started toward the house, then stopped. I'd seen my share of dead bodies, but I wasn't ready to see Robin's.

Detective Irving stepped out of the house and squinted in the sunlight. He made a visor of his hand and spotted me standing in the driveway. He started down the pebbled stairs. "Thanks for coming, Nils." He walked up and shook my hand. "We have some questions to confirm your timeline with Mrs. Rabinowitz last night, but they can wait. What we'd really like your help with is this crime scene."

"I slept here last night."

Irving looked at me. His face soured. "Oh."

"I drove Robin home from the police station, and she asked me to stay. I slept in her bed with her. Fully clothed and on top of the covers. We did not have sex. I left around five A.M. She was fine, and there was no sign of Arndt Kjellgren or anyone else around here. What time did he escape?"

"You slept here last night?"

"Yes. She didn't want to be alone."

Irving scrunched his forehead and squinted in the white-hot light. "Well, I suppose that's none of anyone's business but your own. You know, assuming the M.E. establishes time of death after five A.M. and all that." Irving shuffled from foot to foot and rubbed a hand through his orange crew cut. "Well," he said, "we'll have to check ballistics and DNA and what have you."

"Of course. You have my full cooperation."

"You probably don't have an alibi, considering time of day."

"I don't, but you can check what towers my cell phone pinged. It's not ironclad. But it's something."

"That's a good idea. Thank you. And hey, sorry if what's in there is extra hard to see."

I nodded. "It will be."

"So, are you free now?"

"What do you mean?"

"Can you work for us?"

The heat and humidity magnified the tragedy. The sunlight hurt. I squinted. "I thought you said it was a murder-suicide."

"Yeah. It is. Well, it appears to be. But we still could use your help on Todd Rabinowitz's murder. With no chief, it's just me and Norton and a few uniforms. You would really—"

"Let's talk about it later. I'll see how I feel after . . ." I looked at the house.

"Of course. Yeah. Come on."

I followed Irving up the pebbled steps and into the house. CSU officers took fingerprints, impressions, swabs, and photographs. We walked through the entryway and living room, by the low, flat couches and coffee table. Irving entered the hall toward the bedroom. I followed.

Robin Rabinowitz lay facedown, wearing the same gym shorts and white tank. Her tanned calves had turned gray. A manhole-sized circle of blood soaked the white duvet, Robin's head at its center. It had darkened but not dried. Her throat had been sliced halfway through her neck, a wire still in her flesh.

Arndt Kjellgren lay faceup. It appeared he'd sat on the end

of the bed, put a gun in his mouth, and pulled the trigger. Bits of pink, white, and gray splattered the headboard, wall, and ceiling. A .38 lay on the bed, six inches from Arndt's right hand.

Dr. Melzer, the tall, sexagenarian medical examiner, peered through his tiny, round, rimless eyeglasses at a digital thermometer. His short ponytail bounced as he moved to make a note on a clipboard. He then turned his attention to Robin's fingernails. A CSU photographer snapped photos, the flash making shadows then erasing them.

"You seeing the same thing we're seeing?"

I looked to my right. Detective Norton stood, arms folded, rocking back on his heels and chewing gum like a cow. I'd taken a trip inside myself when I stepped into the room and, during my journey, Irving must have briefed Norton on my whereabouts last night. Norton had a dickish, judgmental look on his face. I stared at him, said nothing, then walked around toward Robin's side of the bed. I squatted to get a closer look at whatever had been used to slice through her throat. It was a wire studded with something coarse, like grains of sand from 60-grit sandpaper. Each end of the thread was tied to a plastic ring.

I said, "CSU take a look at this thing?"

"Not yet," said Irving.

"Get a photographer with a macro lens. And why don't you tell me how Arndt Kjellgren escaped from the Taj Mahal of jails."

Ellegaard and Annika entered the room. Annika stayed back by the doorway, these being the first crime scene bodies she'd seen. When I'd called earlier, I said she didn't have to come, but she wanted to. "I'd rather see my first victims with you and Anders," she said. "I want to be there."

"Well," said Irving, "it's kind of embarrassing, but it appears Kjellgren escaped out the jail cell's window."

"A barred window?" asked Ellegaard.

Norton said, "The thing is—"

I cut him off. "Let me guess. Kjellgren cut out a bar or two."

Norton and Irving looked at each other. Norton rocked back on his heels and took a couple chomps on his gum. "Yeah. How'd you know?"

"That wire in Robin's throat, he cut himself out with that."

"What?" said Irving.

Ellegaard said, "Did you search him before you put him in the cell?"

"Of course we did. Took his belt. Took his shoelaces. I don't know what you're even talking about. You can't cut through metal bars with wire."

"It's not wire," I said. "It's a saw. My guess is it's made of carbon fiber and industrial diamonds. Could have hidden it in his hair, in the sole of his shoe, maybe he ran it through the inseam of his jeans. Don't know if you checked him with a metal detector—"

"Damn right we did," said Detective Norton.

". . . but a metal detector won't detect carbon fiber and diamonds."

"Oh," said Norton.

Irving's face reddened. He looked down, shook his head, and said, "Damn."

Norton kept his arms crossed but no longer rocked on his heels. His friendly, cooperative demeanor toward me was gone. It was about time a cop acted like a cop.

"Where did he get the gun?" said Annika. Norton and Irving

hadn't realized she was in the room. They turned and looked at her, which seemed to catch her off guard. She took half a step back. Unsure, she looked at Ellegaard and me. At Stone Arch, we encouraged Annika to say whatever popped into her head, especially hunches and first impressions, no matter how stupid they seemed. It was hard for her at first, but in the last few months, she'd grown comfortable with it. More than comfortable—it had become second nature. I gave Annika a small smile and nod. She straightened up and said, "I'm just saying Kjellgren didn't hide a gun in his hair or in the sole of his shoe."

Irving and Norton perked up. The gun couldn't have been their fault. They wouldn't have missed a gun before locking up Kjellgren. Irving said, "Maybe last night, he stashed the gun outside the house before he ran."

"Maybe," I said. "Did you have the area searched after we caught Kjellgren?"

Irving and Norton slipped back into their shells of shame. No one said a word. Dr. Melzer put something into a sealed evidence bag and labeled it with a marker.

I told Norton and Irving I'd see them at the station around one, then drove into Excelsior to meet Ellegaard and Annika for an early lunch. I called FBI Special Agent Delvin Peterson on the drive.

I could tell he'd saved my contact information in his phone because he answered with a ho-hum, "What."

"Good day to you, too."

"I'm not in the mood, Shapiro."

"It's D.C. hot and humid today. What are you complaining about?"

"My day started at four A.M. and I'll be lucky to get home before midnight. Karin Tressler has a load of friends in Washington, and every one of them is riding me to find out who blew up Halferin Silver."

"Maybe I can help."

"Oh, really. What's in it for you?"

"One thing. I got a country club police department that wants me to do their job for them. I'm actually doing it right now by making this call. But after I catch you up to speed, you may want to take over for me."

"Let me get this straight. You're calling me during my twenty-hour workday to tell me you want to add to my workload?"

"Yes." I told him about Arndt Kjellgren's escape from Mayberry RFD, Robin Rabinowitz's 911 call, and both of them at her house—dead.

"Got it," said Peterson. "Thanks." He hung up.

Maynards Restaurant sits dockside on Lake Minnetonka looking out on St. Alban's Bay. The water was a gray-blue swash of small chop with sailboats, mostly students piloting white sails from one orange buoy to the next. I watched it all through big windows, opting for the air-conditioning over the outdoor seating with its humidity and panhandling gulls. We sat at a blond oak table preset with paper placemats and cardboard coasters. A waiter took our beverage orders then disappeared.

Ellegaard said, "I don't like this, Shap. We've already pushed the ethical boundaries by working for Halferin Silver and Robin Rabinowitz simultaneously. Working for Halferin Silver and the Greater Lake Minnetonka Police Department is out of the question."

I said, "Yeah. That kind of moonlighting could create trouble. Plus, Halferin Silver would probably be happy if I officially joined Annika working for them."

"So we're agreed?" said Ellegaard. "We turn down GLMPD?"

"We're agreed. What do you think, Annika?"

Annika Brydolf watched the sailboats zigzag across the bay. She said, "Is it always like that? Is there always that much blood and bits and pieces of them all over the room?"

Ellegaard said, "A lot of times, yes. And you never get used to it. You just get better at processing it. Shap's seen a lot more than I have."

I said, "What you get better at is preparing yourself. And focusing on the living. Ellie and I had one hell of an instructor at the Minneapolis Police Academy. He taught us that. Whenever you see a crime scene, remember there are living people who need your help."

Annika shook her head. "But a living person did that. Took those lives with such violence. How do you process that?"

Trite answers popped into my head. About motivation for catching bad guys and other bullshit. I said, "Honestly, Annika, you don't. And you shouldn't. Because the option is normalizing cruelty and evil. And that's the last thing a person should do."

Annika kept her eyes on the sailboats.

Ellegaard watched her, gave her a few moments, then said, "Have you ever sailed?" She shook her head. "There's a great program at Lake Harriet. They teach adults and kids. When yours get a little older they can join the summer program. Olivia has really taken to it. She's going to be a junior instructor next year and wants to race when she gets into high school."

Annika knew what Ellegaard was doing, but it still helped. Not because Annika suddenly became interested in sailing, but because she appreciated the effort.

She asked what age kids could start the sailing program. The conversation drifted to her kids' summer camp and what Ellegaard's kids were doing. Emma's attitude around the house had improved. Watching Ellegaard and Annika talk about their children felt like waking up from a bad dream—it rekindled my anticipation of becoming a father. Then we ordered and ate lunch and moved on with our day, emotionally hobbled but hopeful.

I drove to the GLMPD station after lunch. I could have just called, but I planned to take advantage of their job offer while I still had it. The orange-haired crew cut and big forehead met me in the reception area.

Norton said, "So are you finally ready to consult for GLMPD?"

"First I want to see Kjellgren's cell."

"Uh," said Norton. "Sure."

I followed them down one hall and turned into another. Irving held a card up to a sensor, which buzzed us into the cell area. GLMPD had four jail cells. Each had a three-foot-by-eighteen-inch window, vertical bars inside, with frosted glass behind them. Kjellgren's cell was the last one on the right. Its frosted glass was missing, and two of the bars had been cut clean from the top and bottom. They rested upright in the corner of the cell like unused table legs.

I said, "Where's the glass?"

Irving said, "What do you mean?"

"The frosted glass outside the bars. Where did it go?"

Norton pressed his lips together, wriggled them around, then said, "The window's not glass. It's plexi. And we don't know what happened to it."

"It just disappeared?"

"Appears so," said Irving.

"Huh," I said. "What about metal filings from the saw?"

"That we got," said Norton. "On the cell floor."

"Okay if I go in?"

Norton and Irving looked at each other like parents who couldn't make a decision without the other. Apparently, they'd come to an agreement because Irving said, "Yeah. Go ahead."

I took a few steps into the cell but stopped when I saw the metallic filings gathered on the windowsill and the cell floor against the wall. I turned around and walked out.

"That's it?" said Norton. "You don't want to inspect it more closely."

"No. I've seen all I need to see."

They walked me toward the station's front entrance. I got almost all the way out when Norton said, "Hey. We need to discuss your fee now that you're on board."

I stopped and turned back toward them. "You know, I've decided not to work for you, after all."

Irving and Norton looked at each other in their parental way. I walked out before they agreed on what to say.

20

I walked around back of the police station to the window of Arndt Kjellgren's cell. The ground alongside the building was paved with concrete. I saw no sign of the missing plexi or its surrounding frame and, of course, no footprints on the hard surface.

On the drive downtown I made two phone calls. The first was to Gabriella Núñez. I told her about Arndt Kjellgren's records rant, and that I wanted access to his studio. Ellegaard beeped in on call-waiting. I ignored it. Gabriella said she'd see what she could do. I then got Dr. Melzer on the phone. I had no authority to discuss the case with a Hennepin County medical examiner, and he had no authority to discuss the case with me. But I took a shot and asked if he'd consider meeting for coffee. He agreed, and an hour later we sat in the Dunn Brothers in the Hennepin County Medical Center drinking sweet, frothy ice-cold coffee drinks through thick straws. Heat makes me do crazy things.

Melzer wore khaki pants and a button-down shirt, white with tiny windowpanes of blue. Both garments were wrinkle free, not because they'd been pressed, but because the cotton had been treated with something like embalming fluid. "I shouldn't be talking to you like this," said Dr. Melzer, "but I'm a few months away from retirement. What can they do to me?"

"Make you work a couple extra years."

He smiled. "No thank you. And, I have to talk to someone. I've never seen anything like it."

"Like the murders?"

"Well those, I've seen. Not exactly like the first one, with the vic tied to the dock by a stringer through his jaw. But I've never seen anything like the police work. Or lack thereof."

"I've noticed that, too."

Melzer stirred his caffeinated Slurpee with a straw through the hole in its dome-shaped lid. He took a sip then said, "The Greater Lake Minnetonka Police Department is usually top notch. I've dealt with them quite a bit. Boating accidents and drownings, mostly. People falling through the ice. The occasional homicide. But since their chief went AWOL, they're just rudderless."

"Incompetent?"

Melzer considered my question. I took a big sip of my frozen beverage and got walloped by brain freeze for the first time in twenty years. Melzer said, "Not overtly. They're just not asking enough questions or the right questions and they're not following up. I don't even know if they've read my preliminary report."

I said, "Greater Lake Minnetonka PD offered me a job consulting on the case. Anything I can do to help?" I left out the part about me turning down the offer.

"Well, since you're working with them," said Meltzer, "maybe you could help impress upon them the importance of the water in Todd Rabinowitz's lungs."

"It wasn't lake water?"

"It was lake water," said Melzer.

"That's good, right? It proves Todd Rabinowitz drowned in the lake."

"It proves Todd Rabinowitz drowned in *a* lake. I found milfoil in the victim's lungs. That particular milfoil doesn't live in Christmas Lake. But it does live in Lake Minnetonka. My guess is Todd Rabinowitz drowned across the highway, and then was moved."

"And what did the police say when you told them that?"

"They said, 'Thanks. We'll look into it.' But I got the sense they won't. Maybe they're overwhelmed. And after what happened in the house out there today . . ." He shook his head. "I'll tell you one thing: if you want to kill someone, lure them into GLMPD's jurisdiction. Chances are, you'll get away with it."

I nodded in camaraderie to keep Melzer talking. "What's your gut on the bodies this morning?"

Melzer tucked his upper lip inside his lower then pulled them apart. "It looks like a murder-suicide, at least from a pathological point of view. The powder burns are where they should be, residue on the gun hand, splatter of blood and brain matter, but . . ." He did the thing with his lips again.

"But?"

"When you've seen forty years of bodies and crime scenes, sometimes you develop an intuition. And something feels off."

A voice said, "Nils." I turned toward the door. Anders Ellegaard stood in his Brooks Brothers suit. He wasn't sweating. I don't know how he accomplished that. He said, "I need to talk to you."

I said, "Anders Ellegaard, this is Dr. Melzer, the Hennepin County medical examiner." I gave him a *what-the-fuck are you doing?* look and said, "Dr. Melzer is working the Christmas Lake murders."

Ellegaard nodded then shook Dr. Melzer's hand. "Yes, I saw him this morning at the crime scene. I'm sorry to interrupt, Nils. But it's important."

Ellie was usually discreet and unreadable, but I saw concern. I said to Dr. Melzer, "Excuse me one moment."

"Of course," said Melzer.

I got up and met Ellegaard over by a rack of travel mugs and coffee-cozy grips. I was about to ask how he found me but remembered we at Stone Arch Investigations, as a safety precaution, set our phones to always know one another's location.

Ellegaard said, "They came into the office looking for you."

"They?"

"Two guys. Wouldn't say who they were with. They asked a lot of questions about you."

"What kind of guys?"

"Young, preppy. They're looking for you, Shap. I tried calling but you didn't answer. Saw you were here so I'm telling you in person."

"Sorry, I silenced my phone."

"I got a bad feeling about these guys. We need to deal with this."

I returned to Melzer, explained I had an emergency and had to leave. He thanked me for the coffee, then I went to the counter and asked the barista if there was a back way out.

She wore heavy eyeliner and part of her head was shaved but I couldn't tell if it'd been done by a stylist or a brain surgeon. She scratched the spiderweb tattoo that creeped above the collar of her T-shirt. I wondered where the spider was. She said, "You mean, like through the hospital?"

"Wherever."

"Well, we get deliveries in back, but—"

Ellie and I walked behind the counter and into the stock room, which was lined with shelves filled with shiny bags of coffee beans. A door was marked *Emergency Exit Only*. It felt like an emergency so we opened it and stepped into a large indoor garage. Cars, ambulances, and half a dozen mid-sized trucks filled the parking spots.

Anders Ellegaard half-smiled. The former gold shield at Edina PD was out from behind his desk. It had become a rare occurrence because Ellie focused his efforts on bringing in new business and managing existing business. But my former fellow cadet wasn't cut out for a desk job. That's not why he became a cop. And it's not why he walked away from his gold shield to start an investigations firm with me. Anders Ellegaard was too good of a detective to waste away in the blue light of a computer screen.

Ellegaard said, "Where are you parked?"

"On Sixth Street."

"Let's go up to the skyway level. If anyone followed you they'll be waiting at your car."

We took the stairs up to the second floor and found a skyway over Sixth Street where we could look down on my Volvo parked at a meter. It took ten seconds to spot the guys waiting for me. Khakis and dress shoes under rumpled oxfords with loosened ties. Preppy white boys with quasi-military haircuts and clean-shaven faces. The only two guys on the street not wearing shorts. One was blondish and wore his sleeves long, buttoned at the wrist, a bold show of heat tolerance. The other had a darker complexion, wore wraparound sunglasses, and his sleeves were rolled up above the elbow.

Ellegaard said, "Those are the guys who came into the office."

"I don't know when, but they must have stuck a tracking device on my car."

"How do you want to handle this?"

I said, "Where did you park?"

"Sixth and Portland."

"That will work." I pulled out my phone, searched my contacts, and sent a text. *Long time no talk. Want to make a quick $100?*

A minute later I received a return text. *U r getting cheap dude. What's the job? And how quick?*

Steal my car. Half an hour of work. But has to be right now. Where are you?

The U.

Perfect. I'm on 6th and Park. You in?

$200

If you fill it up with gas.

Fuck you.

:)

I found a dry cleaner on Seventh Street and talked myself into a free coat hanger, then Ellegaard and I met him on Fifth Avenue, two blocks north of my car.

Ernesto Cuellar had grown a sad excuse of a mustache since I'd last seen him in March. He'd lost the Southwest High School insignia–laden clothing and replaced it with baggy maroon basketball shorts, skate shoes, and a gray T-shirt. The sides of his head were clipped tight and the hair on top stood an inch long like brush bristles. He worked hard to suppress a smile when he saw me. I handed him ten crisp twenty-dollar bills, and his smile won. He was seventeen, but with that big stupid grin on his face, looked twelve.

I shook Ernesto's hand. "Good to see you, Ernesto. You taking classes at the U this year?"

"I'll be taking three starting next month. My senior year I'll be there full time."

"A mere high school can't contain your brain, huh?"

"You got that right."

I said, "You think that mustache is working for you?"

"I know it is. Ten thousand college girls can't be wrong."

"How do you even know that reference?"

"I'm smarter than you, Nils Shapiro. Thought you'd be used to it by now."

Ellegaard said, "I like this guy."

"About time," said Ernesto.

Last year, Ellegaard and I met Ernesto Cuellar when we discovered him camped outside my coat factory with his hands in his pockets. He kept his head in his hoodie and said he had a message for Nils Shapiro. When he refused to show his hands, Ellegaard pulled a gun on him.

I said, "I need you to walk a couple blocks up Sixth Street, pretend to use this coat hanger to open my car, get in, and drive away."

"Easy. Where should I drive it?"

"I'll call you and tell you." I handed him the key fob. "Just give us a five-minute head start."

He nodded. Ellie and I walked Seventh Street to Portland Avenue and took a right. I didn't have to worry about Ernesto Cuellar doing his job. The kid was smarter than Silicon Valley. We approached Ellegaard's Lincoln Navigator. I said, "Still got your tailing skills?"

He said, "Like riding a bike."

We got in Ellegaard's oven on wheels. He started the car, pulled into traffic, and a minute later we watched Ernesto Cuellar stick a straightened coat hanger into my car door along the window, jimmy it for a few seconds, open the door, and get in. The neckties seemed stunned and too stupid to realize the alarm should have gone off. They ran to a black Cadillac parked a few spaces back, pulled into the street, and followed Ernesto.

I said, "Idiots."

"How'd you know they'd follow him?"

"I didn't. Just thought they might." I called Ernesto. "Still live by Powderhorn Park?"

He said, "Where else would I live?"

"Drive there. Park in front of your house. Go in. Job done. I'll pick up the key later."

Ernesto said, "So you just paid two hundred bucks for me to drive your wife's station wagon to my own house instead of me taking the bus?"

"I don't have a wife and shut up. It's an SUV."

"It's a station wagon, dude. And why's there a bunch of makeup and shit in the console?"

"That's not makeup—it's lip balm. I'll see you later."

Ernesto Cuellar circled around to Portland Avenue and drove south.

Ellegaard, always the dad, said, "We don't know these guys. Maybe it's safer to send Ernesto to a public place."

"They'd just wait for him to leave and follow him home anyway. We won't lose sight of him. We'll keep him safe."

Ernesto turned left on Thirty-first Street, continued a block and a half, and parked in front of his house. He got out and went inside without incident.

One of the neckties jumped out the passenger side of the Cadillac, used his phone to take a picture of my car, another of its license plate, and another of the house Ernesto walked into. He got back in the Cadillac. It drove off.

"Here we go," said Ellegaard. He followed, hanging two cars behind the black Cadillac. We slugged through rush hour as if gum were stuck to the bottoms of our tires, a slow push and pause to 35W then west on Highway 62, which eventually bled onto Highway 212 and through the streets of Chaska. Ten minutes later, the Cadillac stopped in front of a large iron gate through which I saw an immaculate lawn sprawling to an old-school mansion. The kind with ivy on brick and statues and a fountain and circular driveway with a covered entrance to the front door.

Ellegaard said, "Nice place."

"Eh. The utility bills have got to be murder."

"If you can afford a house like that, utility bills aren't your biggest concern."

I said, "If you can afford a house like that, what is your biggest concern?"

"You might have a few." Ellegaard smiled. "What are the odds Karin Tressler lives here?"

21

We drove a few blocks past the mansion then turned around and parked under the shade of a massive oak. The call came twenty-five minutes later. My caller ID read *BLOCKED*. Of course it did. I answered, "This is Nils."

A man's voice said, "I know who stole your car."

I put the phone on speaker for Ellegaard. I said, "I think you might've dialed the wrong number."

Ellegaard shook his head and smiled.

The man said, "Is this Nils Shapiro?"

"Yes. Who are you? What are you talking about?"

"I'm a Good Samaritan. Your car got stolen, right?"

"I don't think so. Is this a joke? I got to go. I'm visiting a friend in the hospital."

"Did you park your car on Sixth Street?"

"How do you know who I am and where I parked?" The caller hadn't considered the possibility I didn't know my car was stolen. Ellegaard laughed a silent laugh. The caller hesitated. I could hear he'd muffled the phone on his end, probably with a sweaty hand. I said, "Hello? Are you still there?"

Ten seconds later he said, "Uh, yeah. I saw someone steal a car on Sixth Street. I caught the license plate and traced it to you. I'm sorry to tell you the bad news."

"How'd you trace the license plate? Do you work at the Department of Motor Vehicles?" Ellegaard gave me a thumbs-up. It was good to see him back where he belonged. Another muffled pause. Ellegaard found a pen and pad of paper in the driver's-side door pocket and made a note.

The man returned. "I found it online. You can find anything online if you know where to look or who to pay."

Ellegaard showed me his note. Excellent idea.

"Oh," I said, "well, thank you. Did you call the police to report my car stolen?"

"Uh . . . not yet. I'm calling you first."

"Huh. Well, thanks, I guess. But I'd better get off the phone and call the police."

"Wait. I'm calling you because I followed your car when it got stolen. I know where it is."

"But you didn't call the police when you were following my car?"

"No. Listen. You're kind of being an asshole. I'm just trying to help you get your car back."

"Oh. I guess, yeah. Sorry about that. Where is it?" He gave me the address. I said, "Bad neighborhood?"

"Definitely."

"Okay, then I won't try to take it back. I'll let the police do that. And uh, hey. I'd like to thank you. What's your name?"

Another muffled pause, then, "No name. Just a good citizen doing what any other good citizen would do."

I said, "All right, good citizen. Can I buy you a drink or cup of coffee sometime?"

Ellegaard nodded his approval. Another muffled pause, but not well. I could hear fragments of conversation. The man returned and said, "Uh sure, I'll take you up on that. What are you thinking?"

"J.D. Hoyt's at eight?"

Another muffled pause. "Great. I'll see you there."

I hung up.

I suggested J.D. Hoyt's because of its close proximity to Target Field. The Minnesota Twins had a home game that night—the area and Hoyt's would be crowded. Ellegaard drove me to Ernesto Cuellar's then went back to the office. I knocked on Ernesto's door. His mother answered. Late thirties, a kind face. She had just started dinner. She invited me to stay, but I took a rain check. Ernesto stepped out of his room, his noggin sandwiched between big headphones.

He handed me my key and said, "I took it out for a spin and filled the tank."

"You know I was kidding."

"Yeah, I know. But now you owe me." He turned and went back into his room.

I said good-bye to Mrs. Cuellar then got in my Volvo. Ernesto had done more than fill the tank. A pair of red fuzzy dice hung from the rearview mirror, and a tiny plastic Jesus stood suction-cupped on the dash. I left Ernesto's additions where he put them and headed home.

The coat factory was so hot it took five minutes to expel the lukewarm water from the pipes so I could take a cold shower. I changed into fresh khakis and a polo shirt. Micaela bought me a rainbow of them when we were married, but they all featured alligators. Beautiful shirts, but if you want me to advertise your brand, then pay me. Otherwise, forget it. Unless all my other shirts are dirty.

I drove to Arndt Kjellgren's studio in Northeast. Gabriella Núñez had arranged for a uniform to meet me outside Kjellgren's door. The uniform unlocked the place and let me have at it. I started with the albums Kjellgren had first suggested to me: the New York Dolls, Aretha, and Leonard Cohen. None of the discs recorded by those artists contained anything unusual inside the jackets. No documents. No notes. Nothing. I spent another hour spot-checking record albums and found nothing. It would take a full day to check them all. At least. I gave up, thanked the uniform, and left.

When I pulled up to the coat factory's bay door, Susan Silver stood outside my building, looking at the brick, I guessed, for some kind of identifier. A sign. An address. Something.

I rolled down my window and said hello. Susan Silver turned to me and smiled. She wore a peach-colored skirt that fell just below the knee and a white sleeveless blouse. Her long gray hair glinted an eponymous silver when the wind found enough strength to move it.

I pulled into my loading dock and got out of the car. She had entered the bay and smiled something grave then said, "Nils."

"Hello, Susan. Happy coincidence or are you looking for me?"

"The latter, I'm afraid." We shook hands. "I would have called, but I'd appreciate an off-the-record conversation. Do you have a few minutes?"

"I'd ask how you found me but I know too many lawyers." She responded with a nod and nothing more. I said, "It's hotter in here than it is out there. I'm about to head out and grab something to eat if you'd like to join me."

"That would be nice. Thank you."

I wasn't about to grab something to eat. I felt a bit nauseous. Maybe it was the heat. Maybe it was seeing three dead people in the last two days. But we had to go somewhere. I considered a few of my local favorite spots, but sitting down with Susan Silver felt like first-date territory. Not that I felt anything romantic toward her, or her toward me, but it felt like a first date in that I didn't want to be tied to a long meal if it went badly. First dates work best as a drink or coffee. If it goes well, it can push into dinner. If not, you can get the hell out of there. But I'd already brought up food so I suggested a salad place where they make it assembly-line style, and you pay before you sit down. The lighting was a bit harsh, but like I said, it wasn't that kind of first date. We walked a couple blocks then sat down with salads and iced teas. Susan started to say something about giving up artificial sweeteners but must have seen impatience in my eyes.

She said, "You don't care about my relationship with stevia, do you?"

"Not so much, no."

She nodded. "There's something I'd like to share with you. It's probably not important, but I feel compelled to tell you about it."

I don't know why people want to tell private investigators their life story, but they do and it's rarely interesting. It could be worse. I could be a therapist or a priest.

Susan Silver looked down at her salad as if she'd lost her place and what she'd wanted to say was written on a leaf of kale. "I had my babies early. Before I went to law school. Three by the time I was twenty-eight." She looked up from her salad. "My husband worked all the time and left me with the kids then golfed on weekends and told everybody what a beautiful family he had. He was doing it all for us. I used to say the kids and I were a trophy family. He'd take us off the shelf and show us off on holidays but, other than that, we weren't much a part of his daily life."

Susan Silver's eyes looked brown but the brown yielded toward green near her pupils. She probably checked *hazel* on her driver's license. I wanted to ask her but let her continue. She swallowed a bite of salad then said, "So when I was thirty-one, I told him I wanted a divorce. He wanted to stay married. He promised he'd change, but that wasn't the point. The point was he was content, maybe more than content, not spending time with us. I didn't want him compromising his priorities. He wasn't one of the kids. I shouldn't have had to make him do the dishes instead of play video games because he needed to learn how to contribute to the family. So, I held firm and divorced him."

I had no idea why Susan Silver told me all this. Maybe she needed a ramp to get to where she was going.

"My husband went through an angry phase, and during the divorce proceedings, insisted I get a job because—how did he put it?—he wasn't going to fund my lavish lifestyle after getting kids out of him, which, according to him, was all I wanted. He liked to make loud pronouncements like that. I never even got a chance to say I wanted to go to work. And I figured it was better to just let him think it was his will and I was yielding to it.

"He kept negotiating and renegotiating the divorce settlement, dragging it out hoping I'd change my mind. So, I made him an offer. If he'd pay three years of spousal maintenance, I'd put myself through law school and then he wouldn't have to pay any more spousal maintenance. Just child support. He said he'd think about it. I said the offer was good for twenty-four hours, as if I were buying a house. He accepted in the twenty-third hour.

"A year after the divorce, my ex-husband, who was so willing to become father of the year, moved to Florida and out of his children's lives except for one week on Sanibel Island every winter. Then my life got extremely busy and didn't slow down until my youngest went to college."

Maybe Susan Silver told me this to win my favor. It was a hero's story, and she was the hero. I knew that. But it still worked. She'd endeared herself to me. I told myself she was playing me the way you tell yourself you're drunk. You know it, but you're still drunk.

She said, "I went to work for a law firm when the kids were still little. Most of the other lawyers I'd known since I was a kid. They were all what we'd now call liberal elites. And that worldview seemed normal—I was born in the sixties—it's what I grew up with. You couldn't idolize The Beatles when you were a kid and not believe in peace and love. Especially when John sang about it. But then nine-eleven happened . . ." She trailed off and looked down at her salad again.

I said, "Did you lose someone in nine-eleven?"

She shook her head then forked another piece of kale into her mouth. She hesitated then chewed and swallowed. "Both of my parents are Holocaust survivors. They met at Dachau when they were ten years old. They're in their early nineties now and still madly in love with each other. I did lose grandparents, cousins, aunts, and uncles in the Holocaust. I never knew them, of course. But boy oh boy do I feel the loss. Nine-eleven triggered something in me. A protector instinct kicked in. Like how I'd protected my self-worth and my kids from their absent father. And my worldview shifted to the right. Maybe shifted isn't the right word. More like jumped.

"A week after nine-eleven the firm informed me I'd made partner. But I declined. I left the liberal elites and started Halferin Silver with Ian. By day we practice law and by night we fight the good fight for the principles we believe in." She smiled. "I can see by your expression you don't believe in our cause."

I returned the smile and said, "There are two political camps and all the issues get bundled into one or the other. So, you're either an independent or you have to live with some causes you don't care for because they're packaged with the ones you do care for. It's like buying a car. You want leather seats but they're pretty hard to get if you don't take the sunroof, too."

"You're right about that," she said.

"A lot of people believe you have to buy into the whole package or you're part of the problem."

"Yes. And I fear Todd Rabinowitz was one of them."

So that's what this was about. "How so?"

Susan shook her head again. That little head shake meant something—I didn't know what. "I think Todd might have gone too far."

"I'm not sure what that means."

She sighed. "He got very involved, let's say overinvolved, with some radical groups on the right. Anti-tax groups, anti-entitlements groups, and hateful anti-immigrant groups, which was tough for me because, obviously, my parents are immigrants. Robin loathed it. When she attended social events with Todd, I saw her literally roll her eyes on more than one occasion." Susan Silver shook her head again.

"You think he got involved with dangerous people."

"Yes, but I'm not accusing them of killing Todd. There are fringes on the right and the left. They both do ugly things. Bomb buildings. Kill people."

"Yes, they do. But if someone in a fringe element killed Todd Rabinowitz, were they on the left or the right?" She shrugged. I said, "Are you telling me this because you think Arndt Kjell-gren was a fringe lefty and that motivated him to kill a fringe righty?"

"Well, it looks that way to me. That's what the news is practically saying." Her voice grew small and light. Her eyes glistened. She was holding something in. Something that upset her. She looked like she might be reciting a mantra: *Don't cry. A man wouldn't cry.* I'd heard Micaela say it a hundred times. Susan Silver and Micaela Stahl shared some traits. Smart. Hard-working. They steered their own ships at work and at home. And apparently, they both felt emotional expression was an obstacle to achievement. What a tough burden to carry.

I said, "I don't know what you're holding in, but I doubt it has anything to do with fringe elements of an ideology."

She shook her head again then said, "But it does. It does, it does. Because I created the environment in which Todd Rabi-nowitz grew. Like a petri dish for a germ. Like one of those awful cable news channels. A myopic feeding frenzy on its own bullshit. So, no matter whose hand was at work, I killed Todd Rabinowitz. That's what I'm saying, Nils. In a way, *I* killed him. It was me. I'm as guilty as anyone."

Susan Silver looked down one last time, then, without a word, stood from the table and walked out.

22

"Hello, Nils. This is Detective Norton with the Greater Lake Minnetonka Police Department."

"You sound chipper, Detective."

The Minnesota Twins had a 7:05 P.M. start, and I had an hour to kill before meeting the Good Samaritan who spotted Ernesto Cuellar stealing my car. I was scouting outside Target Field for a ticket when Detective Norton called.

"We're closing the Rabinowitz murders."

"Why would you do that?"

"There is nothing to indicate any possibility other than Arndt Kjellgren killed Todd first and then Robin before taking his own life."

"Based on what motive?"

"Our internal investigation is firming up the details. I'm just calling to inform you both cases are closed, and we're no longer interested in your services."

"I declined your offer of employment this afternoon. So why exactly are you calling?"

"To confirm that we'll no longer be interested in your services and because of your uh, uh . . . romantic association with the victim. I thought you should hear it from us rather than on the news."

"I didn't have a romantic association with the victim, and your department has nothing to do other than arrest drunk drivers and boaters. Why are you closing the case so fast? It's been less than a day since Robin was killed."

An African-American man swung a stiff left leg forward while fanning a dozen or so tickets in his right hand and yelling, "Tickets! Who needs tickets?" I let him pass. There's always an upcharge for splitting one off a group.

Detective Norton said, "Closing the case now frees up resources for other ongoing investigations. And they don't all have to do with operating a vehicle under the influence. We have the same problems every other municipality has."

"Bullshit you do."

"You really don't need to—"

"You're bad at your job, Norton. It's amateurville over there." I wanted to bring up the milfoil in Todd Rabinowitz's lungs, but that may have caused trouble for Dr. Melzer.

"Maybe you're a little too close to this one, Shapiro. Let it go. The D.A. and commission agree with the GLMPD. This is our turf. We know it better than anyone else. And based on what we know we've made a decision."

"I don't care if you know every goddamn twig and ladybug on your turf. It has nothing to do with what motivates one person to take another person's life. There's no upside to closing this case now. And if you're wrong, there's a huge downside."

A heavyset man on a mobility scooter rolled in my direction holding a single ticket in the air. A plastic tube delivered oxygen under his nose, a hamburger and fries sat half-eaten in the scooter's front basket, and an orange flag stood tall to alert cars and ticket buyers to his presence.

"Our decision is final, Shapiro. I'm sorry you don't like it. Thank you for your help. And good-bye." He hung up.

I waved down the scooter and bought the ticket, which was for a field-level seat between home and first. My baseball team was having another mediocre year, hovering around .500. But, with six weeks to go, they were only a few games out of first place. Anything could happen. And when anything can happen, things get interesting.

I bought an Able Black Wolf Stout at the microbrew kiosk and found my seat. Even the heavy, wet heat couldn't deter from the beauty of Target Field. Green grass, a limestone façade, and glass buildings over the right-field bleachers reflecting white, billowing clouds.

Two men in their forties sat a few rows in front of me. One wore Eddie Rosario's name on his back. The other wore Miguel Sano's. Their heroes were fifteen years younger than they were. I envied their absence of cynicism.

Some people complain about how slow baseball has become, but I like it slow. The stadium is a place to contemplate. It's expensive, but cheaper than most places of worship. Brief moments rivet between big gaps of time. They are of equal value. The noise of the stadium can insulate you from the noise of everything else. Except when the deplorables participate in the wave. That should carry the same penalty as streaking onto the field.

I had time to think. About dead Todd Rabinowitz. About dead Robin Rabinowitz. About dead Arndt Kjellgren. About Ian Halferin insisting I investigate someone else's investigation and about Susan Silver blaming herself for Todd's death.

The Twins had two outs in the bottom of the first inning when Eddie Rosario ripped a single over the shortstop's head. The fortysomething Sano jersey turned to the fortysomething Rosario jersey and patted him on the shoulder, as if anyone wearing Rosario's jersey deserved credit for the hit. Yet another example of tribalism run amok. The value human beings get from associating with other human beings probably helped our ancestors evolve into the dominant species, but man, has it become ridiculous.

I left Target Field after four innings of 0–0 baseball and walked three blocks to J.D. Hoyt's. It was the kind of place that sold expensive entrees under a cheap suspended ceiling and showed off a lot of liquor bottles and TVs over the bar.

Most were tuned to the game, but two showed CNN's coverage of the bomb blast in downtown Minneapolis. The sound was off, but I read Karin Tressler's name in the crawl. Half the country thought she was the intended victim. The other half thought she was somehow responsible. I wondered which algorithm-wielding assholes figured out how to divide us in half.

A lot of eyes were focused on the report. Two of those eyes belonged to him. He waited for me, seated on one of the stools.

It was the clean-cut blondish one wearing a white oxford shirt, sleeves still cuffed at the wrist, and madras tie, a plaid of blues and pinks, loosened around the collar. I stepped into the bar area and looked left and right to pretend I didn't know who I was looking for.

He said, "Mr. Shapiro?" His voice was clear and smooth, as if he worked in radio or sold investments over the phone.

I turned to him. "Are you my Good Samaritan?"

He smiled and stood. He extended a hand. "Luke."

I took his hand and said, "What's your drink, Luke?"

"Macallen if that's all right."

I asked him how he took it, and he told me. I sat on the bar stool next to Luke and caught the bartender's attention. "A Redbreast neat and a Macallan eighteen, one rock."

The bartender nodded and went to work. Luke laughed and said, "You didn't have to get me the eighteen."

"I got my car back because of you. Intact. That's not nothing."

"Well then," he said, "thank you."

Luke was in his midthirties and had green-gray eyes under white-blond eyebrows, a pale complexion, and red shaving bumps on his neck. His white shirt had a polo pony on the breast and a button-down collar. The garment was heavily starched, which meant he was fastidious or not in charge at home or unaccustomed to wearing dress shirts in summer heat. The stiff shirt was tucked into khaki pants, simple and straight. He wore white bucks on his feet and pink socks. He looked like a man familiar with country clubs and fine cigars, but something money can't buy danced in his eyes. Something wild.

I said, "Pretty crazy someone stole my car off Sixth Street in broad daylight. I don't know what the kid was thinking. And a Volvo station wagon. What soccer moms are looking for black-market parts?"

Luke smiled. "Did the police arrest him?"

"I don't know. I called them right after you called me. They took the kid and the car into the station, found some fingerprints on the dash, then let me drive away. Some detective is supposed to call me with more information."

The bartender set down our drinks. I lifted mine and said, "To neighborhood watch."

He tilted his head, then his brow scrunched. "Hey, I've seen you before. Aren't you like a famous detective?" He was a terrible actor. He knew exactly who I was. And there's no such thing as a famous detective.

But it gave me a chance to play dumb, and playing dumb is one of my favorite pastimes. "Oh, wow. Really? You recognize me?"

"Yeah, yeah! You're the guy who solved the Duluth murders and when that woman got killed in Edina." He sounded like a reality show contestant when they talk to the camera, trying to pretend the producers didn't script every word they say. "This is so cool. I helped a famous detective track down his stolen car. How awesome is that?"

My new friend, Luke, made a mistake. Well, several. But this was his biggest. A small flick of his eyes to our left. I waited a minute while his cascade of flattery gushed on, his ingratiation a neon indicator of his intent. Then I said, "You want anything to eat? Where's a menu?" With that excuse, I looked to my left and saw the other goon who had waited for me earlier on Sixth Street. Same crew cut and dark complexion. His sleeves were still rolled above the elbow, but his wraparound sunglasses were gone. He looked up at a TV, pretending to pay attention to the game. He wasn't all that intimidating, but the guy sitting on his left was. He had a blond-red brush on top of his head and had shaved the sides clean. Though he was sitting, I pegged him for about six feet four. He had broad shoulders and a military tattoo on his right forearm. He seemed to be staring straight ahead at nothing.

"Yeah," said Luke, "I could eat something."

"Great. I got to take a leak. See if you can find a menu."

Luke said, "Another round?"

"Definitely." I left my drink on the counter, got up, and walked toward the bathrooms. I hid behind the line of women waiting to powder their faces. Most wore Minnesota Twins jerseys and glitter tattoos and skipped the cheap seats in favor of drink specials and big TVs.

A six-foot blonde wearing a blue-and-red TC on her cheek and a Harmon Killebrew jersey said, "Hey, you trying to sneak into the ladies' can?" She held a large glass tumbler of green liquid.

"I'm hiding," I said.

"From who?" She sipped her drink, retained a few ice cubes in her mouth, and pushed them around with her tongue.

Luke looked at his colleagues sitting at the end of the bar. The one with the military tattoo made an emphatic gesture to say *what are you waiting for?* Luke pulled something from his pocket then dropped it into my whiskey.

23

The son of a bitch roofied my drink.

"Hey," said Killebrew, "I said, who are you hiding from?"

"That dude sitting at the bar."

Luke grabbed a swizzle straw and stirred my whiskey.

"Why?" said Killebrew. "What'd you do?"

"I didn't do anything. I was just sitting there and he sat next to me. Guy won't shut up. He bought me a drink and now he thinks we're friends."

"He sounds stalkery."

"Yeah. He's something."

"Fuck."

The conversation went on like this as we inched closer to the women's bathroom. My Good Samaritan had just revealed his not-so-good intentions. I needed backup. Luke and company knew me and Ellegaard, so there was a good chance they'd recognize Annika.

"What are you going to do?" said Killebrew.

"How'd you like to earn another one of those green drinks?"

"For free?" Killebrew was all in.

I coached her, keeping things simple, then returned to the bar.

Luke said, "We got wings, rings, and calamari on the way. And fresh drinks as soon as we finish the first ones."

I said, "Perfect. Here's to fried food and fine whiskey."

We raised our glasses and clinked them together. I drew my glass toward my mouth.

"Nils! Oh my God! I can't believe it!" Killebrew stood too close.

"Janice?"

"Yes! Oh my God! I can't believe you remembered! Why didn't you come to the twentieth? Everybody was dying to ask you about that murder in Edina."

"I couldn't make it. Sorry. Janice, this is Luke. Luke, Janice. Janice and I were in the same chemistry class in eleventh grade?"

"It was biology and tenth grade," said Killebrew, improvising. "And oh! Guess who's here? Karen and Gina and Dez."

"No shit?"

She smiled and slugged me on the arm. "Hey, come with me. They will shit in their pants when they see you!"

"Sorry, Janice. Luke and I—"

"Too bad, mister! You're coming with me."

She grabbed my right hand and pulled me off the bar stool— my left hand clutched the roofied whiskey. I looked back at Luke and said, "Be right back," as Killebrew dragged me away and into a private dining room. There, I complimented Killebrew on her acting, ordered her another green drink from a passing waitress, poured my rape juice into a potted plastic plant, and called Ellegaard to bring him up to speed. I hung up just in time to watch Killebrew spot her friends and say, "Hey, fuckers. This dude just bought me another Incredible Hulk!"

I knew from the Somerville case that Rohypnol starts to take effect about half an hour after being ingested. I didn't know what drug I was faking the effects of, but half an hour seemed like a safe play. I waited ten minutes, then returned to my seat next to Luke. "Sorry about that. High school acquaintance."

Luke said, "That's what happens in the biggest small town in the world."

The bartender set down our new drinks as the server brought our food. Luke said, "To another round."

"To another round."

I was pretty sure he didn't bribe the bartender to taint my new drink, so I drank. Just a sip. I needed my wits. Sometimes, being a lightweight has its disadvantages.

We shot the shit for fifteen minutes about where we grew up and the weather and nothing much interesting, then I said, "So Luke, what do you do for a living?"

"I'm a financial analyst for a private equity firm. We mostly buy and sell mid-cap companies."

"Sounds like a good job. What were you doing on Sixth Street when my car was stolen? Don't you have to pay attention to markets all day?"

"I'm not a stockbroker or hedge fund manager. I don't make equities trades in real time. I analyze underperforming companies. When the numbers are right, we buy them, install a new management team, turn things around, then sell them."

He sounded legit. He dressed legit. But something about Luke was far from legit, and that doesn't count my drugged drink or his two thug buddies sitting at the end of the bar. I whipped up a yawn to feign the first effects of being drugged, then said, "I got some buddies in the finance world. Where do you work?"

"Norsk Capital."

I shut my eyes and swayed. "Man, I'm sorry. That drink hit me hard. I'm in danger of losing my he-man credentials. I'll be right back. I'm going to throw some water on my face."

I edged off the stool, but Luke grabbed my upper arm. "No."

"No?"

"I'm getting tired, too. Let's finish up and call it a night." He didn't let go of my arm until I returned to the stool. I smiled and nodded. Luke stole another glance at his comrades.

"Ha! Lookie this!" said a deep baritone. "We got a pitcher's duel in the Twin Towns."

Luke looked to his right and saw a large African-American man standing six feet seven with a full-cheeked face under a tangle of twisted curls. The giant smiled, revealing high-vis white teeth. He wore powder blue sweatpants and a gray T-shirt with the size printed on the chest—5 XL. Jameson White had perfect timing.

"I always say," said Jameson, "if the Twins can hang within five games of first until September, then they still got a chance. This is the American League Central. Nobody's immune to choking in September. Ha!"

I met Jameson White last spring while recovering from an

arrow wound I received while investigating the disappearance of a high school girl. Micaela hired him to be my private nurse even though he was, technically, a nurse practitioner, a fact he reminded me of whenever I called him a nurse. We remained friends after my skewered shoulder healed, enjoying each other's company at sporting events and lazy dinners. Jameson played offensive line for the Montreal Alouettes after college ball at UCLA. Then he became the best trauma nurse in Minnesota, and we entertained each other with stories from the emergency room and stakeouts. Every time I saw him he asked if he could help on a case, as if he were a lion and I was a mouse who'd pulled a thorn from his paw, leaving him forever in my debt. In truth, it was the other way around.

Jameson said, "Why didn't you fellas go to the game?"

"No tickets," said Luke.

"Ha!" said Jameson. "That's no excuse. Tickets are practically falling out of scalpers' butts. Face value when they're playing five hundred ball. No tickets. No excuse." He laughed his infectious laugh.

Luke couldn't hide his annoyance at this stranger infiltrating our twosome.

I said, "Why didn't you go to the game?"

Jameson said, "I'm a conversationalist. Tough to have a good conversation at the game with all the cheering and assigned seats. What if you get stuck between a couple of duds? Where do you go? Don't got that problem at a bar. Plenty of spots to go, but no need now. I found myself a couple of fine gentlemen with whom I can discuss the day's events."

"Actually," said Luke, "my buddy and I were just leaving."

"Oh, come on! We're just getting to know each other."

Luke turned to me and said, "You look tired, Nils. Let's get the tab and get out of here." I handed the bartender my credit card.

I heard a shrieking giggle from the far end of the bar. I looked over and saw her standing between the military tattoo and crew cut, one hand on each of the brutes' shoulders. Annika Brydolf wore a blond wig, pink Twins T-shirt that stopped at the narrow of her waist, and low, hip-hugger jeans. If I didn't suspect she was coming, I wouldn't have recognized her.

We first hired Annika as a distractor. We'd send her into bars to occupy not-so-bright men while we searched or bugged their property. I'd always known she did a good job, but I'd never witnessed it. I'd have to talk to Ellegaard about giving her a raise.

"Yeah . . . ," I said, trying to slur the one-syllable word. "I'd better go." The bartender set down my card and the tab. I looked at it then showed it to Luke. "I'm so out of it. How much should I tip?"

"Well, probably twenty percent . . ."

"I know that. What's twenty percent of ninety-seven dollars and sixteen cents?"

Luke hesitated. He had to think. I knew then he was no financial analyst. He tapped the top of the bar and said, "Well . . . ninety-seven is almost a hundred, and twenty percent of a hundred is . . . twenty. So . . . nineteen? I don't know. Something like that."

"Okay. I'll just make it twenty so it's easier to add." I wrote 20—into the tip area then showed him the bill. "Now how much is it?"

Luke pulled out his phone and opened his calculator app. He pushed some buttons and showed me the answer. I wrote down the total, then signed the check with an even more sloppy signature than my normal one. Then I slid off my stool and stumbled. Luke jumped off his stool and grabbed my arm.

"Whoa," said Jameson. "How many did he have?"

"Too many," said Luke. "Come on, Nils. I'll help you out."

"Thanks, buddy."

Luke walked me out of Hoyt's then led me down Third Avenue toward Target Field. I dragged my left foot into my right, fell onto the pavement, then rolled onto my side to see back toward Hoyt's. No one was following. Luke pulled me up, and just before Bev's Wine Bar, steered me to the right and down a drive that led to a large parking lot along the railroad tracks.

I said, "Hey. Did I park here?"

"I don't know," said Luke. "Let's look for your car."

"Good idea." I panned the massive lot as if I were looking for my Volvo. I did not see Jameson. I did not see Annika. I did not see Ellegaard. I said, "Oh, man. All these cars . . . I'll never find it."

"Sure you will," said Luke. "I'll help you."

I whipped up another stumble, then a black van pulled next to us, and the side panel slid open. Luke threw a fist into my gut then threw me into the van.

24

I lay on the cargo van floor, my lungs void of air. When they managed to draw some in, the van floor smelled of metal, paint, and dirt. I moaned then rolled over, eyes fluttering. The sucker punch hurt like hell, but at least I could stop acting drugged for a few minutes. I got a glimpse of the dark-haired crew cut sitting behind the steering wheel. The tattoo rode shotgun. But someone near me spoke.

"Take his phone."

"What are you doing?" said Luke. "He knows you."

"Doesn't matter. He won't remember any of this."

"Good." Luke pushed my face into the metal floor with his shoe.

"Ease off! We're not here to hurt him." The voice belonged to Ian Halferin, senior partner at Halferin Silver.

Luke said, "This asshole's caused me nothing but trouble. I want to take this van up to ninety and throw him out."

Ian Halferin said, "Get his phone and shut up."

Luke rolled me onto my back and patted me down. He pulled my phone from my right front pocket. "It's locked."

"Use his fingerprint. Probably a thumb."

Luke held my left thumb to the fingerprint sensor on my iPhone. "It's not working."

Ian Halferin said, "Then try the other thumb."

Luke held my right thumb to my phone. "We're in."

"Give it to me," said Halferin. Luke did. As Halferin sifted through the contents of my phone, I feigned grogginess and wondered why our client tried to drug me, had me thrown into a van, and was violating my phone. He either felt I was withholding information from my investigation, or he had something to hide and wanted to know if I'd found it.

"Dammit," said Halferin.

Luke said, "What?"

"He talked to Ellegaard forty-five minutes ago. Did he do that in front of you?"

"No," said Luke. "He was out of my sight a couple of times. He went to the bathroom once. And some drunk chick pulled him away to see friends."

"There's nothing relevant in his texts. Shit. He may have suspected something. Did you make eye contact with Wilson or Pinsky when they came in?"

"I don't think so."

"Do you know where they sat?"

"Yeah . . ."

"Then you looked at them. He could've picked up on it and called his colleague for help."

Luke said, "Did Ellegaard tip him off about our visit this afternoon?"

"Not by text," said Halferin. "But they call each other all the time. Fuck, someone could be watching us. Dump him."

"What?" said Wilson or Pinsky. I didn't know which was who.

"Open the door, take Shapiro out, and let's get out of here. *Now*."

"But we have to question him."

"Too risky."

"But my sister."

"Fucking listen to me!" said Halferin. It got quiet for a moment. Halferin calmed down. "If Shapiro's coworkers find out what we're up to, we'll have more heat on us than we got from the goddamn bomb blast. Now get him out of here."

Luke opened the side panel door and knelt next to me. He slid me toward the opening when Halferin said, "Not that way. Set him down. Easy. I don't want him banged up."

Luke said, "This is bullshit."

Wilson and Pinsky got out of the van. As they lifted me out and set me on the hot asphalt, Halferin said, "And Luke, not a goddamn word about this to your sister. I'll handle it."

The door slid shut, Wilson and Pinsky got back in, and the van crept away. I lay there for five minutes then heard footsteps.

"Hey, mister. You okay?"

"Little tender in the ribs, lady." I sat up and saw Annika Brydolf, blond wig and bare midriff, standing in her high heels.

"What'd they do to you?"

"Played a little rough. I may turn purple in a few spots."

I sat up as Annika said, "I think he's okay," into her phone. Thirty seconds later, Ellegaard and Jameson White joined the party. Jameson helped me to my feet then the four of us got in Ellegaard's Navigator. It still had that new-car smell despite a piece of Fruit Roll-Up shaped like a foot being stuck to the inside of the rear passenger window. It was no doubt put there by Maisy, Ellegaard's youngest.

"Lyle's or Lee's," said Ellegaard.

"Lee's," said Annika. "It's closer."

Lee's Liquor Lounge on Glenwood Avenue has a timeless feel if Time began in 1957. It has an elevated stage for live music, a linoleum dance floor of red and gold checkerboard tiles, a plastering of neon beer signs, and chrome-legged bar stools. The taxidermied cougar, hissing and crouched on a rock, adds a nice touch, as do the year-round Christmas lights, which I find more comforting than melted cheese.

The Twins had taken their 0–0 tie into the ninth inning. Every TV was tuned to the game. A neophyte rock band waited for the game to end so the show could begin. They must have been in their mid-teens—their parents were there and didn't look much older than me. I was going to be an old dad, partaking in preschool drop-offs and birthday parties with younger parents. I'd have to develop a gruff persona so no one would talk to me.

We found a booth in back, and a waitress with Uncle Fester eyeshadow took our orders. On the drive over, I filled them in on the happenings inside the van. Ellie couldn't get over Ian Halferin's involvement. Annika couldn't get over my choice to call for backup instead of text. And Jameson White couldn't get over pretty much the whole thing. Ellegaard and Jameson knew each other from our adventure in Warroad last spring. They were happy to see each other again and picked up where they left off, Jameson asking Ellegaard about his family, and Ellegaard asking Jameson about his most interesting gunshot wound patients. But there was one thing we didn't discuss until seated in Lee's.

"Who is Luke's sister?" said Ellegaard. "Susan Silver?"

I said, "I don't think so. Search Karin Tressler siblings."

Annika pulled out her phone and tapped the screen. I reached for my ribs and must have made a face because Ellegaard said, "Maybe you should get some X-rays."

"No need. I'll just be a little sore for a while."

"Nothing can be done for bruised or cracked ribs," said Jameson. "We can tape 'em, but that's about it."

Annika looked at her phone and said, "Yep. Luke Tressler. Along with Elizabeth and Michael."

"Google just Luke Tressler."

Jameson said, "This is better than a detective show on *Masterpiece*." Uncle Fester Eyes brought us three Grain Belts on tap and a soda with bitters for Ellegaard.

Jameson said to Ellegaard, "You in the program?"

"No," said Ellegaard. "Just don't like alcohol."

"No shit?"

"He doesn't swear either," I said.

"That's fucked up. Ha!" said Jameson. "On religious grounds?"

"Nope," said Ellegaard. "Just made a choice a long time ago."

"You're like a time traveler from Plymouth Rock," said Jameson.

"Weird," said Annika, her face in her phone. "Luke Tressler is barely on the internet."

"He said he worked as a financial analyst for a private equity group called Norsk Capital. Any record of that?"

Annika thumb-typed on her phone. "None," said Annika. "And no Facebook page, no Instagram, no Twitter feed, no Snapchat. Nothing on People Finder or White Pages. No school or job affiliations. Only three hits on Google, all articles on Karin Tressler that reference him as Karin's brother."

"That can't be everything," said Ellegaard.

"It is," said Annika. "I think Luke Tressler never built an on-line presence. Or he's been erased from the internet."

"That's impossible," said Jameson.

"Not impossible," I said. "But expensive."

"It's not the crime," said Jameson. "It's the cover-up." He gave a knowing nod, took a swig of Grain Belt, then looked up at the TV. "Top of the eleventh. Strap yourselves in!"

Annika kept her face in her phone. Ellegaard thought for a moment then said, "The strangest part of this is I called Ian Halferin just after six tonight to say I'd send him a final invoice and to thank him for hiring us. He said he had no idea what I was talking about. We were still on the case as far as he and Susan Silver were concerned."

Jameson said, "The Twins are putting in a baby pitcher they just called up. Welcome to the bigs, and tell the band to get ready!"

Ellegaard said, "I pointed out that GLMPD closed the case. Arndt Kjellgren killed Todd and Robin Rabinowitz before taking his own life. It was as good of an outcome as the firm could hope for. Todd died at the hand of his wife's lover. No shame for the firm in that. But Halferin said they just wanted to make sure all the loose ends are tied up. Nice and neat."

"Hmm," said Jameson, his eyes still on the game. "Sounds to me more like a classic case of keep your friends close, keep your enemies closer."

I said, "You sure are full of well-worn sayings tonight."

Annika looked up from her phone. "How are we Halferin Silver's enemy?"

"They want to know what I know," I said. "That's what tonight was about. Access to my phone. Which means they're hiding something."

"Well, they're not hiding their checkbook," said Ellegaard. "We're billing them for all three of us. And on a closed case. I have no argument with that."

I said, "Even if Halferin Silver had something to do with three deaths at Christmas Lake?"

"That would change things."

"Or what if . . ." I looked up at the game on TV. The rookie pitcher looked young enough to sell magazines door-to-door.

"Or what if what?" said Annika.

"Or what if Karin Tressler had something to do with three deaths at Christmas Lake?"

25

We left the Twins scoreless going into the top of the twelfth inning. Jameson and Ellegaard went their separate ways. Annika drove me toward the coat factory on her way home. She had a 2003 Toyota Corolla. It was silver with a gray interior, and the cloth upholstery shone with wear.

She said, "Sorry you had to see me in this getup."

"I'm sure it's effective. But for the record, I like your natural self better."

"If you didn't I might punch you in the stomach."

"Get in line. But remember, we all have to wear a uniform sometimes."

"Yeah?" said Annika. "What's yours?"

"A leopard-print Speedo. I wear it when working undercover in the Lithuanian mob."

"That's a big business for us."

"And in the circus. And when trying to track down female serial killers who target gigolos. Basically," I said, "I'll take any job where I get to wear it. You know, to amortize the cost. Not cheap."

Annika's phone dinged. A magnet held it to her dash. She read the text. "Shit. Celeste Sorensen."

"What does she want?"

"To meet for a drink. It's after eleven."

"Tell her it's too late."

"I should. But . . ." Annika trailed off and shook her head.

"Work ethic or curiosity?"

"Little bit of both."

"Want help? I still think she knows more than she's said."

"She wouldn't be too talkative if I showed up with you."

"Don't show up with me. Meet her. Get a few drinks in her. Then I'll just happen to bump into you. But only if you don't have to get back to your kids."

"I'm okay. My mom's spending the night. They're all asleep now anyway. You sure you're okay stopping by? I wouldn't mind the tag-team."

"Nice wrestling lingo. You can take the girl out of North Dakota . . ."

"Watch it."

"I'll be there. But go home and get out of that getup first."

"I have everything I need. Can I change at your place?"

We found a parking spot on First Street and walked a half a

block to the coat factory. Annika had never seen my place before and noticed the same things other newcomers noticed. My lack of walls, eclectic furniture, industrial kitchen, and absence of air-conditioning. She commented on the sweaty metal hand railing while ascending the concrete steps from the loading dock to the factory floor. The wood floors were swollen with humidity and creaked less than usual. I suggested she change in the bathroom, pointed in its direction, and off she went. Annika emerged looking like the modest dark-haired grown-up I knew her to be.

I said, "Where to?"

"Bar Louie in Minnetonka."

Someone banged on the door. I flinched. Annika's eyes asked for direction. She pulled a Glock 26 from her purse—it was even tinier than my Ruger. Knock, knock, knock, though more of a rapping this time. I turned toward the door. Annika moved behind me, making sure she was in position to get a bead on whoever might enter.

I peered out the chicken-wired glass then turned to Annika and said, "It's okay." She lowered her gun. I opened the door, and Inspector Gabriella Núñez stood in the opening.

She said, "Sorry if I woke you."

"You didn't. We're working."

"We?"

"Come in."

Gabriella stepped into my loading dock. She wore faded Levi's cut-offs and sandals. Her legs and feet were dark brown and her toenails were clear except for the tips, which were white. She wore a red, short-sleeved blouse that buttoned up the back.

A white band held back her thick black hair. She wore neither makeup nor a smile. This was not a social call.

Gabriella and Annika said hello then I said, "We've had a hell of a night. It started—"

Gabriella shook her head and held a finger to her lips. She said, "It's a hundred and ten in here, Nils. Let's go out for that drink you owe me. Or anywhere with air-conditioning. My God. How do you live like this?"

She pointed to her phone, then my pocket. She held out her hand, and I gave her my phone. She set our phones on my weathered coffee table, then the three of us stepped outside.

Gabriella said, "Oh, I love your car, Annika!" She said this without looking at any car, then shrugged, as if to say, *where is it?* Annika pointed down the street, and the three of us walked the half block in silence. We approached Annika's old Corolla, and Gabriella stuck her hand out for Annika's phone. Annika pulled it from her purse, gave it to Gabriella, then opened her car door. Gabriella tossed Annika's phone onto the driver's seat and shut the door.

We stepped away from the car before Gabriella spoke. "Sorry about all that. Probably nothing to worry about, but I've spent too much time on the JTTF."

The North Loop of Minneapolis was quiet at 11:15 P.M. Ambient city light glowed in the heavy air, and a halo of light floated above Target Field. The only sound seemed to be the game's P.A. announcer and organ, muffled and distant from six blocks away.

I filled Gabriella in on the evening's events. She shook her head and said, "How do you find these webs, know full well they're right in front of you, and still manage to get tangled in them?"

Annika said, "I'd better hit the road for Minnetonka. Give me half an hour head start, Nils. If you can make it, I'll see you there." Annika walked back to her car. A massive roar swelled from Target Field. I turned toward the stadium and saw fireworks light the sky red. Half a second later, I heard them boom. The Twins had won with a walk-off in the umpteenth inning. I wished I could have seen Jameson White's face.

I turned back to Gabriella and said, "Hey, when's the last time you worked undercover?"

We walked the neighborhood for twenty minutes to kill time, then got in her car and headed west. Gabriella said, "I'm hearing through back channels that the FBI is focused on the nature of the bomb at Halferin Silver."

"You mean that it was primarily an incendiary device?"

"Yes. Couple that with Karin Tressler's presence, and the feds are salivating."

"Over what?"

"Let's just say recent events in Washington have left our intelligence agencies extra wary of politicians."

"Extra wary or extra vengeful?"

Gabriella ignored my question. We passed General Mills Corporate Headquarters with its sprawling lawn studded with lit-up trees and sculptures. I wondered if any were made by Arndt Kjellgren. Gabriella signaled to exit at Ridgedale Center Drive. "I spoke to Colleen Milton at the FBI. I suggested they hire you as a C.I."

"Hey, what did I ever do to you?"

"Ian Halferin has brought you into the fold. He wants you

on his team. He's on Karin Tressler's team. That puts you on Karin Tressler's team. It's a logical move."

"Colleen Milton hates me. She won't hire me as a C.I."

"What makes you think the FBI likes any of their C.I.s? Milton's just entertaining the idea right now. But so should you in case you get an offer. And I have a feeling when I tell her what happened in that van tonight, you'll get one."

"You two talk on a regular basis?"

Gabriella pulled into the parking lot in front of Bar Louie. Not a bad crowd for a mall bar at midnight. Quiet downtown. Noisy in the suburbs. What the hell was happening to this world? Gabriella turned off the car and said, "So why are we here?"

I told her about Celeste Sorensen befriending Annika Brydolf, and that we considered a drunk Celeste Sorensen a possible source regarding Halferin Silver.

"Well then," said Gabriella. "Let's go buy her a drink."

26

Bar Louie in Minnetonka featured booths and tables surrounding a big square bar like on *Cheers*. It had more TVs than a Best Buy and served more summer rum drinks than a pirate ship. Food servers carried rectangular white plates filled with rectangular pizzas that some asshole rebranded as flatbreads. There was no shortage of tank tops, shorts, and golf shirts, all in colors normally reserved for Easter eggs. I spotted Annika and Celeste on the corner of the bar. Celeste was drinking cosmos again, so it might be a productive night. Gabriella and I found a table in back. I ordered a Guinness and she ordered a Shirley Temple. It was time for act two in my night of tavern playacting. I was halfway through my beer when I hoisted the mug and headed toward the bar.

"Annika! What are you doing in the burbs?"

Celeste turned and saw the voice belonged to me. She slumped.

Annika said, "Just catching up with Celeste. What got you out of the city?"

"A woman. Turns out some of them live out here. How are you, Celeste?"

Celeste sighed. "Fine. I always enjoy seeing Annika."

"Is the old ball and chain here? I'd like to meet the lucky man."

"He's at home," said Celeste. "Asleep as usual."

"You married a narcoleptic?"

Celeste rolled her eyes. "Not exactly. Just a guy who goes to bed at nine every night." Celeste polished off her cosmo. Her jiggly eyes told me it wasn't her first. "My mother told me not to marry a man fifteen years older than me, but I was in love."

I said, "Love will get you every time."

"Are you married, Nils?"

"Divorced."

"Oh," said Celeste. "You're one of those. The easy path never leads to anywhere worthwhile."

"I beg to differ. Plus, Annika's divorced."

"Well, of course, Annika's divorced. Her husband hit her. He's dangerous. He's in jail. Divorce in that situation is permissible. Not ideal, but permissible." She forced a smile at Annika. "If everyone would just . . ."—Celeste Sorensen's jaw clenched—"get their you-know-what together then this country would be what our Founding Fathers intended it to be."

I said, "Shit?"

"What? The Founding Fathers didn't intend this country to be shit."

"You said if everyone would get their you-know-what together. Did you mean shit?"

"Oh. Yes. Where's that lazy waiter?"

"So, if everyone had a marriage like you, this country would be a-okay."

"That's not what I mean. It's just everything's so goldarn cockamamie. Some people work hard and get no help but do their jobs without complaining. And other people do nothing and complain and get money thrown at them." She gave me a cold stare.

I smiled. It was hard. "Like private investigators who keep getting paid to work on a case that has already been closed?"

"I didn't say those words, Nils Shapiro. You did."

People only use my full name when they're flirting with me, angry at me, or disappointed I didn't send a Mother's Day card. Celeste Sorensen wasn't flirting and she wasn't my mother.

Annika said, "So Celeste, why *is* Halferin Silver keeping us on the case?"

"I have no idea!" said Celeste. "They won't give me a raise, but they'll waste money finding out what they already know. It makes no sense. Except . . ." She smirked and looked at Annika as if Annika knew how Celeste was going to finish the sentence.

But Annika just shook her head and said, "Except what?"

"Hey, waiter!" said Celeste. "Another round, *por favor*! We're dehydrated over here."

A waiter who might have been Latino or might have been a dark-haired Norwegian forced a courtesy smile and said in perfect Midwestern bland, "Yes, ma'am. Coming right up."

Annika looked at me for some kind of direction. I said, "Must be tough for you, Celeste, working at Halferin Silver."

"It's a job," said Celeste. "We all have to work. And Susan has been very good to me."

"How do you like it there? You don't exactly fit the mold."

"I like it just fine. Their heart's in the right place. They're the good guys." She sighed again. "But how many holidays can one religion have? They got the big ones in the fall, of course. But then there's the one they made the Ten Commandments movie about, and the one where the kids wear costumes, and the one with the lemon and the hut. It's a miracle they get any work done."

The waiter brought another cosmo and a gin and tonic for Annika. Celeste snatched her pink martini.

I waited until her first swallow then said, "You must miss Todd."

She kept the liquid down, but with effort. When her pipes were clear she said, "Why did you say that?"

"By all accounts he was a nice guy. Who doesn't like having a friendly face at work?"

Celeste thought a moment then said, "He was a nice guy."

I thought she might elaborate but didn't. I was about to excuse myself to the men's room when Gabriella said, "There you are. I thought you fell in." She walked up, put an arm around me, and kissed my cheek. Then she turned to Celeste and Annika and said, "Hello. I'm Gabriella."

Everyone introduced themselves. Small talk ensued. Celeste didn't recognize Gabriella as a high-ranking Minneapolis police officer. And it's the last thing Gabriella looked like. She'd freed her hair from its binder and swished her Shirley Temple around like a daiquiri. She moved her hips and leaned into me like a golden retriever or girlfriend might do. I felt it in a way I didn't expect, in a way that forced me to concentrate. I played my part and put my beer-free arm around my former fellow cadet, my hand weaving through her hair and releasing a wave of lavender. We talked a little more, then Gabriella and I excused ourselves.

On the drive home, she said, "Think you were any help back there?"

"I think I irritated Celeste, and irritated people like to run their mouth."

"Interesting strategy."

"What can I say? I am interesting guy."

Gabriella said, "Shap, we need pie." We stopped at the Perkins off 394 and joined the crowd of drunks and insomniacs. A hostess sat us at a booth in back. The first thing Gabriella said to me was, "We're ordering eight pieces of pie. We each choose four. And the rule is you have to take at least one bite from every piece."

"Eight pieces?"

"We don't have to eat it all. But we can."

"You can," I said. "You run ten miles every day. I have my boyish figure to consider. I don't want to be single forever."

"What about that?"

"What about what?"

"Why are you still single?"

"Why are you?"

"No, no. Don't do that. I asked the question. Something seems different about you. Lighter. Do you have a new girlfriend I don't know about?"

A waitress with light pink hair and heavy black-framed eyeglasses approached holding a pad of paper and a pencil. "You two ready?"

Gabriella said, "If we get eight separate pieces of pie, can we get the whole-pie price?"

The waitress bit her pencil and said, "What whole-pie price? They're a bunch of different prices."

"Whatever the most expensive slice is, the price of that whole pie."

"No one's ever wanted that before. I have to ask my manager. I'll be right back."

The waitress left.

I said, "Apparently all of your type-A overachieving tendencies go away when you're near pie."

"Don't change the subject."

"All of a sudden, you're fun."

"What's her name?"

"Her name is *nada* because she doesn't exist. Are you working right now? Are you trying to get me high on fun and sugar so I'll go C.I.?"

"I promise I'm not working." She wasn't smiling but her eyes lit up.

The waitress returned. "My manager said you can only order eight different slices of pie if you pay for them per slice. Sorry."

"All right," said Gabriella. "It was worth a shot. For my slices I want banana cream, rhubarb, chocolate silk, and peanut butter silk. Nils?"

"You took all the good ones."

"Don't dilly-dally, pal. You may miss an opportunity."

I got home just before 2:00 A.M. I didn't fall asleep until after 3:00, wondering exactly what opportunity I might be missing.

27

The call came at 8:01 A.M.

"I'm going to give you a chance to make amends, Nils Shapiro." Delvin Peterson used my full name. That was twice in twelve hours.

I said, "What's put you in such a generous mood?"

"Be at my office in half an hour."

"Last time you wanted something from me you had the decency to buy me breakfast."

"I'll still buy you breakfast. But it's coming out of a vending machine." Delvin Peterson hung up.

I showered, threw on a T-shirt, threadbare jeans, running shoes, filled a travel mug with coffee, and pointed my lady station wagon north. I'd forgotten about Ernesto Cuellar's fuzzy dice and suction-cup Jesus. I left them as a special treat for the gate guard at the FBI building.

Delvin Peterson met me in the lobby and escorted me up to Special Agent in Charge Colleen Milton's office. Ellegaard was already there, sitting on a credenza. His choice of furniture and posture signaled all was well. Peterson stood near Milton, who sat behind her desk. A few other agents filled the room on chairs that had been brought in for the occasion. An assistant entered, pushing a cart containing a Dunn Brothers carton of coffee and an assortment of pastries. Peterson had lied about the vending machine. Best use of my tax dollars to date. I half expected an underling to bring me a comfy footstool.

Colleen Milton said, "It's fortuitous, Mr. Shapiro, that our relationship survived the little disagreement we had in Edina a couple years ago."

"Agreed. No sense burning a bridge I may want to jump off one day."

She laughed a little too hard. A key skill to rise through the ranks. "I'll make this quick. Since Stone Arch Investigations is already inside Halferin Silver, we'd like you to work as our C.I., specifically paying attention to the firm's relationship with Karin Tressler. We suspect someone in Ms. Tressler's organization—we don't know who—bombed the office in an attempt to draw attention to and garner sympathy for the candidate for U.S. House of Representatives. How do you feel about the idea of working as our C.I.?"

"Good. I'm in."

Silence. Ellegaard stood. Milton turned to him, and Ellegaard offered a slight shrug.

She said, "Are you being serious?"

"Yes. Why the sad faces? Isn't that what you want?"

Delvin Peterson said, "So that's it? End of conversation?"

"End of conversation." I stood and headed toward the door. "Ellegaard will discuss our fee. Look forward to reporting in." I walked out of Colleen Milton's office and didn't stop until I got into my car, then I headed for downtown and returned a call from Ian Halferin.

"Thanks for getting back to me so quickly, Nils," said Halferin. "I was hoping you could come in today to discuss some details about the case."

"I think I can. Just have to rally. Had kind of a rough night."

"Are you all right? You catch that summer cold that's going around?"

"No. Just had a few drinks on an empty stomach. You'd think I'd learn by age forty. I'm more embarrassed than sick, to be honest. Maybe it's time to take a break from the brown stuff."

Ian Halferin laughed the laugh of the relieved. My story confirmed what he had expected, that the drug had worked—I apparently didn't remember a thing about a parking lot, a van, or him. "You wouldn't be a private detective if you didn't knock a few back, right? Glad to know I hired the real deal."

Whatever Ian Halferin was up to, it appeared not to include Celeste Sorensen. If Celeste had told him about me bumping into her last night, he probably wouldn't have sounded so nonchalant. He specialized in contract law—he was no litigator—so he was no performer.

"I think I can make it around noon. Does that work?"

He said it did, and I went to the office on SE Main Street to meet Ellegaard for an FBI postmortem. But when I walked into his office, someone other than Ellegaard sat at his desk. At least someone other than Anders Ellegaard. Emma Ellegaard, her dark hair bunched on top of her head, sorted a pile of receipts into half a dozen piles.

I said, "I hope your dad's paying you for that."

"He's not," said Emma, her eyes on the piles. She sorted the last few receipts then looked up and smiled. "Hi, Nils." She wore one of her mom's old University of Wisconsin Badgers T-shirts. The red cotton had faded to a dark pink, and only a faint Bucky Badger, chest pumped out, remained. Her parents met at Madison during freshman orientation, married their second year, and both graduated at the end of their third year. Anders then attended the Minneapolis Police Academy with Gabriella Núñez and me. Molly went to law school.

I said, "Are you with us all day?"

Emma rolled her eyes and scrunched her mouth into something between resignation and disapproval. "Yes."

"It's better than babysitting your little sister, isn't it?"

"I guess." She looked out the open door to see if anyone was coming, then said, "Nils, I don't want to start high school next week."

"Why not?"

"It's going to be stupid."

"It's supposed to be stupid. It's high school."

"You said I need to be true to myself."

"There's a difference between being true to yourself and doing whatever the hell you want."

"I want to take classes at the University of Minnesota."

"Is that possible? You're fifteen years old."

"I'll be sixteen next month. Besides, age doesn't matter. I skipped a grade, and any high school junior or senior can take classes at the U if their GPA is high enough, and mine is. Full college credit and totally free. I know lots of kids taking classes there."

"I know one, too," I said, thinking of my Volvo's new decor. "So, what's the problem?"

"My parents said no."

"They must have had a good reason." Emma kept her eyes on me but drifted away to somewhere distant. Her sadness overpowered the corporate blah of her father's office. The air-conditioning's constant exhale inflated a long silence.

I said, "Do you want me to talk to them?"

"Nils, you're here. Good," said Ellegaard, walking into his office, his attention on a sheet of paper. "Annika will join us in ten. She wants to fill us in on her evening with Celeste Sorensen."

Emma Ellegaard flipped a switch. She was happy and present and said, "I sorted all your receipts."

"Thank you, honey."

"One of those piles is your lunch receipts. Dad, you eat at Chipotle way too much."

"You're right. I do. So, take this credit card and walk over to Lunds and get us stuff to make sandwiches. And Emma—"

"I know, Dad. Keep the receipt."

Emma took Ellie's credit card, gave me a look that said *don't say anything,* and traipsed out of the office. Ellegaard handed me the document and said, "Interesting turn of events this morning."

I said, "You finally found a conflict of interest you like."

"Let's just say I trust the FBI."

I read the FBI confidential informant agreement, or at least enough of it to know that's what it was. I handed it back to my partner, wondering if I should say something about Emma's wish to leapfrog high school, but let it go. I sat in one of the chairs opposite Ellegaard's desk and said, "Ian Halferin doesn't want Karin Tressler to know about what happened in the van last night. Is that because he doesn't want her to know they supposedly drugged me and looked at my phone, or is it because she ordered them to do so, but they didn't find what they were looking for?"

"If Karin Tressler's brother is involved then I'd guess she is, too."

"Will you vote for her in November?"

Ellegaard hesitated. He rested his left ankle across his right knee. Politics didn't get in the way of our friendship. We agreed on almost everything but had somehow found ourselves on different teams. The teams and their noisy mouthpieces are bullshit, of course. He knows it. I know it. Any person who's honest with the world and themselves knows it. Party over politics. Every issue. Every day. Every party. Two-dimensional characters make great heroes and villains. And who doesn't love a great hero or villain? More fundamental untruths than in a superhero movie.

Ellegaard rubbed his black-socked ankle and smiled. "She's one I won't vote for."

I laughed. "No wonder you're so excited about working for the FBI. You help bring her down, someone else will step in. Someone you can vote for."

Ellegaard smiled and nodded, a rare admission of ulterior motive. Hell, a rare occurrence of ulterior motive for my friend with adult-onset Boy Scout syndrome.

Annika entered, sleepy-eyed and slow. "You're lucky you left last night," she said, "the party was just getting started."

I said, "Does Celeste Sorensen ever sleep?"

"Apparently not. We were the last people out of there at two A.M. I started drinking coffee at midnight. Celeste kept sucking down cosmos. She wouldn't stop talking. It's like she's never had a friend before."

"Anything interesting?" said Ellegaard.

"Yeah," said Annika. "I think she's having an affair."

I said, "Really? The woman who shamed me for being divorced?"

"That very woman."

"But you only think she's having an affair? She didn't admit it."

"Not directly, no. But she talked a lot about sex. She said she used to think it was normal men didn't want to do it very often. I asked what she meant by *not very often*. She said three or four times a year. I agreed that wasn't very often. And then she said she used to think men could only achieve climax—her words— if they did it from behind. She thought everything she saw on TV and in the movies was fake. But then she found out it wasn't fake. Of course, I asked how she found out, but all she said was she had her ways. But it was the grin on her face when she said it. You know when people are getting it. And a lot of it. They all have that stupid grin."

"Like on Ellegaard's face?"

Ellegaard laughed. "Hold on," he said. "If Celeste is having an affair, is that relevant to our investigation?"

I said, "Depends on who she's having an affair with. Or had an affair with." I looked at Annika. "Was it with Todd Rabinowitz?"

"I don't know. She was pretty drunk, so I playfully asked her if she had a new man in her life. But her grin disappeared and she denied it, saying she was a married woman."

Ellegaard said, "How do we find out if she had an affair with Todd Rabinowitz?"

"Oh," I said, "you know, the usual way. Stake out Todd Rabinowitz's grave, see if she shows up. Take photos of Todd and Celeste around to romantic restaurants, ask if anyone recognizes them as a couple. Hack into Celeste's email—"

"We're not hacking into anyone's email," said Ellegaard.

"What about Todd's email? He's dead."

"No," said Ellegaard.

"Who's going to complain? He's d—"

"No."

"We could," said Annika, "ask Ian Halferin for access to Celeste and Todd's work emails. Halferin Silver owns them, not its employees. It's a long shot, but you never know."

Ellegaard made a *that's an idea* face then looked to me for confirmation.

28

Arndt Kjellgren's sculpture was no longer in the Halferin Silver reception area. If he'd written a book they would have burned it. But he'd made a big metal kinetic sculpture so they hired someone to take it away.

Construction workers carried out charred debris and carried in new boards of Sheetrock, presumably rebuilding the mail room. The sprinkler system had limited the damage, but it smelled like you were sitting on the downwind side of a campfire.

The receptionist on the rolly chair swiveled behind her cherrywood desk. She wore a sleeveless lime green blouse that looked neon parked under her jet-black hair. I avoided staring too long because she might have been watching me. I couldn't tell. She wore plastic film over her eyes, the sunglasses-shaped kind the eye doctor gives you after administering dilation drops. Apparently, she'd had her retinas looked at and wanted everyone to know.

"Mr. Halferin will be with you in a few more minutes," she said.

"Thank you."

She smiled and kept her face pointed in my direction, pleading for me to mention her eye protection, but I didn't feel like giving her the satisfaction of repeating whatever the doctor said about macular degeneration or glaucoma and the importance of getting your eyes examined every year. That didn't stop her. She sighed loudly enough to be heard across the swollen Mississippi. "Well . . . ," she said, "one more hour and I can lose these ridiculous glasses."

"You sure? They're kind of awesome."

She said, "Oh, you . . . You're just being a smart aleck." I hadn't been called a smart aleck since the last millennium. "Where did you go to high school, Mr. Shapiro?"

"Armstrong."

"My cousin, Dana Glass, is about your age. She went to Armstrong. Do you know her?"

"I don't think so. But I'm older than I look. Maybe we missed each other."

"She's forty. How old are you?"

"Huh. Apparently, my looks are catching up with me."

"Ian is ready for you now," said Celeste Sorensen, who had appeared from nowhere like a ghost or speed trap cop. She looked bright and cheerful despite her night of drinking and said nothing about our conversation at Bar Louie. I trailed in her wake of soapiness, past the signed prints to the big office at the end of the hall. She wore a sleeveless frock and her arms looked like she'd just done a thousand push-ups. We entered Ian Halferin's office. He stood with his back to me, looking out one of his floor-to-ceiling windows. The city of green and blue looked like a soft-focus photograph, the water in its lakes, streams, and lawns evaporating into haze.

"Can I get you anything?" said Celeste.

I used my nice words to say no. Ian thanked her for bringing me in. Then Celeste Sorensen left, closing the door behind her.

"Maybe we'll get that thunderstorm they keep promising," said Halferin. Gray pants, white shirt, and his suit jacket draped on the back of his chair. He turned around to reveal a minty green tie with tiny red dots. I don't know much about fashion, but I would have gone with something different. He stepped forward and shook my hand. "Feeling better?"

"Much. Thank you."

He returned to the window and said, "I never get tired of this view. This city pulls us all back. Even the ones who make it big in New York or L.A. or London or Paris—we all come back. Why do you think that is?"

"I don't know," I said. "I never left."

"Really?"

"I got busy then hit a few bumps and then got busy again. Maybe someday."

Ian sat at his desk. I walked over to the window. He said, "You should. You'll appreciate this town that much more after being away."

"Where did you go?"

"Duke University for undergrad, then lived in Israel a year, then went to law school at Northwestern. I worked in Chicago for a couple years, took the Minnesota bar, and came home. Married a girl I met in second grade. I was gone ten years, and I'm a better Minnesotan because of it."

"You came back because of the second-grader?"

He laughed. "No, no. I came back because Minnesotans are like salmon. We return to where we were born to create young of our own. Then I met the woman who happened to be my classmate in second grade. Do you have kids, Nils?"

The heat had boiled the blue out of the sky. It was a cloudless grayish white, dormant and stagnant, like if you put your head in a white pillowcase and breathed that all day.

"Not yet," I said. Explaining Micaela, who she is, who she was, and her pregnancy felt too complicated. "Hopefully soon."

"Your outlook changes when you have kids. You get less forgiving of the world and its ways because you want it to be better for your kids. Do you know what I mean?"

"Not really."

"I suppose that makes sense. You don't have kids. But take my word for it, you want them to have the same opportunities you had. You want to make sure the world doesn't go bad before they get a chance to make their mark."

I turned away from the window. "Is that what you wanted to see me about?" I sat in the chair across from Halferin. "Because it hardly seems worth paying our rate."

Halferin smiled. "No, Nils. I want to talk to you about Arndt Kjellgren."

"The killer."

"Yes. His sculptures are all over the city. Kjellgren is a local hero. You know how this town is. Anyone who makes something of themselves, they're heroes for life, regardless of whatever transgressions they commit." He pushed back in his chair. "Charles Lindberg, Nazi sympathizer. Still a hero. Kirby Puckett, alleged groper, still a hero. I want you to find so much dirt on Kjellgren that he doesn't have a chance of going that route."

"Huh," I said. "Some shrewd brain out there might think you're trying to devalue Kjellgren's sculptures so you can pick up a few on the cheap."

"I wish it were that simple. The truth is I want to bury Kjellgren in so much stink he can't be revived."

"So dig up more dirt on him?"

"Exactly."

"That's what we're already doing. And wouldn't you rather let this one fade away quietly? Every time one of his sculptures disappears, people will start talking about him again."

"I want him gone, Nils. For good."

"Kjellgren's a double-murderer. At least that's what the police are saying. And the press. He can't be convicted, of course, being inconveniently dead. But 'Arndt Kjellgren Did It' is front-page news. And all over TV. How much more dirt do you want on him?"

"I haven't seen any news about Kjellgren bombing our mail room."

"What?"

"Well, come on. Who else would have?" *You,* I thought. Digging up more dirt on Kjellgren felt bizarre. Halferin said, "And there are just as many news stories from Kjellgren's supporters speculating he didn't commit those murders. Conspiracy theories. Insane stuff like that. We need proof that would stand up in court."

"Why?"

Halferin shouted, "To clear this firm's name! And to clear the crazy rumors out there about Karin Tressler being involved!"

Halferin's face reddened through his olive skin. Why was he so anxious to pin the bombing on Arndt Kjellgren? What did he expect me to find, a manifesto and bomb-making kit? I said, "You seem pretty worked up about what people think. Maybe you should hire a P.R. firm, not a detective agency."

"Of course I'm worked up. Who wouldn't be if their livelihood was at stake? No, Nils. I need you on this. I need the best. Find me the dirt, and I'll give that to a P.R. firm."

I let him catch his breath, then said, "All right. I'll see what I can do. And maybe you can help me."

"How so?"

"I'd like access to Todd Rabinowitz's emails."

Halferin shook his head. "I can't do that. They're full of information covered by attorney-client privilege."

"Okay," I said. "What about Celeste Sorensen's emails?"

Halferin looked like he might laugh or throw up. "What about them?"

"Can I see them?"

He opted to laugh. "No."

"Why not?"

"For the same reason. Everything in this office runs through Celeste. Her emails are full of confidential information."

"All right," I said. "Can you look at them?"

"Yes," said Halferin. "They're property of the firm. But why would I? What exactly would I be looking for?"

"It's possible Celeste was having an affair with Todd Rabinowitz."

"What?" said Ian Halferin just shy of a shout. "Where did you come up with that? It's ridiculous, even as a possibility."

I let Halferin's voice bounce around the mostly glass-walled room then said, "How do you know?"

"Robin Rabinowitz was the one having an affair. That's what the police said. As far as Todd knew, he was happily married."

"Not true," I said. "He and Robin were about to separate. That is not conjecture. It's a fact."

Ian Halferin sank in his chair. He looked down in thought but it didn't take him long to look back up for confirmation. I nodded. He said, "I don't believe it."

"Don't or won't?"

Ian looked at nothing. "A little of both, I guess." He remained in his trancelike state then said, "Even if that's true, Celeste Sorensen is born-again. Marriage is next to godliness to her."

"It is for a lot of people. She wouldn't be the first believer to stray."

Halferin rubbed his forehead as if he could smooth out the creases. "But neither Celeste nor Todd would be stupid enough to communicate anything illicit over company email."

"I agree," I said. "But there might be some flirtation in the beginning. Little salutations and sign-offs. Jokes. Sharing of personal information. The precursor to something illicit that even they weren't aware of at the time. That could be in the company email."

"And if something illicit was happening between Todd and Celeste," said Halferin, "then so what? Arndt Kjellgren killed Todd. Arndt Kjellgren killed Robin. Arndt Kjellgren blew up our mail room. I'm sure of it. Even if the highly unlikely is true, that Todd and Celeste were romantically involved—No. Let me restate that. Even if the impossible is somehow true, what difference does it make?"

I was thinking how absurd this conversation was the day after Ian Halferin had me drugged and slugged and thrown in a van when his office door opened without the courtesy of a knock. I looked up and saw Celeste Sorensen with a crooked smile on her face. She threw an aggressive look my way then stepped to the side.

Karin Tressler walked in. She said, "Hello, Nils Shapiro."

29

Karin Tressler didn't wait for my reply. She walked toward me and didn't stop until she'd violated my personal space. I looked up at her tanned, taut face. Even from my low angle, she was attractive. Like a once-famous actress hawking skin creams or an evil queen. She sported a slight, playful smile the way people can when feeling invulnerable. I stood, shook her hand, and said, "Nice ambush, Ms. Tressler."

She sat in the chair next to me. Celeste Sorensen's crooked smirk remained. The office manager swung her eyes toward Ian Halferin, swung her hips around, then swung the door shut as she left. Ian Halferin had not just wanted to discuss Arndt Kjellgren. Ian Halferin wanted to set a trap. He succeeded.

He looked at his watch then said, "I'm sorry. I'm late for a meeting." He stood and left his office. I considered getting up and saying *Dammit, I'm in that meeting, too,* then following him, but curiosity kept me put. Karin Tressler wanted an audience with me. When her underlings had failed to get it, she stepped in to do the job herself just like Darth Vader would have done. I had to find out what was so goddamned important.

I said, "Maybe you should sit in Halferin's chair. It feels a little awkward being on the same side of the desk with you."

She looked behind us and said, "Let's sit back there." She stood, and I followed Karin Tressler to the boss of any company's obligatory couch, chair, coffee table area. The furniture was upholstered in blue-gray leather to reinforce or establish Ian Halferin's manliness. The coffee table was natural cherry. On it: one cut-crystal dish of M&M's and another of almonds. Karin chose the chair because chairs are where bossy people sit. I kept my distance and sat in the middle of the couch.

She said, "I'm not going to bite."

"I've heard otherwise."

She laughed. "I'm sure you have. I'm quite the demon lady according to some." I looked at her but said nothing. She tilted her head to steer the conversation in a new direction. "Why did you make that comment about traffic lights the other day?"

"It's the kind of thing I would have said to the TV if I'd seen you on TV. But you weren't on TV. You were right in front of me so I said it to you."

"Were you trying to pick a fight with me?"

"You know, I think I was."

"I'm not an anarchist."

"Too bad. Anarchy is way better than fascism."

"Ouch." She smiled and crossed her legs.

I felt furious because I wasn't furious. With her, anyway. I found Karin Tressler charming, informal, and smart. Kind of unfair when you're trying to hate a person. I said, "I think you only have a problem with me saying government has no business regulating intersections because I'm me. What if it was one of your wealthy donors? Or a working-class person who'd vote for you? Then would it have bothered you?"

"Did I say it bothered me?"

"No, you didn't. But your question implied it."

"You sure do jump to a lot of conclusions when it comes to me, don't you, Nils Shapiro?"

"I'd say take logical steps, not jump. And if you don't want me to come to my own conclusions, maybe you'd like to be more forthcoming about things like, for example, why you and Halferin just set me up."

"All right," she said, "I will." She grabbed a few almonds from the dish and popped them into her mouth. "The M&M's are tempting, but I'm on that damn caveman diet."

"Why? Cavemen had a life expectancy of eight."

Karin Tressler burst into laughter, choking on her almonds. She had a sense of humor. An evil queen isn't supposed to swirl levity in her cauldron of nastiness.

She said, "I'm fascinated by how you solved the Duluth murders and that murder in Edina. And I have a friend in St. Paul who relayed a story from the St. Paul chief of police about what you did in Warroad. You seem to have a knack for understanding what makes people tick."

"There are a few women out there who would beg to differ." I helped myself to a few M&M's.

"Oh, really? Romance isn't as simple as solving murders?"

"Romance has too many variables. In murder, at least one variable is fixed because it's dead."

She laughed and fingered a thin gold chain on her neck. What in the hell did this woman want? "Do you know," she said, "my late husband used to spend ten hours a week working on his fantasy sports teams."

I'd forgotten Karin Tressler was a widow. I was surrounded by them lately.

"That was on top of the seventy hours a week he worked. And yet studies have shown that he would have done just as well flipping a coin when choosing his players. Ten hours a week when he could have spent ten minutes coin flipping. Ten hours a week wasted. He got nothing for his efforts."

"You know that's not true."

"I do not know that. Please tell me what he got." The joy on her face was gone. She let go of the gold chain.

"He got ten hours of joy. Or at least pain-numbing focus. But I know what you're saying. That's ten hours he could have spent with you." I threw more M&M's in my mouth and tried to suck off the candy coating before biting into them.

Karin Tressler said, "You have a way of cutting right to the matter at heart, don't you, Mr. Shapiro."

"I suppose."

"Well, let me do the same. I don't believe in surrounding myself with yes-men. I want to hire you to help me understand my opposition."

"Excuse my language, but holy shit—I've had more job offers in the last week than I've had in the previous forty years."

"My campaign manager wants me to sit through focus groups and read left-wing position papers. Sounds like a boring waste of time. Why not hire one highly intelligent individual who really understands people?"

"Are you equating what motivates a person to vote for a particular candidate to what motivates a person to commit murder?"

"That's exactly what I'm doing. A person feels disenfranchised. Disempowered. Wronged. Cheated. A terrible sense of injustice. Those feelings send people to the polls. And they also motivate people to commit crimes."

"Whoa, whoa, whoa. That's no way for the law-and-order candidate to talk."

"Of course, I'd have to put up with your sarcasm."

I said, "What makes you think I'd have any interest in helping you get elected?"

"You will if you get to know me. I'm much more complex than the way I'm portrayed. I want to understand my opposition not so I can beat them but so I can include them."

"Include them in what?"

"My constituency. My policy. How I vote on legislation."

"Bullshit, Ms. Tressler."

"It's the truth. I don't want to win if I can't represent the vast majority of my district. And I can't do that if I'm partisan."

"Do you remember your primary campaign?"

"That was the primary. The general election is different."

"Sounds like a game."

"A candidate needs her base, that thirty percent of the electorate who will stick with her no matter what. After securing her base, she just needs to sway relatively few of the undecideds out there."

I took some almonds to round out my balanced meal and said,

"Why are you talking about yourself in the third person and why are we having this conversation? Politics are boring."

"I'm sorry."

"You should be."

"Well, what do you think?"

"The almonds are terrible compared to the M&M's."

She smiled and shook her head. "Will you accept the job?"

"I need to ask you some questions first."

"Of course."

Karin Tressler uncrossed her legs, pressed her knees together, and sat up straight as if she were interviewing for a job. Then she giggled—this *was* a game to her. But she wasn't going to find it as fun as she'd imagined.

I said, "Did you have Todd Rabinowitz killed?"

"What?"

"Simple question," I said. "Did you have Todd Rabinowitz killed?"

"No." Her feminine voice boomed. She looked all business. Eyebrows vee'd, mouth small, eyes intense, nostrils flared.

I kept my tone light. "Were you sleeping with him?"

Her mouth opened, and her eyes went wild. "God no. What is this about? That case is closed."

"Have you had any conversations with GLMPD about the case?"

"What?!"

"Quit making me repeat my questions. Have you discussed Todd Rabinowitz, Robin Rabinowitz, or Arndt Kjellgren with anyone from the Greater Lake Minnetonka Police Department?"

"Of course I haven't. Everything I know I've heard on the

news or from Ian Halferin and Susan Silver. What are you implying?"

We locked eyes. She didn't look away. She was either telling the truth or was an excellent liar. Her interest in politics made me favor the latter. Then she looked away and in a businesslike tone said, "I hope you'll consider my offer. Thank you for listening."

She stood and walked out of the room.

30

I waited for Halferin to return, but after five minutes, he didn't. So I got up and left. I made it into the reception area when a voice said, "Hold it right there, Nils Shapiro." It was my friend on the rolly chair, still wearing the optical film on her face. She said, "I called my cousin, Dana." She set down a can of Diet Coke stabbed by a bendy straw tipped with lipstick. "Dana said you two dated all of junior year and you were the first boy who she let touch her you-know-where and make her you-know-what. So I find it a little hard to believe you don't remember her." She frowned the frown of the bamboozled, arms crossed over her torso. I didn't respond. She said, "Well?"

I walked over to the reception desk and said, "Can I be honest?"

"That would be refreshing."

"Of course I remember Dana Glass. But if I admitted it, you would have asked me about other people we might know in common. Then we would have discussed summer camp. Then you would have asked what line of Shapiros I come from. And the conversation would have gone on from there. And on. And on. And on."

"And that's bad?"

"Not in and of itself. But as of late, I'm not a huge fan of tribalism. And you can't hate on tribalism without scrutinizing your own. Now, if you want more details on my adolescent sexual exploration with your cousin, I'm happy to give them, but otherwise, I don't have much to say."

The receptionist listened without expression. When I finished, she lifted her Diet Coke and sucked on the bendy straw. I second-guessed my outburst. Rule #1: Always ingratiate yourself to support staff. But I'd made a mess of that with Celeste Sorensen and then again with—I looked at the nameplate on the desk—Sheryl Glass.

Sheryl Glass set down her Diet Coke and sighed. "Well, I did ask you to be honest. And you know what? You're right. That is how the conversation would have gone. I didn't know it bothered some people. Guess you learn something every day." The phone rang. She answered the call and talked into her headset, sent the call on to wherever it needed to go, and vacuumed more Diet Coke into her gullet. "And, since we're being honest, Dana never did marry. She has quite the reputation."

"I blame myself. She was the first girl I got past first base with. And I was terrible. Dana dating a lot of men is probably just her way to erase my fumbling hands from her memory."

"You *are* honest." She offered a smile and said, "Hey, you want a pop or a water to go?"

"I'll take a water, thanks." She reached down behind the desk and opened a mini fridge. She handed me a cool plastic bottle. It had a custom label—the Halferin Silver logo. I don't know why they felt the need to advertise to people who were already in the office. I said, "How long have you worked here, Sheryl?"

"Since the beginning."

"What'd you think of Todd Rabinowitz?"

The receptionist swiveled on her rolly chair to make sure the room was clear. It was. "Todd Rabinowitz was the best. A mensch. I cry every night thinking about what happened to him."

"Did you know Robin?"

"Of course." She looked around the room again. "I didn't like her so much. But it's still terrible what happened to her."

"Are you comfortable talking about this?"

"Not really."

"Then I'll talk. This place you work, Sheryl, something's rotten about it. You might not know it or see it because you're used to it. Business as usual, like a musty-smelling house you don't notice anymore. But if I were you, I'd polish up my résumé."

Sheryl Glass looked at me and said, "Thank you. That's probably good advice."

I said, "Anything you want to tell me about this place?"

She shook her head. "I know who signs my checks, and it's not you."

"Fair enough. Thanks for the water."

I almost made it to the door when Sheryl Glass said, "I'm going to find out if Dana's still interested in you. If she is, will you talk to her?"

"Yeah. Why not?"

The receptionist got solemn and looked dead at me. "I can't tell if you're being serious. Because if you are, I'll play yenta. You two would make an excellent couple."

"Sure, I'm serious. Got to swing the bat, right?"

She thought for a moment then used her feet and hands to propel herself alongside the reception desk toward the entrance side. When she ran out of desk she stood but her head didn't gain much height. She towered at four feet ten inches—her chair had created a pneumatic illusion of height.

Her solemn expression amped up to grave. She waddled closer, looked up at me the way a child looks up at the minimum-height-required mark to ride the roller coaster, and said, "These are good people at this firm. They love their families and their community and their country. They get involved because they care. They—or should I say *we*—are not the problem. *We* are trying to make the world a better place. It's important you understand that."

My plastic bottle of water had started to sweat. I could feel the Halferin Silver label softening in my hand and said, "You're trying to make the world a better place for whom?"

Sheryl Glass thought about that for a good ten seconds, adjusted the plastic film over her eyes, then said, "For the good people. That's *whom*." She nodded and smiled then returned to her chair. I opened the door to the elevator lobby and the receptionist said, "Expect a call from Dana. And answer it. Do not make me look foolish!"

I rode the elevator down to the lobby. The door opened, and I stepped into a man-made canyon of granite and glass. Detective Irving of the Greater Lake Minnetonka Police Department leaned against a polished pillar, waiting for me.

His orange hair had been cut, and his newly exposed skin beamed white, as if he needed any more beaconlike features. He wore a suit. Not a sport coat and pants but a suit. And a tie. He looked ridiculous. He peeled himself off the pillar as if some grown-up had told him no loitering. If he'd had a toothpick in his mouth, he would have been in 1940. He approached and said, "Nils."

"Detective. Little out of your neighborhood, aren't you?"

"I thought we could talk if you have a minute."

"There's got to be ten thousand elevators in this town. What are the odds you'd be standing outside the one I stepped out of?"

He smiled. "I made some calls."

I smiled. "You sure some calls weren't made to you?"

"No," he said. "I made the calls. Took a few, but I found you."

"Why didn't you come up to Halferin Silver?"

"Can we go somewhere and talk? Get a cup of coffee or something?"

"No, Detective. We can't. Because I'm getting tired of everyone wanting my attention. That's not how this job is supposed to work. That's not how my life works. I chase people down. Ferret things out. It takes days, weeks, even months just to get a grain of sand. But the last few days, everything and everyone are coming at me. Nonstop. Dead bodies and government agencies. I just got baited by a lawyer, ambushed by Karin fucking Tressler, and accosted by a receptionist who wants me to go out with her goddamn cousin. I step into an elevator and finally get some peace and solitude. A twenty-floor descent of bliss. I step out ready for a tranquil walk home, but guess who's waiting for me? You, you son of a bitch. So no. No to coffee. No to conversation. No to everything and anything. I'm leaving. Alone."

Irving's face turned pink under his orange hair. Bashful, ashamed, impish. He looked like a caricature on a kid's cheap Valentine's Day card. I walked away. Two steps later I heard, "Nils, please. This is important."

He broke into a jog. I considered taking the skyway but opted for the August swelter. He'd almost caught up when I stepped into a quadrant of revolving door. The door spat me out onto Ninth Street. Irving followed in the quadrant behind me.

"Nils! You have to let go of Christmas Lake."

"Fuck off, Detective." I picked up my pace. Ninety-nine degrees radiated off the concrete. I wore a T-shirt, but Irving was all dressed up. Advantage me.

"I was given an order to tell you in person." He was right beside me, matching my stride. I'd always liked Irving. Now I liked him more.

"By whom?"

"What?"

"Who gave you the order?"

The walk countdown on the Hennepin Avenue traffic light flashed 3 . . . 2 . . . I accelerated into a jog to make the light. Irving kept pace.

"The chief of police," said Irving.

I ramped back up onto the sidewalk and said, "I thought your chief ran off with a woman."

"He did. That chief did. But the committee just appointed Detective Norton as the new chief. Interim, anyway, until they find a new one or decide to make him permanent."

"Oh, I get it. He's trying to start with three closed cases so his board is clean. Tell him you gave me the message and I said fine."

We passed three young men, corner boys if I wasn't mistaken. They made a not-so-subtle exchange right in the open. In the middle of downtown, like I was watching *The Wire*.

Detective Irving didn't seem to notice. He said, "So that's it, you're done?"

"Hell no I'm not done." I stopped for the light on First Avenue. "But tell him I said I'm done so he thinks you did your job and gets off your ass. You'll be happy. I'll be happy. We'll go our merry ways."

The light turned green and I resumed my pace. Irving kept stride. "But he'll find out."

"I know. But maybe he'll get one good night of sleep. And then it's all on me because I double-crossed you. My word is shit. Lesson learned."

I looked over at Irving for the first time since we revolved out of the building. His face was grapefruit pink and shiny with sweat. His collar was soaked, as was the knot of his necktie. The front of his shirt was splotched with darker patches of blue. His eyes begged for mercy, maybe from the physical discomfort but more likely from the trouble I was making for him. He looked like a kid who'd been sent to the store to buy milk with the last of his family's money but had lost it along the way. I thought of stepping into some air-conditioning but couldn't risk Irving taking a moment to think straight.

I said, "What's going on, Irving?"

"I told you. I need you to—"

Irving broke eye contact. Frustration flowed out of his pores along with the sweat. He started to say something then stopped and peeled off his suit coat. Then he struggled with the sweat-soaked knot to loosen his tie. He had to pinch his jacket in his chicken wing and use both hands. With effort, he slid the knot to the dry part of the tie and pulled it off.

"Holy shit, Irving. You're a wet hot mess. What's the problem? What are you afraid of?"

Irving shut his eyes. The sweat had condensed into drops and ran down his jaw. He took a breath and said, "There's a tool."

"Yeah there's a tool. He's your new chief of police."

"No. The plexiglass window outside Kjellgren's cell. It was held in place by screws. But not normal screws. They have a special-shaped indent. Not a slot or a square or a star. This other shape that's hard to explain." He wiped his forehead with his crumpled-up suit coat. The sweat trickled into his eyes. It must have stung. He blinked hard. "When Kjellgren escaped, Detective—Chief Norton . . . Well, I guess he was Detective then . . . Norton said Kjellgren must have somehow used his string saw to cut his way out of the plexiglass, too. But if he did that, the bolted parts would still be in. Even if he somehow cut through the bolts, the body of the bolts would still be screwed into the exterior wall. Do you know what I'm saying?"

Detective Irving hated telling me what he just told me. He looked nauseous.

I said, "Yeah. You're saying someone unscrewed the screws from the outside then removed the plexiglass from the window."

He nodded. "There's a special tool to take out the screws. We keep it in a toolbox in the maintenance room. Sometimes things get slow. Especially in winter when the lake is quiet. So I nose around the station. That's how I knew what we had in the tool kit. After Kjellgren escaped, I looked for the special tool. But it was gone. Someone had taken it."

"Do you know who?"

He shook his head. "It drove me crazy that night. Kjellgren didn't escape. Someone broke him out."

"I know someone broke him out. That's why the metal shavings were on the inside. If he'd used the saw, they would have been on the outside."

"Whoa," said Irving. "You're right. Why didn't you say anything?" I answered his question with a blank stare. He said, "Doesn't matter now, I guess. Anyway, whoever broke him out must have used our special tool. But that's impossible. So I went back the next day to look again, thinking maybe I'd missed it. I opened the toolbox and there it was, right in the top tray next to the Allen wrenches."

"So you did miss it."

"No. I didn't. I looked there. I removed everything from the tray. It wasn't there. Someone put it back after I'd checked for it. And whoever did it had the sense to wipe it clean, because I dusted it for prints and found nothing. Absolutely zero. Which doesn't make sense. Someone had touched it at some time. It's a tool. But it was spotless."

"Did your runaway chief take it?"

"I didn't say that!" said Irving. "I'm not accusing anybody. I'm just saying some person took it then put it back."

I started walking First Avenue toward the North Loop, but at a more humane pace. Irving stayed at my side. I said, "Did you tell Norton?"

"Yes."

"What'd he say?"

"He said he disagreed with my conclusion. That I must have not seen the tool the first time I looked for it, and Arndt Kjellgren cut his way out of the plexi then figured out a way to remove the screws."

We walked a bit more then I said, "If you cut your way through two steel bars and then a plexiglass window, would you then take the time to remove a bunch of screws that didn't make a damn difference?"

"Of course not," said Irving.

"Neither would I."

31

I left Detective Irving at the corner of First Avenue and Second Street near The Red Cow. The sweat-soaked Irving backtracked into downtown, and I took a left into the North Loop, where my coat factory remained one of the few buildings yet to be renovated. I showered in a lukewarm spray and didn't towel off, hoping the water would evaporate and pull some heat from my body. I called Ellegaard, told him Ian Halferin entrapped me into meeting with Karin Tressler, about my conversation with the rolly chair receptionist, and my walk/talk with Detective Irving featuring the tool that disappeared then reappeared. But Ellegaard seemed preoccupied.

He said, "Sorry. Emma just told us she's taking all her classes at the University of Minnesota this fall."

I played dumb. "My buddy Ernesto Cuellar is taking some classes at the U. It's good, right?"

"It's not good. Emma forged our signatures on the application."

"Did she ask you and Molly about it earlier?"

"She did," said Ellegaard. "We said no. I didn't want her going to college at sixteen years old. Didn't see any reason to rush that part of her life."

"Does Molly feel the same way?"

There was a long pause. My wet body was still wet. Maybe the air held too much moisture to take any more. Maybe I was sweating again. Ellegaard said, "Molly and I disagreed about it when Emma asked. But Molly's pretty upset because Emma went ahead anyway and lied and forged our signatures. Listen, I'll make some calls about the new Chief Norton of the Greater Lake Minnetonka Police Department, see if he has a history of questionable ethics."

"Smooth topic switch."

Ellegaard said, "I got to go. I'll talk to you later, Shap."

The call ended as my phone dinged with a text from Micaela. She'd sent a movie taken on her phone. It was of a screen in a doctor's office that showed the heartbeat of our baby. I'd seen them before with our first in-utero child, the one who didn't make it out alive. It didn't look much different than those, though the technology has improved. Better resolution and all that. And one other difference: I knew about the doctor appointment with the first pregnancy. I was there. I didn't see it via text.

Micaela had been upfront and direct. She would be the baby's mother. I would be the baby's father. She did not want a partner. We would not be parenting together. I didn't respond to her text. That's a non-partner's prerogative.

I called Annika and updated her on the day's events. She said she'd just got off the phone with Celeste Sorensen. "She asked me if I wanted to go to the range," said Annika.

"The driving range?"

"No. The gun range. I forgot to tell you about this earlier. After you and Gabriella left last night, Celeste asked me if private detectives carry guns. I said some do some don't, but I did, not so much for the job, but for general protection in case I ever ran into another man like my ex. She gets this weird little smile on her face, looks around to see if anyone is watching, then opens her purse and tips it toward me. A pistol is in there. This tiny gun."

"Probably a .38 special."

"No. Much smaller than that. I looked it up. It's called a Derringer."

"Two barrels? One over the other?"

"That's it. It's puny. You saw how drunk she was. I was freaking out. Then she asks if I want to see something cool. I asked her if the gun was loaded, and she said yes. It couldn't do any good if it wasn't loaded. I told her to shut her purse—she could lose her permit if anyone saw the gun. Or worse, someone could get hurt. But she got this impish look on her face, reached into her purse, and next thing I know a laser beam is shooting out of it."

"What an idiot."

"I stood up from the table and said I'd leave if she didn't stop it. She called me a party pooper and closed her purse, but not before she splayed the laser around the room like a high school kid at fucking assembly. It was crazy."

"So are you going?"

"To what?"

"The target range with Celeste?"

"I don't know. I said I'd call her back. What do you think?"

"I think you should go."

"Shit. I knew you'd say that."

"Hey, Annika."

"What?"

"Do you realize you never swore until you became a full-time investigator?"

"Fuck. I'd better watch it around the kids."

She hung up.

I texted Gabriella and asked if Celeste Sorensen had a permit to carry. She said she was in a meeting but would check and get back to me.

I was still on the Halferin Silver payroll, so I headed back to Northeast Minneapolis. Arndt Kjellgren said *I have records. I know. I have records.* I'd searched dozens of record albums inside and out and found nothing. I didn't have time to search all two thousand then, but I had time now. I pulled into the rear parking lot. It was empty. Strange for midafternoon on a workday. Yellow police tape blocked off the loading docks and service door. A Minneapolis Police cadet sat on a folding chair. I knew she was a cadet because I once wore the same uniform. I drove within a few feet of her and rolled down my window.

"Hello."

The cadet was a young African-American woman wearing red horn-rimmed glasses. "Sorry," she said. "Building's sealed off."

"What happened?"

"There was a gas problem. Something toxic. Sent a few people to the hospital. No one's allowed in."

"You mean a gas leak?"

"Not a gas company gas leak. A leak from a tank. That's all I know."

I looked at the cadet. She knew more than that. I said, "Was the leak from a welding tank?"

The cadet shrugged.

My phone rang. I looked at the Volvo's screen. Gabriella. "What's your name?"

"Denise Franklin."

I pressed the call-answer button on the Volvo's steering wheel and said, "Would you quit hassling me, Chief Inspector Núñez. I told you I don't like Latin women. Too spicy for my white-boy Minnesota blood."

The cadet sat up in her chair. Her head tilted and her eyes narrowed to say *Are you bullshitting me?*

I cranked the volume as Gabriella said, "Shut up, Shap. I said I'd call you back and I am. Celeste Sorensen does have a permit to carry."

"Thank you. And hey, do you know anything about a gas leak in Arndt Kjellgren's studio at Hennepin and Stinson?"

"I just got a report on that. One of the welding tanks inside Kjellgren's studio was filled with chlorine gas. The valve had a slow leak. The levels inside Kjellgren's studio were lethal. But we didn't know it until other people in the building started getting sick."

"Huh."

"Hey, I got to go. Call me later."

"Will do. And Gabriella, you got a hell of a cadet in your ranks."

"I do?"

"Denise Franklin. She's on post outside Kjellgren's building. Wouldn't tell me a goddamn thing."

"That's what I like to hear."

We hung up. Denise Franklin had a big smile on her face. I rolled up my window and drove away. I had just crossed back over the river and taken a right on First Street when I saw him. He walked out of Askov Finlayson, a men's clothing boutique that sold clothes I'd actually wear. The man wore shorts and a tank and every square inch of his left leg was covered in tattoos. But his right leg didn't match—it was covered in a shiny swirl of scars.

I might not have noticed if I hadn't just been to Kjellgren's studio, because the man was insignificant. At least to me. But his leg was not. His leg told me everything.

I looked for a place to pull over, but finding a parking spot in the North Loop is like finding a leprechaun—you can't. So, I continued a few more blocks and pulled into the coat factory's loading dock.

I didn't know who to call first. I tried Ellegaard. He didn't answer. I tried Gabriella. No answer. I tried Annika.

"Hey, Nils. What's up?"

"I know who killed Todd Rabinowitz."

32

Two security cameras sat atop the gateposts, which were not so much posts but square columns faced with limestone. I stopped outside the iron gate and reached for a call box, but the gate moved before I could push the button. I drove in and onto a driveway of stone pavers. The grounds looked time-consuming. Chemically induced green grass, beds of flowers, sculpted hedges, pools, and fountains. Someone, apparently, had tamed the great outdoors. A flagpole rose from a circle of white rocks. A United States flag no smaller than Kansas hung limp in the August doldrums.

I drove on the pavers toward a house of red brick, black shutters, and ivy crawling up its sides. Everything about the place felt expensive and traditional. I became conscious of how dented and dirty my Volvo was—I'd cleaned my windshield with the wipers—a film of something barely translucent lined the edges.

I wasn't sure where to park. The pavers formed a circle. I stopped under an overhang near the front door, hoping to see a *Do Park* or *Don't Park* sign, but instead the front door opened and a man of about sixty emerged wearing a wedding-quality black suit and threadbare combover. He smiled and nodded and with those two gestures managed to convey he would take the car from there.

I got out of the Volvo. He said, "Good afternoon, Mr. Shapiro. My name is Hawkins. I will be happy to take your car."

Hawkins. That's butler nomenclature. I said, "Thank you, Hawkins. The keys are in the cup holder."

"Excellent. Thank you, sir."

Another man, maybe fifty years old, with a marine crew cut and athletic physique, pink-faced and clean-shaven, as if he shaved before breakfast and lunch, stepped outside. He wore a gray suit, white shirt, and black tie. I recognized him as one of the three men with Karin Tressler when the bomb threat cleared Halferin Silver.

"Hello, Mr. Shapiro. Blake Lamb. I'm Ms. Tressler's chief of security." I shook his hand. He had a firm, exploratory grip coupled with probing eye contact. "I'm sorry, sir," he said, "but I have to ask: Are you in possession of a firearm?"

Since my Ruger was in the car I said, "I am not."

"Any other weapons?"

I said, "Just my wit," holding my arms out.

He looked like he was about to pat me down, but then nodded and smiled. "Thank you. Come on in."

I followed him into a cavernous foyer. A polished marble floor and a bajillion-jeweled chandelier overhead. The molding and millwork were detailed with panels inside panels all painted white and looking like cake frosting. The furniture was antique. Walnut and oak, accented with marble and ceramic. The décor alone—heavy-framed paintings, carved benches, an armoire so big Paul Bunyan could hang his coats inside—sent me into detail overload, and I stopped noticing minutiae. Not a good thing in my business.

Blake Lamb led me through what I guessed was the living room, or probably *a* living room, and into a large corridor, passing what looked like a dining room, other sitting rooms, and a room I didn't see but sounded like it might be a kitchen. We made our way toward the back of the house and into a somewhat more casual room lined with windows looking out on the grounds behind the house. There was a swimming pool with its own not-so-small house, putting green, tennis court, gardens, and several outbuildings. It looked like an exhausting place to live.

Karin Tressler appeared from another entrance. She smiled and said, "Nils Shapiro. Thank you for considering my offer." She wore a white dress to the knee under a cardinal red blazer, an oversized American flag pin on its lapel.

I said, "I just wanted to see if the rumors were true."

"What rumors?"

"That you live at an all-inclusive resort."

She smiled. "You're starting with an insult?"

"Come on, look at this place. You gave me no choice. But here I am. I thought about what you said. I want to hear more."

"Good."

We sat in chairs that looked like they had been upholstered in one of Sherlock Holmes's tweed suits. Blake Lamb disappeared. Then a woman who last worked at Downton Abbey, wearing a battleship gray dress under a white apron, carried in a silver tray filled with hot and cold beverages, cakes, cookies, crudités, and pistachios. There were half a dozen mini silver tongs to transport the food from tray to plate. Karin Tressler tonged herself some radishes, celery, pea pods, and nuts.

I said, "Sticking with that caveman diet, huh?"

"The results are undeniable."

Downton Abbey disappeared. Karin Tressler poured me a glass of lemonade and said, "You mentioned there are some things you'd like to clear up before you agree to work for me."

"Yes. I've done a little homework. Not easy. You're squeaky clean, or someone's covering your backside well."

"Squeaky clean, I'm afraid. Hope that doesn't bore you."

"Boring is good. I don't have much, but I do have a reputation. I don't want to throw it away by associating with someone who could go down in scandal. Or worse."

Karin Tressler's smile faded. "Worse?"

"Ethics are one thing. The law is another."

"You're worried I'm involved in something criminal?"

"I'd be an idiot not to look into the possibility." I bit into a tiny white cake of thin layers sandwiching pink jellylike mortar. "As far as I can tell, you're not asking me for investigative work. You're asking me to help you understand the electorate and broaden your support."

"That's correct."

"I like the bipartisan notion, but if you're dirty—"

"Excuse me. I don't appreciate that word. I've worked hard

to play by the rules. I may have inherited a great deal, but, like you, I've earned my reputation."

"As far as I can tell, that's true. But it's not true of everyone you're associated with. And that's what concerns me."

"Ah," said Karin Tressler. She munched a pea pod. "That's why you asked for my staff to be here today. Not to introduce you so we could hit the ground running, as you said."

"You ambushed me. Now I'm repaying the favor. Could you bring them in, please?"

Karin Tressler reached for her phone and did something I couldn't see. I reached for mine and did something she couldn't see, then slipped it into the breast pocket on my shirt. A minute later, fifteen people had joined us. Some women, some men, including Blake Lamb and the two other men who'd accompanied Karin Tressler on bomb blast day. After they'd all entered Karin said, "Now what?"

"Some are missing."

"No one's missing," said Karin Tressler, "except for possibly Ian Halferin and Susan Silver, but you know them."

"I do. But I'm not talking about them. Two men in their thirties work for you. They dress eighties preppy. Polo ponies and madras and white bucks. That kind of tomfoolery. Where are they?"

Karin reached for a radish. "I don't know who you're talking about."

"I think you do. One of them is your brother Luke."

If my life had been a movie, a murmur would have swept the room. A cacophony of woe. Concerned faces. Shared glances of outrage. Not-so-subtle whispers. But my life wasn't a movie. These people were pros. You had to look for the anxiety to see it.

Karin Tressler did not blink. She said, "No one in my family works for me."

I said, "That's not what I hear."

"Then you're hearing wrong. Someone is lying to you."

"Maybe," I said, "but I won't move forward without meeting your brother Luke." She opened her mouth to say something but I cut her off. "And if that's a deal breaker, then fine, we'll go our separate ways."

I'd put Karin Tressler's self-made reputation front and center. She'd either bring her brother in or she'd refuse. Either way, she had to make a move. She thought for a moment then turned to one of her bombing day associates and said, "Please ask Luke and Gregory to come in."

Luke and the man I now knew to be Gregory Wilson or Pinsky entered less than a minute later. Luke wore a seersucker suit, tan stripes on an ivory field, suede bucks, a white shirt, and an aquamarine tie. Gregory Wilson or Pinsky wore khakis, a navy blazer, a pink shirt, and a yellow bow tie. They looked like polo mannequins. Their clothing, combined with using their full names, was like applying burl maple veneer over a rusty tin can.

Luke said, "Hello, Nils. Nice to see you again."

"Nice to see you, Luke."

Karin said, "You two know each other?" Her question seemed genuine.

I said, "Luke witnessed someone stealing a car. He followed the thief, made a call to trace the license plate, learned it was mine, and called to tell me where it was. Small world, huh?"

Karin looked at her brother and said, "Is that true?"

"It is," said Luke.

"When did this happen?"

"A couple days ago."

Karin looked at me and said, "Why didn't you mention it to me?"

"I didn't know he was your brother until I ran a background check on you." That was a lie, but a plausible one. "But aren't you going to ask Luke why he didn't tell you?"

Karin shook her head in small, subtle oscillations. Then she turned to Luke and said, "Why didn't you tell me, Luke?"

"I didn't think it was a big deal. Just witnessed a crime and reported it."

Karin looked confused. I said, "Except you didn't report it. To the police, anyway. You called me."

"Yeah. It's your car. Why get a bureaucracy involved?"

"Really? The police are a bureaucracy? A dispatcher would have had a squad car behind my stolen vehicle in five minutes."

Luke reacted like a scolded child. "Yeah, well, I didn't think about that."

Karin Tressler waved her hand to stop Luke or maybe the whole conversation. She said, "Okay, Nils. Luke and Gregory are here. What do you want?"

I looked at Luke, Gregory, Blake Lamb, then back to Karin. I said, "I want every man in this room to remove his jacket and roll up his sleeves."

Karin's mouth popped open. It took her a while to say, "What? Why on earth?"

"Someone in this room killed Arndt Kjellgren and most likely Robin and Todd Rabinowitz, as well. I know this dramatic intervention is a little weird, but I couldn't see another way."

No one said anything for a moment, then Blake Lamb said, "It's a dangerous way. There are over a dozen of us, some armed, and one of you."

"Yeah, well, I don't believe much in conspiracies. I've run checks on all of you and all of you have spotless reputations. I just don't buy this group colluding to commit murder. Not most of you, anyway."

Now there were murmurs and audible gasps and shared looks of incredulity. That was more like it. The only calm one in the room was Luke Tressler, who had inched toward a pair of French doors that opened to the patio.

I said, "I've taken precautions. I'm live broadcasting right now to law enforcement and my partners at Stone Arch." I tapped the phone in my breast pocket, its camera sticking above the top of my pocket. "Local police are cooperating with the FBI, Greater Lake Minnetonka Police, and Minneapolis PD to watch all roads and fields around this estate. I've tipped off a few reporters to join them."

Blake Lamb looked like he wanted to strangle me. He placed his right hand inside his suit jacket.

A woman wearing Chanel and smelling of it, too, said, "You've opened yourself up to countless lawsuits, Mr. Shapiro, civil and criminal. We will see this prosecuted to the full extent of the law."

"I know. But only if I'm wrong. And I'm not wrong. So, if the men could please remove their jackets and roll up their sleeves."

Luke Tressler darted to the French doors, swung one open, and reached for the screen door behind it. A wire flew toward him. I followed the other end of the wire to Blake Lamb, who held a stun gun. Luke Tressler crumpled into a convulsing mess. Karin Tressler screamed. The room of dignified professionals lost their shit. Blake Lamb threw Gregory up against the wall and zip-tied Gregory's hands behind his back, led him to an empty chair, sat him down, and zip-tied Gregory's feet together. Blake produced two more plastic strips and bound writhing Luke's wrists and ankles, though it was hardly necessary.

Karin Tressler lost most of the blood in her face. She looked ghostly, and her eyes dimmed. She said to herself more than anyone else, "I knew this day would come. I knew you would drag me down."

33

We gathered around a big table in a small room at FBI headquarters in Brooklyn Center. The table was so big in comparison to the room you could barely get around it without walking sideways, as if you were traversing a narrow ledge, your back to the wall. Luke Tressler sat with his team of lawyers, who were led by the woman wearing and smelling of Chanel. Luke's seersucker jacket was gone, the sleeves of his oxford rolled up to his elbows, exposing swirled scars on his forearms, the same scars I'd seen in Arndt Kjellgren's building wheeling a dolly of welding gas tanks. Luke's bound wrists rested in front of him on the table.

Special Agent in Charge Colleen Milton and Special Agent Delvin Peterson sat at the opposite end of the table. I took the chair next to Peterson, who gave me a *you can't sit with the FBI* look but said nothing so I stayed put. Ellegaard sat to my left.

Detective Irving from the Greater Lake Minnetonka Police Department was there. His old partner and new chief, Norton, was absent.

Officers from Chanhassen PD, Chaska PD, Eden Prairie PD, and Minneapolis PD filled out the room, including Inspector Gabriella Núñez, who wore her dress blues and her hair in a tight French braid.

The gathering was a formality, and an unusual one. The FBI invited municipal law enforcement agencies because each had jurisdiction in one of the crimes. They included me for no reason other than I had witnessed a man delivering welding gas the day I met Arndt Kjellgren. That man directed me to Kjellgren's studio. He wore a cap, had long dark hair, brown eyes, and a hoarse, weak voice. He also had scarred arms. That man delivered poison gas in a leaky tank that would have killed Arndt Kjellgren if Arndt Kjellgren had spent much time in his studio after it was delivered. He had not. I spent less than an hour there looking at record albums and felt sick.

The kind of scarring on Luke's arms is sometimes the result of laser tattoo removal. That's when my newfound friendship with the FBI paid off. I shared my suspicions with Agents Milton and Peterson, and they put the FBI computers to work analyzing photographs.

The algorithms found it in less than ten minutes. Luke Tressler, a full sleeve of tattoos on each arm, carrying a tiki torch in Charlottesville, Virginia, two years prior, marching with other men wearing polo shirts and chanting, "Blood and soil! Blood and soil!"

That's why Karin Tressler had her brother Luke scrubbed from the internet.

Before we gathered in that room, Luke Tressler had confessed to killing Todd Rabinowitz by drowning him in Lake Minnetonka then moving the body to Christmas Lake, where Luke tied Todd Rabinowitz to the dock. Luke confessed to breaking Arndt Kjellgren out of jail, then killing him and Robin Rabinowitz in the Rabinowitz home. And he confessed to planting the bomb in Halferin Silver's mail room by posing as a UPS delivery person, using the same disguise he used when delivering the poison gas.

"Luke," said Colleen Milton, "we're going to ask you some questions. We appreciate your cooperation, but of course, you don't need to answer. You can consult with your attorneys. Or you can just remain quiet. But I advise you not to lie. That will not make your road any easier."

"I've told you everything," said Luke. "I killed them. I planted the bomb. What more do you want to know?"

"Quite a few things, actually. For example, why?"

"Why what?" said Luke.

"Let's start with why did you kill Todd Rabinowitz?"

Luke Tressler looked at the Chanel woman. She nodded. He looked at Colleen Milton and said, "He knew about my past. About Charlottesville and other things that could hurt my sister politically. He planned to leak it to the press."

Colleen Milton scrunched up her face, then said, "How do you know he knew?"

Luke Tressler shook his head.

Colleen Milton said, "Who are you protecting?"

"No one."

"All right. Why did you kill Arndt Kjellgren and Robin Rabinowitz?"

"Because," said Luke, "it made Arndt Kjellgren look guilty for killing Todd."

"It did," said Colleen Milton. "But you made a mistake delivering the poison gas. How long ago did you have your tattoos removed?"

"Over a year ago. The person who gave me the tattoos didn't do it right. That's why I have all this scarring."

"Uh-huh. So you thought to cover your hair in a hat and disguise its color with a brown ponytail. And you thought to cover your blue eyes with brown contact lenses and your face with a beard. Our witness says you disguised your voice to sound weak. But you didn't think to cover the most distinguishing physical characteristic you have?"

"It was hot that day," said Luke. "I rolled up my sleeves. I forgot."

"You forgot about your scarred arms?"

Luke said, "Yes, because it was hot."

"But the day you were waiting for Nils Shapiro at his car, you were wearing long sleeves. I guess you thought of covering up your tattoos that day."

"I guess I did."

"You know," said Colleen Milton, "whether you spend the rest of your life in jail will depend on how cooperative you are from this point forward. That's how a judge is going to look at it. And I got to tell you: right now, you're not being all that cooperative."

"I confessed," said Luke. "What more do you want?"

"I want to know who else is involved."

"No one."

"Right. No one. Stick with that. You, Luke Tressler, may never see another snowfall. Another Christmas. Another warm spring day. Another—"

"That's enough," said the Chanel-clad lawyer. "My client has told you what he knows. There's nothing left to tell."

I whispered something to Delvin Peterson, who repeated it to Colleen Milton. The special agent in charge of the Minneapolis FBI office leaned in front of Peterson and gave me a nod. I said, "Luke, why were you waiting for me at my car the day it was stolen?"

Luke consulted with his lawyer. They whispered back and forth for half a minute. The room was so small we could all hear snippets of "Do I have to answer?" and "No, you don't have to say anything" and "Any information you can give is helpful" and "I want to stop this now." Then Luke turned to me and said, "I just was."

I said, "Okay. Did you try to break into Robin Rabinowitz's house the night Arndt Kjellgren was apprehended outside?"

"Yes."

"Why?"

"I thought Todd Rabinowitz might have kept more evidence of my past in the house."

"How did you break Arndt Kjellgren out of jail?"

Detective Irving from the GLMPD rubbed a crease in his forehead.

Luke said, "I was wearing the same disguise I used to deliver the gas. When I met him at his studio, I raved about his sculptures. Kind of bonded with the guy. So when I showed up outside his cell window, I told him I'd come to rescue him. That I knew he had to be innocent. So I sawed Kjellgren out with a string saw."

"But the bars were covered by plexiglass. How did you remove the plexiglass in order to pass the string saw through the bars?"

"With a screwdriver."

"What kind of screwdriver?"

"I don't know. Just a screwdriver."

"That's impossible. The screw heads had a proprietary indentation. Removing them took a special tool. Who gave it to you?"

Luke Tressler said, "I'm done answering questions. I want to leave now."

"That's up to Agent Milton. And get used to it, Luke, because everything you do from now on will be up to someone else. When you eat. When you sleep. When you take a shit. And that's too bad, because I don't know if you did any of the things you've confessed to."

"I did all of them," said Luke. "You should know. You saw me in Kjellgren's building right after I delivered the gas. I told you how to get to his studio. You saw my arms."

"Scars are easy to fake."

"The FBI found my ponytail and beard and brown contacts in my condo. It was me. They found my fingerprints on fragments of the bomb. Because I made that bomb." The Chanel lawyer whispered something into Luke's ear. He said, "No. They need to know. I bought the fishing stringer I used on Todd with a credit card. You can look it up. I did all of it. And I don't regret any of it. This country is going to hell. It needs martyrs like me to make things right. I'm proud to go to prison. Hell, I'm proud to die for my cause if that's what it takes."

"Martyr," I said. "Interesting word."

We went back and forth a bit longer, but Luke said nothing more of value. The interview ended. Everyone went their separate ways, except for Ellegaard, Gabriella, and me. At Colleen Milton's request, we met with her and Agent Peterson in her office as rush-hour traffic clogged the tangle of freeways below.

Colleen Milton looked at me and said, "I think it's possible Luke Tressler worked alone. But you don't?"

"No. For no other reason than he's too stupid."

Ellegaard agreed.

Delvin Peterson said, "So you think Luke is working with Ian Halferin or Karin Tressler?"

"Or both?" said Milton.

I stood by the window and looked down on the main gate to the FBI building. A maroon Lincoln was parked around the corner on James Circle. Hiring the most loyal people does not mean hiring the most intelligent. I said, "Ellie, take a look."

Ellegaard looked out the window, then said, "Can we please borrow a pair of binoculars?"

I said, "I don't know who Luke is working with. But I do know Ian Halferin is keeping me close for no good reason. Karin Tressler is, too."

"Well," said Gabriella, "since you're close, you know what to do."

"Do I have the full cooperation of Minneapolis PD and the bureau?"

Colleen Milton and Gabriella Núñez huddled in a cloud of whispers as an underling entered the room and handed me a pair of binoculars. I aimed them at the maroon Lincoln. The windows were too tinted for me to make out who was inside. But I could see the license plate. I fed the number to Agent Peterson. He opened his laptop. Then I handed the binoculars to Ellegaard.

Special Agent Coleen Milton said, "You have our cooperation, Shap. But only because you're already on the inside with both Halferin Silver and Karin Tressler."

"You called me Shap," I said. "That's cozy."

"You have our cooperation to a point," said Milton. "Don't push it."

34

I pulled out of the FBI parking lot with Ellegaard riding shot-gun. We spotted the maroon Lincoln just after merging onto Highway 100—the driver should have been ashamed. I signaled to exit on Bass Lake Road, and the Lincoln followed. Just before the exit, I jerked back into traffic. So did the Lincoln. I repeated the process at both the Forty-second Street exit and then again at the Duluth Street exit. The tail fell for it both times. If I were driving the maroon Lincoln I would have accepted defeat and backed off, but as I'd already guessed from my vantage point in the FBI building, the driver wasn't all that concerned with stealth.

We continued south on Highway 100 then I cloverleafed east

on 394 and headed toward downtown. The Lincoln was right behind me.

Ellegaard said, "I'm sorry, Shap."

"About what?"

"I've laid back on this case. Let you and Annika do everything."

"What are you apologizing for? You're running the company."

Ellegaard said, "That doesn't excuse my absence. I should have been more hands-on."

"You're hands-on right now. I can't pull off this little trick without you."

"I mean before now."

I said, "I don't know how you could have been hands-on. Robin Rabinowitz asked for me specifically. Annika befriended Celeste to work that angle. Ian Halferin assumes I'm his friend because I was bar mitzvahed. And my big mouth somehow endeared me to Karin Tressler."

Ellegaard smiled. "Now you're making me feel not needed."

"The company would fall apart without you. Besides, it all evens out in the end."

"I suppose."

"If you really feel like you're not contributing, you could straighten up my office."

Ellegaard laughed as I moved into the left lane for the downtown exits. Then a quarter mile before the Dunwoody-Hennepin Avenue exit, I cut right, straight across four lanes of traffic, drawing no less than three one-finger salutes, accompanied by horns honking and screeching brakes. The Lincoln followed. I accelerated down the exit ramp.

I said, "Ready?"

"Ready," said Ellegaard.

Fifty feet before the awaiting green light, I slammed on my brakes, and the Lincoln rear-ended me.

I jumped out of the Volvo and turned around. Ellegaard joined me, one hand on his body-holstered Glock. Whoever was driving the Lincoln had a face full of airbag. I ran back, yanked open the driver-side door, pushed down the airbag, hot to the touch, and saw a broken, bloody nose. It belonged to Blake Lamb.

Karin Tressler's head of security said, "You fucking asshole, Shapiro!"

"You could have just called if you want to talk to me."

Blake Lamb touched his nose and said, "Fuck!"

Ellegaard said, "I see cartilage."

"God dammit!"

I said, "Uh-oh. The cops are here. Better have your license and registration."

The cops were already there because they expected us. It was Gabriella's idea. And an excellent one. Blake Lamb jerked his head around and saw the flashing cherries of three Minneapolis PD squad cars. "Good. You're fucking toast, Shapiro."

"Toast? What's wrong with toast?"

Ellegaard said, "I like toast."

Blake Lamb said, "Fuck. You. Both."

A uniformed officer leaned into our talk space. She stood about six feet tall, had short hair, and a broad face. She said, "Sir, are you able to talk?"

"You're fucking right I am." Blake Lamb pointed to me. "And

this fucking asshole slammed on his brakes in front of me for no reason."

"Well, sir, that's why we recommend you follow at one car length for every ten miles per hour." The officer turned to another uniform. "Call an ambulance. This one's going to the hospital."

"I'm fucking fine!" said Blake Lamb. "I'm not going anywhere!"

"Sorry, sir. Not your call. You're going to the hospital, then you're coming downtown."

"Downtown? What the hell for?"

"Careless driving, sir."

"What?! It's Shapiro's fault! Take him downtown!"

It went on like that for another minute, then two police officers escorted Blake Lamb to an arriving ambulance. When it pulled away, the tall, broad-faced officer handed me Blake Lamb's keys and said, "I don't know what this is about and I don't want to know." She looked at Ellegaard. "Is this gentleman taking your Volvo?"

"I am," said Ellegaard. "Thank you, officer."

"Don't thank me. This did not happen." The officer went back to her car.

Ellegaard put a hand on my shoulder. "You sure you're okay doing this next bit alone?"

"I don't see any other way. They need to think I'm him, at least for a little bit."

Ellegaard nodded. "Be safe. There's a baby who needs you."

Blake Lamb's maroon Lincoln smelled of expensive leather and cheap cologne and whatever exploded to inflate the airbag. I pushed the coarse fabric down between my knees, started the car, and pulled into traffic. One of the front tires rubbed on something when I made a hard right, but other than that, it drove fine.

I turned south on Hennepin to Franklin then turned right and caught Lake of the Isles on its northern tip and passed its mansions old and new, turned off at Dean Parkway, then headed west on Lake Street at Bde Maka Ska, the lake formerly known as Calhoun. I meandered south and west, taking turns for no reason other than they were in one of those two directions.

My indirect route gave the sun time to set and me time to think. Law enforcement wanted the mastermind bomber. I wanted the mastermind killer of Robin Rabinowitz. They wanted a closed case. I wanted to avenge the death of a person I liked and ease my guilt over leaving her bed before the sun rose. If I had stayed, Robin Rabinowitz might still be alive. Arndt Kjellgren might be, too.

To achieve both our ends, the FBI and Minneapolis PD gave me access I wouldn't have otherwise had. Driving away from the "accident" in Blake Lamb's Lincoln was unethical and probably illegal and just what I needed to get where I wanted to go.

It was all one big transaction. An exchange of currencies. But every relationship is. Professional and personal. Love for security. Sex for love. A need to lead for a need to follow. A deal is made but not voiced in words or even conscious thoughts. But it's there, and its contract holds the parties true. I will protect you. I will love you. I will sleep with you. I will be amazed by you. I will worship you. I will let you hurt me.

A swarm of news vans and their people blocked the mansion's entrance. I hit the horn and hoped Brian Lamb's sunglasses and Hazeltine CC hat would do their jobs. The press parted, and I pulled into the driveway and stopped before the iron gate. The camera mounted on the limestone post saw what someone wanted it to see. The iron gate opened. I pulled forward. On the right side of the house, the ivy parted, exposing what had to be a ten-car garage. I drove between the greenery and parked the Lincoln in an open spot.

I entered the house through the garage service door and passed through a room with a limestone floor and walnut lockers. A mudroom for people who never step in mud. I continued through and into a large kitchen that looked like what you'd see in a restaurant. Stainless steel industrial appliances, overgrown metal bowls and pots. The maid from Downton Abbey filled a silver tray with dainty teacups and a matching pitcher. Karin Tressler must have had another, more residential-looking kitchen for her late-night bowl of meat sticks or whatever paleo dieters snack on.

Hawkins the butler, napkin tucked into his collar, ate his dinner standing at a counter. He said, "Mr. Shapiro. My apologies. I wasn't expecting you."

"No need to apologize. I drove in with Blake Lamb. He's around here somewhere but I seem to have misplaced him."

Hawkins smiled knowingly, as if I'd referred to something that happens often. "Perhaps I can help you find Mr. Lamb."

"He was a bit steamed about something. I'd rather let him go wherever he went. Besides, Ms. Tressler is expecting me." Hawkins's scrunched forehead said that was news to him. I said, "There's some kind of P.R. emergency. She sent Blake Lamb to fetch me. Then he dumped me in the garage and told me to find her."

Downton Abbey carried the tray out of the kitchen.

"I see," said Hawkins. "I'll be happy to—"

"No, no. Don't interrupt your dinner. I'll find her."

I strode out of the kitchen and heard Hawkins jumping off his stool behind me. "But sir . . ."

I spotted Downton Abbey's gray-clad backside turning a corner. I followed and saw her descending a wide, carpeted staircase.

The basement level of Karin Tressler's mansion was as presentable as the above-ground levels, the only difference being it lacked windows. I guessed she was down there to avoid the probing cameras camped outside her gate. Downton Abbey passed through a large party room. It had a long bar with a dozen bar stools and a nine-foot billiards table. There were leather couches and chairs clustered in groups and it all sat on carpeting of red and green plaid. Oil paintings featuring English hunting scenes hung on the walls in heavy, gold-painted frames. It reminded me of the casual space in a country club in that it was formally informal.

The tea carrier passed through the party room toward a pair of double doors. As she pushed her way in, the sounds and flickering light of a movie escaped. I hid behind the massive bar and waited for her to leave. A minute after she did, I entered Karin Tressler's home theater.

"Blake?" said Karin Tressler. My eyes hadn't adjusted to the dark. A black-and-white movie flickered on the screen. Something with Gary Cooper and Patricia Neal at a construction site. "Blake, why haven't you responded to my texts?"

The home theater had twenty seats, each a heavy recliner with cup holders in the armrests. Karin Tressler sat in the second-to-last row. No one else was in the theater. Just before I sat in the seat next to her I said, "I'm not Blake, Ms. Tressler. I'm Nils."

"Oh." She sounded surprised but not upset.

"I called but couldn't get through to you."

She grabbed a remote and pushed a button. I expected lights and an alarm, but the movie disappeared, replaced by a screen showing the home theater's options. Colored icons on a black background. The room was now even darker.

Karin Tressler said, "I haven't taken any calls except from lawyers, politicians, and donors."

"Well, I'm certainly none of those."

She laughed. "No, Nils. You are none of those." She took a sip of tea, only it wasn't tea. It was gin. Ice tinkled in the glass, and it smelled like a pine tree. She said, "Can I offer you a drink?"

"Eh, boy. I'd love one, but I probably shouldn't."

"You're working."

"Unfortunately."

She said, "Some private detective you are."

"No shit."

"Well, I can't be in too much trouble or the police would be here."

"That's to be determined."

"So *that's* why you're here."

The door opened and two men entered. One spoke. It was Hawkins. "I'm terribly sorry to interrupt, ma'am, but we have a situation. It seems that private detective who was here earlier has breached the house. We're searching—"

"It's all right, Hawkins. I found him."

"Ma'am?" Hawkins's eyes hadn't yet adjusted.

"He's here. Right beside me. We're chatting."

"Would you like me to—"

"No, Hawkins. Please leave. Everything's fine."

Hawkins hesitated.

Karin Tressler held up the remote. "I'll buzz you if I need anything."

Another pause, then Hawkins said, "Very well, ma'am." Hawkins and his muscle turned around and exited the theater.

Karin Tressler took a sip of gin then said, "You're not here to hurt me, are you?"

"Not my style."

"That's good. Because I suppose I deserve to be hurt."

"Why's that?"

"Something's wrong with Luke. Something's been wrong with him since he was a boy. My family didn't make him like that. He was born that way." She took another sip of gin. The big screen went into screensaver mode, a swirl of shifting shapes, all some shade of blue. Karin Tressler said, "When you get a puppy who grows up to be an aggressive dog, one that's not safe even around its owner, you give it to someone who lives on a farm so it can run wild and do what it does. Or, more likely, you put it down. Because you can't take the risk it will hurt someone. You write it off as crazy or evil or whatever you want to call it and you take it out of this world. But what do you do when it's not a dog? What do you do when it's your brother?"

"What you did was keep him close."

"Luke's crazy, but not clinically. He didn't do well in school. He's never held a job. Can't make a relationship work. And of course, he blames everybody else. It's all just one big conspiracy to keep him down. He can't face the fact he's not capable. And it doesn't help that our father bought Luke into private schools and a good college. That just made him a bigger failure compared to his friends."

The screensaver shifted to purple shapes. I said, "What you're talking about right now is why I'm here."

"You think I should have had Luke put down?" She laughed at her joke. The gin was doing what gin does.

"Maybe, but I'm referring to his lack of capability. He's capable of killing and did, I'm sure. But he's not capable of conceiving all that's happened. Someone directed him."

"And you think it's me?"

"It's possible. It depends on why Todd Rabinowitz died. I will tell you this: the FBI thinks the bomb at Halferin Silver was planted as a publicity stunt in your favor."

"I'm sure they do."

"Luke says that's why he did it." The screen shifted to orange. Karin Tressler said, "Orange. Yuck. Who likes the color orange except when it's on an orange?" She sounded like a snotty teenager, not a tightrope-walking politician.

I turned toward her and said, "I think Todd Rabinowitz was having an affair. If that affair was with you, you'll have to answer some questions."

"It wasn't with me. Do you want to know something personal?"

"I don't know. Do I?"

"I have been celibate for five years." She held up her right hand and spread her fingers. "Five years. What do you think of that?"

Karin Tressler was drunk, which for some reason made me believe her. But she was also a skilled politician. She won her primary campaign by making people believe what she wanted them to believe. And some affairs are never consummated. A good percentage, from my experience. So even if she were telling the truth about her celibacy, it didn't mean all that much.

I said, "Did you know Todd Rabinowitz?"

"Of course I knew him. He was one of my lawyers."

"What did you think of him?"

She smiled. "There was something decent about Todd. He worked hard. He was kind. Thoughtful and straightforward. I liked him. A lot. And it's true what they say, you know. All the men like him are taken. Too bad for women like me. And you know what else is too bad?"

"Are we talking about your dating life now?"

"Yes we are. What else is too bad is our society is so fractured that a person can only date half the eligible men because the other half hate your guts."

"I agree."

"Hey, that wasn't very nice. Are you saying you hate my guts?"

"I used to. But now that I've gotten to know you a little, I find your guts at least tolerable."

"Thank you."

I said, "Do you know neurological differences affect the way people think? About families and countries. About inclusiveness and homogony? Our brains are different. Those differences predict a person's political disposition even more than what family the person grows up in. So, all the talking and arguing in the world means nothing. Almost no one's going to change their mind, because they can't change their mind. Their frontal lobe or amygdala is what it is. Just like with introverts and extroverts. We're born the way we're born."

Karin Tressler said, "That sounds hopeless."

"And dangerous. At least with introverts and extroverts, the biggest argument is whether to go out on Saturday night or stay home. And yet, I remain an optimist. Because what's the point of being a pessimist?"

Karin Tressler smiled and said, "I agree with you on that."

"Hey. We have one thing in common."

I have friends and relatives, people who if I met today, I would dislike. But I've known them for decades. I met them when I was less formed and less self-aware and less critical. So I had time and space to appreciate the good in them, their qualities that balance their faults. It's a plague on humanity we can't know everyone like that.

Karin Tressler stared straight at me and smiled, lost the smile in thought, and then found it again. Her eyes twinkled. She said, "I like to stay home on Saturday nights. What about you?"

"Stay home. Always."

"Huh. Two things in common." She burst into laughter, and I summoned a Lyft. It took half an hour for my ride to get there. I spent that time getting to know Karin Tressler. I liked her more than I thought possible, but was certain I would neither work nor vote for her. I was equally certain she had nothing to do with her brother's crimes.

35

I called Detective Irving on the way home and set the meeting for 9:30 P.M. at a semi-equidistant restaurant called Bacio.

Someone had parked my Volvo in the coat factory. I found my keys on the counter and a sealed envelope between wiper and windshield. It was a handwritten note on Gabriella Núñez's personal stationery. I didn't know people still had personal stationery. The note said: *Call me ASAP. I have a problem –Gabriella*

Gabriella obviously wasn't afraid to communicate by phone, otherwise the note would have said *Leave a note on my windshield ASAP*. But there's something personal about a handwritten note. Something urgent. I would not forget to call Gabriella Núñez.

I showered, dug one shirt deeper into the well-creased polo

shirts, got in my twice-dented Volvo, and headed west for the thousandth time that week.

I called Gabriella. She answered on the second ring. I said, "I don't think Karin Tressler is our man."

Gabriella said, "I don't want to talk about Karin Tressler right now. Can we meet?"

I told her about my 9:30 at Bacio.

She said, "Go to Bacio. My place after?"

"You have a place? I thought you lived at the first precinct."

She said she'd text me the address and to call when I was leaving Minnetonka because she'd most likely be asleep.

I said, "Sounds like maybe it should wait until tomorrow."

"No," said Gabriella. "It shouldn't."

I hung up and received her text. Ten minutes later I exited 394 at Plymouth Road and got that creepy feeling I get around shopping malls. I have nothing against commerce but when two hundred stores are under the same roof, you get marketed at from every angle. It's unnatural and disconcerting.

Bacio was in the smaller Bonaventure mall connected to the main Ridgedale mall by a sea of asphalt. Bonaventure was Ridgedale's moon that didn't rotate but sat there waiting for spillover shoppers who weren't ready to go home. The restaurant abutted a Marshall's discount store, and it brightened my mood to think plenty of day-drinkers had tottered next door and left with ridiculous outfits.

I parked the Volvo a hundred feet from the restaurant. The day's heat held firm in the pavement and cooked my feet through my Rod Lavers. I stepped into a full blast of air-conditioning and the calliope music made by alcohol, conversation, knives and forks on plates.

Bacio was full of men with haircuts from sports-themed barber shops wearing wrinkle-free khakis and tucked-in golf shirts. Most of the women wore sleeveless frocks and preferred their wine sweet and their husbands out of town on business. The restaurant itself was decorated in faux castle complete with fake stone arches with no supporting columns, leather booths, and a huge, curved bar that's greased plenty of quadragenarian make-out sessions in minivans.

I found Detective Irving in wrinkle-free khakis and a tucked-in golf shirt sitting on a bar stool, his back to the bar. He sipped on a glass of water then raised it in a toastlike gesture when he saw me. I approached and said, "Where's Norton?"

"Not here yet."

"Is he coming?"

Irving shrugged. "He's had a rough day."

"Yeah?" I sat on the stool next to Irving and ordered a soda with bitters.

"The committee relieved him of his chief duties."

"What for?"

"You know what for. He closed the Christmas Lake cases too soon. That M.E. with the ponytail, what's his name?"

I said, "Melzer."

"Yeah. He copied the committee on a bunch of emails he'd sent Norton."

"About the water in Todd Rabinowitz's lungs containing milfoil not found in Christmas Lake?"

Irving said, "Yeah. How'd you know?"

"Just paying attention."

Irving cast me a dubious glance then said, "So when the news broke that Luke Tressler confessed to the killings, the committee wasn't too happy with Norton. Karin fucking Tressler's fucking brother. Jesus. Committee members got news vans camped outside their houses. And I'm not talking just local news. It's a freak show and GLMPD are the freaks."

"Did the committee demote Norton or is he on leave?"

"Leave. Unpaid. He's pissed."

"Who's the new temporary chief?" Detective Irving shrugged. Even in the dim castle light, I could see he was blushing. "Well, well, Chief. Let me buy you a drink."

"Thanks, but I don't drink unless I'm home for the night. You know in Utah, a blood alcohol level of point zero five is the max. Anything more and you go to jail."

"We're not in Utah, but I get your point. Did the committee question you?" Chief Irving nodded. "Did you tell them what you told me about the missing tool?"

He drained his glass of water. The remaining ice cubes clung to the bottom, loosening their grip enough to twist and turn but not fall. Irving said, "Yup."

The bartender brought me my soda with bitters. I gave him a ten and said, "Sure you don't want a drink, Chief? It's on Halferin Silver."

"Yup. I'm sure."

I said, "This has worked out pretty well for you, hasn't it?"

Irving shrugged. "For a little while. I just turned thirty-six. They'll bring in someone else to be chief by the end of the year."

"Thirty-six isn't too young."

"Me being permanent chief is not going to happen. The best thing about all this, to tell you the truth, is Norton's on leave and out of my hair. Guy's kind of a dick. I didn't like working with him and I hated working for him. I hope he's gone for good. Or at least gets bumped back down to patrol."

"Do you think Norton will show up tonight?" Irving shook his head. "Are you sure you told him about it?"

Irving said, "I texted him."

"Did he respond?"

"He did not." A blonde with short, teased hair wearing a sleeveless white blouse said hello and sat on the stool next to me. She ordered a Riesling and set her red Coach purse on the bar. Not that I know my purses, but it said *Coach* on the side in gold letters.

I thought of asking Irving to show me his text to Norton, but Chief Irving seemed a little too confident and comfortable, and I wanted to keep him in that place. I said, "So do you think Norton did it?"

"Did what?"

"Do you think Norton gave the tool to Luke Tressler so Luke could remove the plexiglass window and break Arndt Kjellgren out of jail?"

Irving shrugged. "Someone did."

"Do you know where Norton is right now?"

"Home, I'd guess."

"Anyone keeping an eye on him? Making sure he doesn't join his old boss in Nicaragua?"

"Not that I know of."

"Well, Chief, maybe it's time you showed some leadership skills." I got off my stool and told the bartender to keep the change he'd laid on the bar. I turned to the woman, put a hand on Irving's shoulder, and said, "See this guy here? He was just promoted to chief of police of the Greater Lake Minnetonka Police Department."

"Wow," said the woman. "Congratulations."

"Pretty impressive for a young buck. And he's single." I had no idea if that was true. "And he's celebrating." I looked at Irving and said, "Chief Irving, you're a big shot now. Act like it and pay for this young lady's grape juice. I got to run. And hey, I'll let you know how it goes with the committee tomorrow."

"What are you talking about?" said Irving.

"The Greater Lake Minnetonka whatever committee. They asked me to come in tomorrow."

A mixture of concern and surprise swept across Irving's face. Why would the committee want to talk to me? What did they know? Did they suspect Irving of setting up Norton? Those were good questions and they would not be answered because the committee didn't want to see me. I just told Irving that to see his response. I walked out of Bacio and onto the lava parking lot.

I'd known Gabriella Núñez eighteen years and I'd never been to a place she called home. Most cops lived in a suburb because they couldn't afford Minneapolis. But Gabriella was frugal, invested well, and worked her way up to a top paygrade. She owned a one-bedroom condo near the northeast edge of Loring Park across Hennepin Avenue from the Walker Art Center's sculpture garden. She had a view of it from her balcony, and that's where we sat at a bistro table drinking añejo tequila garnished with a slice of orange.

"Do you like the tequila?"

"I do."

"Good," said Gabriella, "because this might be a two-drink conversation. At least."

The humidity hung still and heavy, softening the edges of everything in sight. Gabriella said, "I've spent a lot of this past year with the feds. The Joint Terrorism Task Force has met more frequently. Not because the threat of terrorism has increased, but because the destructive bullshit in Washington has led to an increase in cooperation between agencies."

"Like when Mom and Dad are fighting, the kids get along better?"

"Exactly like that. So, when Halferin Silver got bombed, the wheels were greased for Minneapolis PD and the FBI to work together."

I looked over at my fellow cadet. When we made eye contact, she glanced down. Her swagger was gone. When a strong, confident person misplaces her swagger, even for a second, its absence leaves a vacuum that can suck your heart out.

I said, "What's going on with you?"

Gabriella said, "They offered me a job today, Nils."

"The FBI?" She nodded. "I thought they didn't take anyone older than thirty-six."

"Thirty-seven," she said, "but they make exceptions. In my case it's because of my work at JTTF."

I said, "Why does this feel more like bad news than good news?"

"I don't know what it is."

"That's unlike you."

"No shit."

"Do you want the job?"

"Yes. And because I'm thirty-nine, it's a one-time offer. But if I take it, I'll have to go to D.C. for a while then most likely be sent to wherever they need me, which is unlikely to be here."

"Tough view to give up."

Gabriella nodded. "Tough job to give up. I could be chief here in the next ten years."

"Sooner than that. I hear your boss wants to retire."

"But if I take the FBI job, who knows how high I can go?"

"Is that what you want? To go high?"

She smiled something worried and lifted her glass—it was empty. "See what I mean? Two-drink conversation." She got up and left the balcony. The crickets and frogs were at it again. They sang about how Ellegaard and I had rekindled our friendship after over a decade of infrequent contact. Now Gabriella and I seemed to be doing the same. All from a bond forged in a few months at the police academy. I didn't have that bond with any of my other fellow cadets. But Ellegaard and Gabriella and I complemented one another like chamber music instruments.

She returned with a tequila bottle in one hand. It looked like a short baseball bat. She sat, poured, and lifted her glass toward mine. "To old friends."

We sipped and looked out at the sculpture garden and listened to the croakers and leg rubbers for a minute then Gabriella said, "We've both had a long day, so I'll just say this: Do you ever think about you and me? You know, in a romantic way?"

I kept my eyes on the giant cherry and spoon in the sculpture garden and said, "Of course."

In a steady, calm voice she said, "You son of a bitch. Why didn't you say something?"

"Because." I turned and looked at her. "Because I've never felt it reciprocated and even if I did I would have fucked it up."

She nodded and looked away then said, "I had the same fear. But—and I know this is going to sound strange—but in the last few days something has changed. I don't know how to explain it. I don't even understand it. But something is different, Nils. I've been feeling it in a big way. And thinking about it. Too much. Like nonstop. Then I get this job offer from the FBI today and it just turned up the volume on all of it. Because if I accept it I not only ruin any chance with you, which is an absurd notion because all of a sudden, I'm thinking about a chance with you, but being a fed would probably keep me single until I retire. Which big fucking deal, right? Being single never bothered me before. And yet all of a sudden, it does. I don't know why. I don't fucking need a relationship. I don't fucking need you. No offense. And yet, for some goddamn reason you're pulling at me. And don't you dare say it's my biological clock because I don't want kids. Of that I'm sure. It's just *something*. Do you feel it?"

A wave of sadness ran through me. It came from that part of my brain I can't access. Or worse, from my heart. I said, "Yeah." I stopped, but felt she was about to say *yeah what?* So I started again. "I've felt something. I think for a long time. But I've never given myself permission to acknowledge that feeling for you. You're too . . . I don't know . . . out of my league, I guess."

"Well, thank you. But I'm not. And why now? Why is this happening now? Why do you seem different *now*, Nils?"

I was about to answer when Gabriella Núñez leaned across the tiny bistro table and kissed me. A slow, soft kiss. An introduction. A kiss that stood on its own and needed nothing else to complete it. She pulled back and looked at me. Just looked at me.

36

Gabriella said, "Don't say anything." She poured more tequila, refreshed the orange slices, then tossed the spent ones over the balcony. "It's not littering. The squirrels eat them."

"Uh-huh."

"So what's different, Shap? What am I picking up on?"

I said, "I wasn't free before. Now I am."

"How did that happen?"

"It finally ended with Micaela."

"Ah. And how did *that* happen?"

"She's pregnant."

Gabriella nodded as if she understood. "She got married."

"No."

"She's in a relationship."

"No."

"Someone just got her pregnant."

"Yep."

"Do you know who?"

"I do."

"Who is it?"

I took a sip of tequila and looked up at the starless sky awash in city light. "It's me."

"What?!"

"We'd sleep together sometimes. That was the extent of our relationship. We didn't think she could get pregnant. But she did."

"Jesus Christ, Shap. What the hell is wrong with you? You think you two having a baby together is going to end your relationship? What the fuck?! Seriously. How could you even let me say what I said? What the fuck, Nils. Fuck!"

"I know. It's counterintuitive."

"It's counter *reality*. You need to see a doctor. The kind with a couch you lie down on. Dammit, Nils. I can't believe I talked to you about us. This is so embarrassing. *So* fucking embarrassing. You need to leave."

Three police cars, sirens flashing and whining, sped south on Hennepin Avenue, cars pulling over to let them pass then filling back in behind them.

I let the sirens fade until the regular night sounds returned to their rightful place. I said, "You're wrong."

She had scorn in her voice. "You're being cruel now."

"No. You are wrong. You can't tell me what I'm feeling. I know what I'm feeling. It took me a long time and a lot of pain to understand what I understand now. You don't have to believe me. You can believe anything you want. But I know." I stood. Gabriella did not. "Do what you have to, but I hope you turn down the FBI."

She spoke with almost no volume, as if to herself. "Fuck you."

I set down my glass. "You can't lie your way through a kiss, Gabriella. No one can." I slid open the sliding door and showed myself out.

I couldn't feel the alcohol. Even a little. So I got back into my battered Volvo and drove south on Hennepin, half expecting to get involved with what those police cars were racing to. But I didn't. Just another random wrong that had nothing to do with me. I continued through uptown and took a right when the road dead-ended into Lakewood Cemetery. I followed Bde Maka Ska to Lake Harriet then parked below Micaela's penthouse.

She hated when I dropped by unannounced. But Gabriella's pushback had sparked doubt. I needed to deal with it. Not because of Gabriella but because I'm bad with loose ends. They're unavoidable at times. But when I can cut them off, I cut them off. In my personal life and in my work.

I woke Micaela and she wasn't happy about it. She buzzed me up, I entered the building and stepped into her private elevator. When I stepped out she waited, leaning against the wall, sleep in her eyes.

Micaela Stahl said, "What is it, Nils?"

"I need to know how you're feeling."

"A little nauseous. And really fucking tired. But that's good. It's a good sign."

"Okay. All right. I wanted to hear it directly from you. Not in a text. Not over the phone. I wanted to see your face when you said it."

"I'm happy to tell you more." She folded her arms. "Tomorrow."

"I get it. I'll go. But can I use your bathroom? Kind of rushed out of my last thing and haven't had a chance."

"Please."

"Thank you." I skipped the powder room, walked down the hall and into Micaela's master suite. I passed through her bedroom, her blanket and sheets barely disturbed from her effortless sleep. I continued through her master closet that had more shoes than a Nine fucking West, then into her master bathroom.

Micaela's master bathroom was bigger than some garages. White marble made up most of it. The shower was in one corner, surrounded by one continuous piece of glass. It had several showerheads in different positions so you could get blasted clean like a car in a car wash. The bathroom also had a separate clawfoot tub, antique porcelain, the kind Louis IX soaked his ass in. It had a TV, sound system, wall of built-in cabinets, and shelves for towels and whatever else people keep in their bathroom. It had a toilet and a bidet, and a chaise lounge for kicking back in the same room you shit in. It had a regular mirror, full-length mirror, and magnifying mirror. It had everything a luxurious bathroom could have. Except for one thing.

Consideration for another person.

There was enough square footage, of course. But Micaela Stahl's master bathroom did not have a second closet. It did not have the greatest amenity, separate toilet areas. It didn't even have a second sink. When she bought the penthouse, she gutted it. Rebuilt it from the exterior walls in. When she built the master bathroom, she spared no expense other than omitting what every other luxury master bathroom had: design for a couple. Because Micaela Stahl knew a partner would never come along. Never join her. She knew that because she didn't want a partner. Not even the possibility of one.

I didn't need to hear how Micaela was feeling. I didn't have to go to the bathroom. I needed to see that bathroom. One more time. One last time. To know we were done. Forever.

I looked at myself in the mirror. A smile found my face. I didn't put it there. Micaela did. The heartbeat inside her did.

I was free.

And then I felt it—the lightness—it usually happened on cases. The lightness told me I was near something significant. It's what some people called being psychic, but it has nothing to do with the supernatural. It's just math, an equation that gets calculated in the part of my brain I can't reach. That part of my brain reaches me sometimes, but I can't reach it.

The lightness wasn't triggered by my smile in the mirror. It was triggered by the mirror itself. Check that. Not the mirror. What was behind the mirror. It was a medicine cabinet. I kept a toothbrush head in there. I'd used it dozens of times so I'd seen what else was in that cabinet. And the unreachable part of my brain had done the math. It just hadn't clued me in until now.

I opened the medicine cabinet and there it was in the lower left-hand corner. A pill bottle. The opaque white kind. That was the problem. Because Micaela didn't take pills. She didn't take them and she didn't shut up about it. If she'd get a headache, she'd take a nap. "You don't need chemicals when your body is telling you to rest." She thought if you had sleeping problems you didn't work hard enough during the day. "If you can't sleep, your body is telling you there's more work to be done and it can't wait." If you get a fever, your body is raising its temperature for a reason. "The high temperature is to kill the infection. The last thing you should do is lower your temperature with aspirin or acetaminophen or ibuprofen."

I picked up the white pill bottle and turned it around. No label. I opened it and looked inside. White pills in foil blister packs. I dumped some into my hand. On the back of the blister pack, in a clear blue font, were the words *Clomiphene Citrate.*

I walked over to the toilet, flushed it as if I were actually using the bathroom for its intended purpose, and Googled clomiphene citrate.

I put everything back in its place, then returned to Micaela, who sat in the leather chair that was once part of a pair before our divorce. She got one. I got the other. The chairs, like us, lived separately.

She said, "Nils, I have to go to bed."

"Go. Sorry to bother you."

I pushed the elevator button.

Micaela said, "Nils."

The elevator opened. I stepped inside and pushed another button.

"Nils, I'm sorry. I'm exhausted."

The elevator door started to close.

"Nils!"

I descended.

37

I woke to a lightening sky and a text from Ian Halferin asking to meet for breakfast at seven. I thumb-typed I would be there, then stayed in bed thinking about my vacuous flaws and the trouble, disappointment, and heartache they'd sucked into my life, all masquerading under the name Micaela Stahl. It would be easy to demonize her, but I wasn't any better. We both knew our path and obliterated obstacles that stood in our way, *who* stood in our way.

I cast aside rational thought, convention, and stability to free the inaccessible part of my brain to solve hard-to-solve problems. Finding those solutions didn't make my life any better but gave it direction. Direction is focus. Focus is a free, legal anesthetic.

Micaela Stahl lone-wolfed it, which kept her on a path to

excellence. She'd achieved it in her personal and professional life. I would have held her back. Anyone would have held her back. But I would have most, because she loved me.

And so she figured out how to keep part of me without the burden of me and add the one jewel missing from her crown. A baby. She got pregnant with chemical help. And me. I hated and loved her for it. I always would. But we'd never again share a house. Or even a bed. Our relationship would live on playgrounds and at school conferences and at birthday parties. If whoever was in there made it out alive, there would be three of us, but we three would never be a family.

I drifted back to sleep for another hour and dreamed nothing worth remembering. Then I started my day with coffee and internet news plastered with headlines about Luke Tressler's past and Karin Tressler's attempt to cover it up. I especially enjoyed an op-ed arguing Karin Tressler is not her brother's keeper. It was chock-full of biblical references trying to restore her credibility with her base. The comments section was full of tirades and misspellings. I tried to wash off what I'd read in the shower.

I called Gabriella Núñez, Special Agent in Charge Colleen Milton, then left my coat factory and walked from the North Loop to the skyway system entrance near the parking ramps on Third Avenue. I snaked my way through air-conditioned glass bridges to the Soo Line Building to meet Ian Halferin for breakfast.

He waited in a booth wearing a white shirt and royal blue tie. He stood, shook my hand, then we sat facing each other.

"Let me just get this off my chest," he said. "I'm embarrassed. Nils, I'm telling you. I am mortified. Was I so gung-ho for Arndt

Kjellgren's neck I didn't think clearly? Absolutely. I should have let the investigation play out naturally instead of trying to push it forward."

"All right," I said. "But what you're saying makes no sense."

"What? You think I'm not ashamed?"

"I don't care how you're feeling. The fact is if you hadn't kept us on the case after Robin died, Luke Tressler would have got away with it."

A young waitress with hair dyed gray and rhinestone-studded cat-eye glasses took our order. She was friendlier than her stand-offish look. She was trying to tell us something by dyeing her hair and surrounding her eyes with a cinema marquis—I just didn't know what.

After she left, Ian Halferin shook his head and said, "I read in the paper this morning that Luke Tressler has a huge swastika tattooed on his back. And that he was one of the tiki-torch carriers in Charlottesville a couple years ago. In Sunday school when I was a boy they taught us *never forget. Never forget.* They were right."

"You say that as if it's new information. As if you haven't raised millions of dollars to fight that battle."

"Well, it's one thing to support organizations. For the old and disadvantaged. For people who live in other countries and don't have the freedoms we have. We all have a responsibility—"

"Stop. Please. Just stop talking."

Ian Halferin stopped. He looked hurt and confused. Two women and a man walked by looking like Brooks Brothers mannequins. They said hello to Ian. Introductions were made. They moved on.

Ian Halferin tried to change the subject. "Sorry about that.

Too many lawyers breakfast here. I should have suggested someplace else."

I said, "Remember that morning I said I drank too much the night before? I was embarrassed because I'm too old for that. Remember when I said that?"

He nodded. "Yes. But what's that have to do with anything?"

"Well, turns out I didn't drink too much that night. The reason I didn't feel well is someone drugged my drink."

The lines in Ian Halferin's forehead contorted from confusion to concern, as if they were a seismograph measuring his emotional state. Marquis Eyes came back with a coffeepot, filled our cups, and said our food would be out shortly. Her eyes smiled in their rhinestone frames then she and her coffeepot drifted away.

Ian Halferin shook his head but his forehead lines held firm. "Drugged? Nils, that's terrible."

"It was some kind of rape drug that wipes your memory of the evening. You wake up the next morning and wonder how you ended up where you ended up."

"Oh my God. You must have been terrified."

"I was." The lines in Ian Halferin's forehead disappeared. He wasn't thinking this through. But that was good. I wanted him relaxed.

He said, "You blacked out? That's why you thought you drank too much?"

"Ian, I never thought I drank too much."

"But—"

"I met Luke Tressler that night to thank him for reporting my car stolen. I didn't know he was Luke Tressler. And he didn't know I'd hired a friend to steal my car."

"I don't understand."

"No, you don't. While I was with Luke, I saw him drop something into my drink." Ian Halferin's forehead lines fired up again. "I know, right? A murderer dropped something in my drink. I didn't know he was a murderer at the time, but still. I had gone to the bathroom and—well, I really didn't have to go to the bathroom. I just told him I did because I'd noticed these two goons at the other end of the bar and I'd seen one of them with Luke casing my car before I paid a friend to steal it."

Ian Halferin sipped his coffee and said, "I'm not following this at all."

"Don't worry," I said. "You will."

Ian Halferin unbuttoned his sleeves at the cuff and began to roll them up.

"So obviously, I didn't drink my drink after what I'd seen. I went back to the bar, picked up my glass, then walked away. When I returned, my glass was empty. Luke Tressler just thought I drank it."

I looked hard at Ian Halferin. He shrank. He reached for his water and picked it up. His hand shook.

Two uniformed police officers walked past. One of them was a young woman I'd never met before. She said, "Hi, Nils."

I smiled. "Good morning, officer." They sat in the booth directly across the aisle. Ian Halferin's seismograph turned bright red. It glistened with sweat. I said, "I pretended I was under the influence of whatever drug Luke had dropped into my drink."

Ian Halferin looked at his watch and said, "Nils, I'm sorry, but I need to get to the office." He slid toward the edge of the booth.

I said, "If you get up from this table, those two officers will arrest you. Right here. Right now. Up against the wall. Cuffs behind the back. The whole shebang. In front of all your lawyer friends."

Ian Halferin forced a smile and said, "The police won't arrest me. They have no reason to."

He slipped out of the booth. The two officers stood to block his exit. Ian Halferin looked back at me.

I said, "It's your choice. We can keep talking and see what happens, or you can get hauled out of here in front of everyone."

"I would sue this city for every penny it has."

"You were in the van that night. You thought I was drugged. By the way, you're probably not in the mood right now, but at some point, I'd like a little kudos for my acting chops. Not bad, huh?"

Ian Halferin sat back down. He said, "I had nothing to do with Todd's murder. Or Robin's. Or Arndt Kjellgren's."

"That's hard to believe."

"It's the truth. I . . . what . . ." He stopped. He opened his mouth to say something then closed it, shook his head, and pressed his lips together. Goddamn lawyers. Sometimes they know when to shut up.

Marquis Eyes brought our food with a lovely smile. I reciprocated. Ian Halferin did not. She left.

I said, "Luke Tressler confessed everything."

Halferin said, "His word is worthless."

"Maybe. But there were two other people in that van. You referred to them as Wilson and Pinsky. Both are in FBI custody."

"FBI?!" Ian Halferin shut his eyes, opened them, then shut them again. "Why would the FBI be involved in this?"

"Because someone exploded a bomb in your law firm. And

that someone was Luke Tressler, your van buddy. Domestic terrorism is a federal offense."

Halferin's head dropped forward. He shook it from side to side, chin against his chest, his bald spot pointing right at me. He stayed in that position and said, "I will tell the FBI everything. Absolutely everything. I had nothing to do with the bombing or anyone getting killed. I was just trying to protect Karin Tressler. I overstepped. I made mistakes. I may have broken the law. But I did not know of any plans to kill anyone or blow up anything, much less have any involvement." He lifted his head. His face had returned to its normal color. "I will call my lawyer. From this booth. And I will cooperate fully with the FBI and Minneapolis PD and anyone else who wants my cooperation."

I ate some toast then said, "Can I ask you something?"

"You can ask, but I probably won't answer."

"You can't get in any trouble answering this. It's just to satisfy my own curiosity. Why the fervent support of Karin Tressler? What's so wrong in this world that she's so capable of fixing?"

Ian Halferin forked a piece of omelet, lifted it from the plate, then put it back down. He said, "Two things: I don't like paying taxes—Karin Tressler is for less taxes. And Karin Tressler is good for Israel."

"Is she?"

"Without question. She's anti-Iran. She's pro-settlement. She's anti-two-state-solution. She'll increase sanctions with any state or nonstate actor that supports terrorists. Directly or indirectly. And she bases her policy positions on Judeo-Christian values."

I said, "Huh. I have nothing against Karin Tressler as a person. I actually like her. And maybe she's good for Israel and maybe she isn't. I don't know enough about those things to say. But here's what I do know: the same people who hate you and me because of the religion we were born into, they love Karin Tressler. That's who you've aligned yourself with. A lint filter that catches the worst of the worst. They fucking hate you, Ian. Because you're Jewish. They simultaneously deny the Holocaust happened and would love to perpetrate it again. Luke Tressler, Karin's brother, has a swastika on his back. He's your colleague. He's your political ally. How does that happen?"

Ian Halferin pounded his fist on the table. "Nothing's all good or all bad. You're being naïve, Shapiro."

"When you work with them, you become them."

"Nice catchphrase, but it's not true."

"You kidnapped me. With Luke Tressler at your side. Seems pretty true to me."

"I was trying to protect Karin. And to do that I had to protect the firm. The firm represents her interests. I wanted to know what you knew. Who you were in contact with. And how it reflected on the firm. I needed *you* on our side. But you betrayed us. You betrayed our people." Ian Halferin lifted his fork and ate. The son of a bitch still had an appetite. He said, "How can the Jews survive hatred and prejudice if we can't stick together? You're a bad Jew, Shapiro. In fact, you're not even a Jew. You're the enemy."

I lowered my voice to just above a whisper. "Karin Tressler's brother carried a tiki torch in Charlottesville and chanted, 'Jews will not replace us.' And I'm the enemy? You'll have to tell me how that works."

"I would, Shapiro, but you're incapable of understanding."

"Am I? A monster open fired inside a Pittsburgh synagogue and killed eleven Jews, including a ninety-seven-year-old

Holocaust survivor. On Shabbat. Luke Tessler is no better than that subhuman piece of shit. And that's who you associate with to protect your interests. Maybe you can explain that. But not now. You have to go."

"What are you talking about?"

I stood and nodded to the police officers. They came over to our booth. The young woman officer looked at Halferin and said, "Sir, please step out of the booth and put your hands on the table."

"What? We made a deal!"

"No, we didn't. You just heard what you wanted to hear. You're good at that."

One of the police officers said, "Sir, if you do not stand and put your hands on the table, we will use any force necessary to remove you from the premises."

The restaurant had gone quiet. All eyes were on our booth. Ian Halferin stood, turned his back toward the officers, and placed his hands on the table. The older officer patted him down, and the younger one said, "You are under arrest for kidnapping. You have the right to remain silent—"

Halferin said, "I know my fucking Miranda rights. Let's just get this over with."

The young cop pulled Halferin's arms behind his back and cuffed his wrists together.

Ian Halferin turned to me and said, "You're what's wrong with this world, Shapiro. You and every self-hating Jew like you."

They turned him around to leave the restaurant. I saw more than one smartphone held high, recording video. I could hear Halferin breathe like a panting cat. I said, "You know that saying you just touted? *Never again.* Well guess what? You are the *again,* and Anne Frank is rolling over in her mass grave."

38

Ian Halferin would be out on bail in hours, and I had no intention of easing the conscience of his bailor. I walked up Marquette, took a right on Ninth Street, and entered the building I'd grown sick of. When I stepped into the lobby of Halferin Silver, the receptionist on the rolly chair threw her eyes my way.

She said, "Hello, Nils Shapiro. You haven't called my cousin yet."

"I've been busy."

"We're all busy, but we find time for the important things."

"Really?"

She nodded, then grabbed the reception desk to roll herself toward the lobby entrance. "That was good what you did, catching Luke Tressler. But poor Karin. She's devastated. It's over for her. Over."

"You sound pretty sure about that."

She shrugged. "I hear things."

"I bet. Is Susan in?"

"Ms. Silver has an appointment this morning. She'll be in shortly."

"I'll wait."

I was about to sit down when the air smelled soapy. A second later, Celeste Sorensen entered from the corridor. She saw me and stopped cold—the muscles in her ripped arms tensed. A long silence filled the reception area. Sheryl Glass watched as if it were riveting TV.

Celeste broke first and said, "Mr. Halferin isn't in yet."

"I know. I just had breakfast with him. I'm here to see Susan Silver."

"She's not—"

"I know that, too. I'm waiting."

"Why didn't Ian come back with you?"

"He wanted to but his hands were tied."

Celeste pivoted toward the rolly chair but Sheryl answered before Celeste could even ask. "I don't know anything about it. I expected Mr. Halferin to be in by now."

"Mr. Shapiro, why don't you wait in Ms. Silver's office. It's more comfortable, and I'm sure she wouldn't mind."

I followed Celeste Sorensen through the corridor of framed prints and into Susan Silver's office. I hadn't seen it before. Susan Silver had a glass desk with glass sides holding it up. Her seating area featured a love seat and chairs upholstered in matching fabric of black-and-white houndstooth. The coffee table was also made of glass and mimicked the desk in style, only shorter and smaller. It all whispered that Susan Silver had taste if you cared to notice but she wasn't going to shove it down your throat. I chose one of the houndstooth chairs and saw, mounted on the wall, something that seemed out of place in Susan Silver's decor.

A trophy fish mounted on the wall. Only it wasn't a trophy, but rather a young northern pike, a foot long and not much thicker than a bratwurst. An engraved brass plate was affixed to the plaque, but I couldn't read it from where I was sitting.

Celeste said, "Can I get you anything? Coffee? Water?"

"No, thank you."

"Let me know if you change your mind."

I said, "Can I ask you something?"

"Of course." She forced a smile.

"Were you romantically involved with Todd Rabinowitz?"

Her smile faded. She said, "Why would you ask that?"

"Because I know your marriage is rotten. And so was Todd's. You two worked together every day. Sometimes that's how affairs happen."

Celeste Sorensen leaned to her right to look into the hall. She apparently saw no one because she said, "Todd and I were friends, but we did not have an affair. I forget Annika works with you and probably tells you everything I say. I just . . . I haven't had a real friend in a long time. . . . She's a good listener. And you're right—I don't have a good marriage. But God wants us to have what we have and withholds what He doesn't want us to have."

"So, God doesn't want you to have a good marriage?"

Celeste Sorensen smiled. "You don't believe in God, do you, Mr. Shapiro?"

"To tell you the truth, I don't think about it all that much."

"Why is that?"

"The Golden Rule covers a lot of ground, and I don't waste my time asking questions that can't be answered. Not for me, anyway. What anyone else believes is their business, and I'm happy for them. As long as their beliefs don't lead them to harm someone else."

"It's hard to have faith. But it's worthwhile. You should try it sometime."

"Faith in what?"

"In a God who loves you. Who put you on this earth to serve Him. Who does battle with the devil every day and needs your help to win."

"Well," I said, "if I ever meet that God, we'll have a talk and see if we're on the same page."

"You will meet that God," said Celeste, "but by then it will be too late." She smiled. "Why does it matter if someone was having an affair with Todd? I mean, to you, why does it matter?"

"Because Luke Tressler wasn't working alone."

"You're sure of that?"

"Pretty sure."

"And you think whoever was sleeping with Todd might have helped Luke kill Todd and Robin and that artist?"

"It's possible."

She looked down and kept looking down then said, "I think Todd was involved with someone but that person is incapable of hurting anyone. Especially Todd."

I said, "Well, it must be someone at the office or you wouldn't have an opinion about it."

Celeste Sorensen said nothing.

"And there aren't a whole lot of women working here. You.

My friend on the rolly chair. One associate. A few support staff. And Susan Silver."

Celeste hesitated then said, "Are you sure I can't get you coffee?" I nodded. She smiled then walked out of the office. I texted Ellegaard and Annika. They needed to know what I now knew, and I needed their help to prove it. I'd just hit Send when Susan Silver walked into her office.

She said, "Hello, Nils. I heard you were waiting for me." She wore a pink summery dress and a simple string of pearls around her neck. Her silver hair was pushed back by a tortoiseshell set of teeth on top of her head. The teeth matched her glasses. "So, how can I help you?"

"First I'd like to help you. You're going to get a call from Ian Halferin within the hour. He's been arrested and will ask you to bail him out."

"Arrested? That can't be true."

"I was there when it happened."

Susan Silver walked over and sat on her houndstooth loveseat. She looked sick. It took her a while to form the question. "Arrested on what charges?"

"Kidnapping."

"What?! Who did he kidnap?"

"Me." I told her about my stolen Volvo, drinks with Luke Tressler, and my adventure in the van. She buried her face in her hands. Her breathing grew arrhythmic, and tears squeezed their way between her fingers. I said, "It's interesting."

She took a moment to regain her composure, then said, "What's interesting?"

"You're just a person right now. Not one bit a lawyer."

She lowered her hands. Her eyes were red. Mascara smeared

her face. She looked like an evil clown. She said, "Of course I'm a person."

"All the lawyers I know would have jumped into action when hearing their partner had been arrested. They would have called the bank or their broker to liquidate funds for bail. They would have sent someone to the precinct if not gone themselves. They would have kicked into lawyer mode immediately."

"I'm sorry I've disappointed you."

"You haven't disappointed me. I don't care what happens to Ian Halferin."

"Well then, I'm sorry if my emotion makes you uncomfortable."

"No need to apologize. It doesn't make me uncomfortable. But I am curious who you're crying for."

"What is that supposed to mean?"

"Are you crying for Ian because his career is over? Are you crying for you because your firm is over? Or maybe you're crying for Todd Rabinowitz because his life is over."

"I've cried plenty for Todd Rabinowitz."

"You were in love with him."

Susan returned her face to her hands. Her shoulders heaved.

I said, "Why the big secret? What was the problem? You're not married. His marriage was ending. Why couldn't you just be together?"

She took a few breaths to compose herself. She stood, walked to her glass desk, picked up a remote control, and pressed a button. Her office door shut. She set down the remote, lifted a box of tissues in a leather tissue box cover, walked it back to the love seat, and sat. She wiped her face and looked at what had collected on the tissue. "Oh my God, I'm a mess."

I said nothing that confirmed she was, indeed, a mess.

Susan Silver said, "Todd insisted we keep our affair secret."

"Because of Karin Tressler?"

Susan nodded and pulled her knees up onto the couch. "Todd said any perception of marital infidelity in Karin's campaign would reflect badly on her. He wanted her to win the primary. It was important to him. I'm glad he lived long enough to see that happen."

"Was it important to you?"

"Yes. It was important to me for the same reason it was important to Todd." Susan Silver grabbed a few fresh tissues, blew her nose, then shut her eyes. "I wanted to tell you something the other day when I walked to your place, but I lost my nerve—I couldn't risk it. Now it doesn't much matter, at least for the reason it did then."

"All right . . ."

"Todd and I worked hard to help Karin Tressler win the primary. But we wanted Karin Tressler to lose the general election. We shared this with no one. Todd didn't even tell Robin."

"Let me make sure I'm hearing you right. You want Karin Tressler to lose in November?"

"More than want. We actively plotted for her to lose."

"Was that in the best interest of your client?"

"No. Of course not. It's the main reason I stopped myself from telling you this the other day. I could get disbarred."

I said nothing.

"Two years ago, before this firm worked for Karin Tressler, her people scrubbed her brother, Luke, from the internet. Almost impossible, but they did an excellent job. But Todd stumbled across Luke's history. It was by accident. He was in D.C.

representing our firm at a fundraising event. One of the attend-
ees at the event was a journalist who had been in Charlottesville.
She had taken pictures. They were in her personal collection, and
some of those pictures were used in a presentation. Todd recognized Luke Tressler as one of the tiki torchbearers chanting
those horrible things. Todd told no one. Except me.

"Then we did a little digging and found more dirt on Luke
Tressler. So we quietly investigated all of Karin Tressler's inner
circle. Her campaign has a number of white nationalists. They're
anti-black. Anti-brown. Anti-LGBT. Anti-Semitic."

"Did you discuss it with Ian?"

"I tried. But without telling him what I knew about Luke. I
just told him I was concerned that some of the people in Karin's
camp had swung too far right. They weren't conservatives. They
were fascists."

"And?"

"And Ian Halferin had drunk the Kool-Aid, so to speak. The
more conservative the candidate the better. I considered present-
ing him with the Luke Tressler information, but Ian had dug
in. He wasn't going to budge. He would have pushed back. We
have a business to run. It cannot tolerate that kind of conflict at
the top."

There was a knock on the door. Susan Silver told whoever
it was to come in. The door opened. Celeste Sorensen entered.
She said, "I'm sorry to interrupt. Ian's on the phone. He says it's
urgent."

"Thank you, Celeste. Send it in. And please shut the door on
your way out."

Celeste Sorensen left. Susan went to her desk. The phone
rang. She answered it. "Hello? . . . My God, that's terrible . . .

Of course. I'll send David right away with bail. As soon you're arraigned, we'll get you out . . . Okay, hang in there. I'll see you in a few hours."

She hung up and returned to the houndstooth couch, phone in hand. She dialed and held it to her head, "Hi, Celeste. Could you please bring David into the office?"

Twenty seconds later Celeste Sorensen entered with a young man wearing a bow tie and suspenders. I don't know why young men sometimes dress like old men, but I like it. Time feels less linear, and that's comforting.

Susan Silver said, "Celeste, please take David into Ian's office. David, you know the combination to the safe, right?"

"I do," said David.

"Ian has been arrested. Get down to the courthouse ASAP and bail him out. Take fifty thousand in cash. I don't want any delays if they make a stink about verifying funds."

Celeste said, "Arrested? What for?" The soapy-smelling woman with sinewy arms looked hard at Susan, but Susan revealed nothing. Then Celeste looked at me, as if I'd tell her.

Susan said, "Celeste, I need your discretion right now. Please keep this between us. We'll have a company meeting about it this afternoon. David, could you please go now?"

"Yes, of course. I'm on it."

"Thank you."

Celeste led David out of the office. The door closed behind her.

I said, "You always keep that much cash in the office?"

"Ian worries about the grid going down. If it does, he wants the firm and his family to be taken care of."

"Ah. A doomsday survivalist with means."

Susan paused for a moment then said, "Where were we?"

"You tried to tell Ian about the fascists in Karin Tressler's campaign, but he'd dug in."

"Right. And in the process of learning more about Luke Tressler and some of the others, Todd and I found ourselves moving away from the right."

"You mean to the left?"

"I'd say the right moved to the right of us."

"And you were on the inside of Karin Tressler's campaign. A saboteur's dream."

"Yes," said Susan. "So we assembled a goody-bag of information about Luke Tressler and Karin's efforts to cover her brother's past. We intended to release it to the press ten days before the general election. We wanted to change the outcome of the election, and possibly weed out other anti-Semitic incumbents and candidates. We wanted conservatives. Not reactionaries. Not crazies. We wanted to make a real difference. Just me and Todd Rabinowitz, a couple of lawyers no one's ever heard of."

I said, "What do you mean *wanted to*, as if you've failed? Luke Tressler's past is front-page news. Karin Tressler's candidacy is in real trouble."

"Thanks to you. Not Todd and me."

"Doesn't matter. Luke's behind bars for three murders and bombing this place. Kind of seals the deal, don't you think?"

"You're naïve, Nils. Karin Tressler has all of September and October to recover. That's plenty of time. She could still win this election."

I stood and walked over to Susan Silver's window. I looked

out on the city and counted eleven construction cranes. All the people who would fill those new office buildings—what in the hell would they do in there all day?

Susan said, "Todd and I each had electronic copies of the damaging information on Luke. I stored a copy of the files on my computer. Todd stored a copy of the files on his. But both disappeared. Could have been an inside job. Could have been an outside job. We considered having our I.T. people investigate, but that could expose what we knew. Fortunately, we'd considered the possibility our computers might be compromised, so we made plenty of hard and digital copies. There are more thumbdrives hidden around this country than you can imagine.

"But the situation had grown dangerous. Whoever erased those files from our computers knew we had dirt on Luke and the campaign. We were concerned for our safety, so we tried to bait the person who erased our files into exposing themselves."

"And how did you do that?"

"We played dumb. We pretended we didn't know our computer files were missing, which was plausible because we'd each buried them deep within our hard drives—it's not like they were sitting on the desktop or in our documents folders. Then Todd sent me emails about having hidden a hard copy in the mail room, where he had set up security cameras. The cameras weren't online. They were self-contained because our network had been compromised. The night after Todd set up the cameras, he was murdered. And all that awful business with the fishing stringer through his jaw, I believe that was a message for me."

"Because you're a master angler," I said, pointing to the tiny pike mounted on the wall.

Susan nodded. "Actually, I love fishing. I know, I know.

Everyone's surprised. I learned at summer camp when I was a kid and have fished ever since. But that little guy is a practical joke. We had a company retreat up at Grandview Lodge. I was fishing with a live minnow and caught the baby pike. Unfortunately, he'd swallowed the hook. By the time I got it out and put him back in the water, he was dead. One of our lawyers scooped him out when I wasn't looking, had him stuffed, and presented me with that plaque."

"What's the inscription say?"

"It says *Susan Silver Killed Me*." She shrugged. "I don't know why I kept it, but it's a running joke in the office. Whenever I go on vacation I get an earful about not killing baby fish. That's why I think Todd's gruesome death was a message for me. Back off or I'd be next. So I decided to lie low until I could retrieve the video footage from the mail room, but the mail room was blown up, and the cameras were completely destroyed."

"Blown up by Luke Tressler."

"Yes. And now he's in custody. Which is a huge relief. Thank God this is all over, even if Karin Tressler wins in November."

"Except for one thing," I said.

"What's that?"

There was another knock at the door. Celeste Sorensen entered. "Susan, some police officers are here to see you."

39

Susan Silver left with the police. When they were gone, I walked into the reception area.

My friend on the rolly chair said, "What's happening?"

"It's not my place to say."

"Is Susan in trouble?"

"I wish I could tell you but I can't."

Sheryl rolled herself toward me and said, "After all we've been through together." I couldn't tell if she was kidding or not.

I said, "All right. Maybe we can make a deal."

"What kind of deal?"

"Do you know where they put the Arndt Kjellgren sculpture that used to be in here?"

"Yes." She said nothing more.

"Well," I said, "if you can get me access to it, I'll share what I know about Ms. Silver."

Sheryl Glass looked at me long and hard. Then she pushed herself along the reception desk, disappeared underneath, and popped back up with a Diet Coke for herself and a Halferin Silver bottle of water for me. She said, "All right. Follow me."

I followed her out of Halferin Silver and down the hall. She used a key to open a door near the elevators. We stepped into the dark until she found a light switch that revealed a storage room full of desks, chairs, lamps, and dead computer equipment. Some framed prints were stacked against one wall. A muslin tarp covered something large. Four-feet-ten-inch-tall Sheryl Glass waddled toward the tarp and said, "I'll need some help."

I found a chair, carried it over, stood on it, and removed the tarp. Arndt Kjellgren's sculpture was underneath and intact. I said, "Can I have a few minutes alone with it?"

Sheryl said, "My answer should be no. But you promise to tell me everything about what's going on with Susan?"

"I promise."

She thought about that then said, "All right. But you'd better keep your end of the deal, Nils Shapiro."

"Of course I will. My reputation is all I have."

"Yeah. That's what I'm worried about. Just turn the lights out when you leave. The door will lock behind you."

"Thanks." She started toward the door. I said, "Hey, you wouldn't happen to know if there's a tool kit in here, would you?"

"Oh boy, you are going to get me in trouble." She found a plastic orange case on a shelf. She walked it over and handed me a cheap IKEA tool kit that contained a crescent wrench and screwdriver with multiple tips.

I said, "This should do it."

Sheryl Glass left, and I started my search. Ten minutes later, I found it. A small, inconspicuous door on top of Arndt Kjellgren's sculpture. It was invisible from the ground and held in place by four sheet metal screws. I had to replace the chair with a stepladder to get a look at it. I removed the door and used the flashlight on my phone to peer inside. Arndt Kjellgren's word was good. He had done something he wasn't proud of.

I refastened the door onto the sculpture and returned to Sheryl Glass to tell her about Susan Silver.

By the time I walked into Arndt Kjellgren's studio, they'd dropped the needle on over two hundred records. Ellegaard, Emma, and Annika had formed an assembly line to pull records from the shelf, remove each sleeve from its jacket, remove the vinyl from the sleeve, place it on the platter, give it a listen, then out of respect for what human beings make, carefully reverse the process.

It took another three hundred plus records and an order of sandwiches before we found the first one. They were scattered randomly throughout his massive vinyl collection because Arndt Kjellgren knew if anyone found out what he'd done, his career would be over, he'd be sued into poverty, and he'd probably go to jail. That's why he could only drop hints at the Greater Lake Minnetonka Police Station—I wish I'd figured them out sooner.

We found Arndt Kjellgren's confession on a disc pulled from the sleeve of Yes's *Close to the Edge*. I wouldn't find out for days where he'd had the vinyl pressed. And it took two weeks to find where he'd hidden the original discs.

His voice amplified through McIntosh vacuum tubes and projected out Klipsch horned speakers, complete with the pops and hisses you'd hear on any vinyl record. In his recorded confession, Kjellgren admitted to hiding voice-activated recording devices in his sculptures. He was spying on his customers. No way around it. He said it started as market research but morphed into an audio scrapbook of how art is perceived in private collections. Because his sculptures were kinetic, they had to be maintained. Kjellgren said patrons were surprised the artist did the routine maintenance work himself, but he told them he insisted because his sculptures were an ongoing, fluid creation.

That was a lie. The frequent maintenance allowed Kjellgren to refresh batteries and remove high-capacity SD cards filled with voice recordings and replace them with new, blank cards. He combed through the recordings. When he heard something worthwhile, he had it pressed onto vinyl discs. He put a fake label on the disc to make it look like a real record album then erased the SD card so he could use it again. At the end of Arndt Kjellgren's confessionary monologue he said, "I have not documented what recordings are on which discs. I have not documented which album jackets have fake discs inside. Whoever discovers this is on their own."

The day felt like a treasure hunt.

At one point, Annika said, "I can't believe you figured this out, Shap."

"Right place at the right time. The night Kjellgren was arrested outside Robin's house, he told me he'd done things he wasn't proud of and that he had recordings. He emphasized and repeated that word—*recordings*. I didn't know what it meant at the time, but it stuck with me. So did a nagging question: How did Kjellgren know Luke Tressler planned to break into the Rabinowitz house that night? Couple that with Kjellgren maintaining his sculptures himself. Eventually the idea of Kjellgren bugging his sculptures not only made sense but seemed a likely explanation for Kjellgren's seemingly crazy accusations and erratic behavior."

Ellegaard smiled. "This is why I keep you on the payroll."

Emma said, "Yeah, right."

Around 6:30 P.M. we discovered it on what looked like Elvis Costello's *This Year's Model*. Arndt Kjellgren's voice said, "The law firm of Halferin Silver purchased a sculpture for their reception area in 2009. Nobody in the reception area talked about it much. I guess they were there for lawyer business and didn't give much of a shit about art. My sculpture was just another thing in an office building. Something to impress somebody and show wealth and taste. To them it was anything and everything except what it was, a piece of art made by an artist. Something someone had put their soul into to create beauty or find beauty or say something. Whatever. And the receptionist was in there answering phones so the voice-activated recorder picked up everything except what I wanted to hear about, which was my sculpture, which every motherfucker didn't mention 'cause you got to play it close to the vest in the business world. So I stopped servicing that sculpture and stopped listening to those recordings.

"But then I fell in love with Robin Rabinowitz. And she told me Todd had been acting weird. So I started up again listening to the recordings from Halferin Silver, especially after business hours when he'd stay late sometimes. Or at least that's what Todd said he was doing. Robin was hoping she could find out he was having an affair so that she wouldn't have to be the bad guy ending the marriage. Problem was it wasn't Todd who said the interesting stuff.

"I pressed those recordings onto another disc. Maybe you already found it. Or found it and didn't know what it was. Now you do. Sorry for the runaround but I'm trying to cover my ass here."

Annika said, "That motherfucker."

Ellegaard said, "Pizza and salad good for everyone?"

We continued our search. The food came. We ate and searched some more. Then shortly after 10:00 P.M. we found it.

40

It was on a fake disc of Joni Mitchell's *Blue*, side B. They spoke freely in the Halferin Silver reception area.

A woman said, "He thinks I'm on his side. I told him I have more incriminating evidence on your past. That you didn't just attend Charlottesville, but you led a local group of white nationalists. That you planned to assassinate our Muslim congresswoman."

"Did he believe you?" Luke Tressler spoke in a soft voice. He was not the leader of these two. The record turned but we only heard the needle on vinyl. Then the soft smack of a kiss.

"Yes," she said. "He agreed to meet me at my boat in St. Alban's Bay at midnight."

"All right. But . . . does it have to be this way?" said Luke Tressler.

"What do you mean?"

"Do we have to take him out? We can't just make him disappear until after the election?"

"No, Luke. Think. I set him up. Even if he somehow thought you weren't involved, which he would because this is all about you, but even if he didn't, he'd know I set him up. You have to kill him. And you have to make it ugly and frightening when you do."

Another long silence, then Luke Tressler said, "I know how to do that."

"Of course you do. But you'll run it by me. Two brains are better than one."

Luke said, "I want to touch you."

"Give me your hand." Another soft smack of a kiss. "Here? Do you want to touch me here?"

Luke said, "Yes."

"And . . ." the record popped and hissed ". . . here?"

"Yes."

"I like that."

"Me, too."

I texted Gabriella: *Please confirm police officers have eyes on Susan Silver.*

The woman on the record said, "Do you feel how happy you're making me?"

"I do," said Luke.

Ellegaard blushed and didn't dare look at his daughter.

The woman said, "Midnight tomorrow night."

Luke Tressler said, "Yes."

She said, "Undo your belt."

It was quiet for a little while then Luke said, "Celeste?"

"Mmm?"

"You'll leave him, right, Celeste? You'll leave him and marry me?"

"Yes, Luke," she said, "I'll leave him the day they swear Karin into office."

The recording ended.

Gabriella returned my text: *Yes, Susan is with two uniformed officers.*

Keep them with her. Celeste Sorensen conspired with Luke. She has a gun.

Around midnight, a uniform led us into the Halferin Silver office. Ellegaard stayed outside with Emma. But Annika and I headed toward the offices.

Gabriella emerged from the corridor. She said, "This way."

We followed her down the hall and into Ian Halferin's office. He lay dead on his back, his eyes staring at the fluorescent lights in the ceiling like Todd Rabinowitz had stared at the night sky. Ian had two little holes in his chest. Blood leaked onto his white shirt. But not much.

The safe door was open. Celeste Sorenson had taken everything. She was gone.

The photographs of Ian's wife and two children smiled. They couldn't see what I could.

I said, "It's been almost three weeks. We should have found her by now."

She said, "Is that why you can't sleep? Celeste Sorensen is still out there?"

I turned onto my side to face her. My left shoulder was up and over the sheets. The plastic surgeon had done a pretty good job on my arrow wound thanks to Jameson White keeping it clean, but there was still a scar. I didn't mind. It was about time I had a scar on the outside. I wished it would hurt like Harry Potter's so I'd know when evil was near. If it was that kind of scar, Celeste Sorensen would be in custody. But it was just a regular scar—no magic in it whatsoever. At least we helped bust Detective Norton for giving his fellow white nationalist, Luke Tressler, the tool.

I watched her eyes drift toward my scar. It did something for her. At least it had that going for it.

I said, "Are you jealous of my scar?"

She smiled and shook her head. "No. I'm just not used to it. And every time I see it I think how close I was to losing you. It reminds me how fragile everything is."

"I prefer the word delicate. I am delicate. Never forget it."

"Oh," she said, "you make it impossible to forget how delicate you are." She paused and stared at nothing. "I pretend I'm strong. It's an act. I just move forward regardless."

"You've accomplished so much. Whatever lie you're telling yourself seems to be working."

"For some parts of my life. But it almost ruined a chance for this."

I had a big smile on my face. A kid's smile. Then I grew conscious of it and killed it. We were quiet for a long but comfortable minute and had a conversation with our eyes that seemed to go well. Then I said, "I'm sorry if I'm a little preoccupied."

"Occupational hazard," she said, and reached over with her right arm to run a fingertip over my non-magical scar.

"What Ian Halferin did seems so stupid," I said. She put the flat of her palm on my chest, not pushing but just there. "He overlooked Luke Tressler's past and character because he thought Luke supported his interests. Ian saw only what he wanted to see because he thought he was getting what he wanted. Instead, he got killed."

She moved closer and held my face in her hands. This side of her was new to me. Touchy and affectionate. I tried to act as if it didn't blow me away.

I said, "We all do it. I did, too, with Celeste Sorensen, by having Annika befriend her in hope of getting information on Halferin Silver. I could see who Celeste was from day one. But I thought she could help me so I looked the other way."

She removed her hands from my face. "Is that what we're doing right now?"

"What do you mean?"

She said, "Are we ignoring character for the sake of what we want?"

I shook my head, reached out, and pulled Gabriella Núñez's hands back toward me and kissed them. "No," I said. "This is not a mistake. Even if it doesn't work. This is an honest attempt at something good."

Gabriella's eyes shined but she didn't cry. She just nodded her head and said, "I think so, too."

Acknowledgments

This novel-writing business plops a writer on an uncharted island and says, "Make something from nothing, then deliver it to the world." So a novelist needs help. For that I thank my agent, Jennifer Weltz; my editor, Kristin Sevick; and everyone at Forge for their wisdom and hard work. I thank the booksellers and librarians and journalists for their passion and helping readers find the books that will speak to them. I thank the mystery community, readers and writers, whose kindness and inclusiveness make me wish I had written my first mystery decades ago. I thank Steven Selikoff and Bob Getman in Los Angeles for their support and friendship and patience. My family is everything. Every day. To my wife, Michele, like book-writing, I found you midlife, and what a find you are. Thank you for your love and loveliness and for the beautiful people you've brought into my life.

As for the subject matter of this book, I hope for an alien invasion so the 99 percent of people on Earth who share 99 percent of the same values will unite and force the alien invaders to retreat, taking with them the 1 percent of humanoids they left behind the last time they were here. Maybe with that 1 percent gone, the scar tissue in our ears will heal, and we can listen to one another.